The Long Table Dinner

A Novel

Also by Dennis Frahmann

Tales from the Loon Town Cafe

The Finnish Girl

The Devil's Analyst

The Long Table Dinner

A Novel

Dennis Frahmann

 LOON TOWN BOOKS

Loon Town Books
www.loontown.com

Publisher's Note: This is a work of fiction. Names, characters, places, and incidents are a product of the author's imagination. Locales and public names are sometimes used for atmospheric purposes. Any resemblance to actual people, living or dead, or to businesses, companies, events, institutions, or locales is completely coincidental.

Book Layout © 2017 BookDesignTemplates.com

The Long Table Dinner/Dennis Frahmann.
ISBN 978-0-578-42994-6

Library of Congress Control Number: 2018915143

For all those who love to tell stories

CONTENTS

A NEW EVENT...11

TEDDY: THE DAY BEFORE......................................13

THE GUESTS: THE MORNING OF THE DINNER......................67

TEDDY: THE COCKTAIL PARTY.................................119

THE SEATED GUESTS: DINNER................................163

TEDDY: AFTER DINNER......................................213

ABOUT THIS BOOK..247

A NEW EVENT

The Long Table Dinner is pleased to announce plans to host its first ever dinner at the famed Massetti Abalone and Cattle Ranch. Nestled on a picturesque stretch of California's Central Coast, this is the perfect setting for one of our famed outdoor dinners. Featuring local provisions and wines, a famed chef from San Francisco, and outstanding scenery, our event this fall is one that no fan of the Long Table Dinner program will want to miss. Make your reservations now.

PART ONE

TEDDY:
THE DAY BEFORE

Early on Friday

My name is Teddy Massetti, and soon I will turn seventy. Almost all of my years have been spent in this same spot—the place I like to call the vale of my youth. I don't think of myself as a hermit or a curmudgeon. Still I like things my way and don't care much for many people hanging around my ranch. How can I justify what I am about to suffer?

It all starts with my ranch. To understand me, you need to understand why I love this place so.

My land is home to the perfect bluff, and this bluff overlooks a perfect beach. This spot is at the edge of the continent at a point where the Central Coast of California dashes headlong into the Pacific Ocean, where a dark green line of Monterey pines nearly reaches the white froth of a sea, which in the stormy winter takes on its own shade of green. But during those hot days which mark the turn of summer, when the rains of the previous season have become a distant memory and the first hints of upcoming clouds of November remain an unsuspected portent, orange creeps into both the green sun-stressed succulents atop the cliff as well as the water-stressed needles of those pine boughs, while just beyond the bluff and out into the bay, bobbing on the ocean surface, the kelp forest blooms with its own peculiar yellowish hue. To the untrained eye the heads of the kelp skim so convincingly atop the ocean waves that one can become convinced that he has spotted a sea otter . . . only to have those hopes dashed, because in a moment, as one pauses to listen for the distinctive clink of rock against shell that would confirm this is a floating otter trying to open its dinner . . . there is heard only the rush of the wave, dashing away your fantasy.

Okay, say it. I am ridiculous in my overwrought description.

But you have to understand how this spot is the soul of my youth. It is also my adulthood home. Sometimes it seems all that I know of the world is found in this small valley, more of a ravine or a minor arroyo. In one way, it is all I know and yet in another way, can I ever know this place? In every way, it has trapped me into being the person I am.

In under twenty-four hours, my Eden is about to be invaded by scores of people, maybe even hundreds, most of them strangers. Permitted, but not invited by me, they will appear, each carrying a special fancy plate. Together we will sit down in a communal dinner at a long table that will curve along my bluff. We will dine as the sun sets over the Pacific. People call this a Long Table Dinner.

If we are lucky in this day ahead, the fog banks will stay well to the west, lingering as just a smudge along the evening horizon. If we are lucky, we will be blessed with one of those clear fall days where the sun is bright, the colors vibrant, and only the lightest of cooling breezes will flow from the west as we count the minutes down to a darkened sky. If we are truly lucky, the evening ebb tide of warm fall waters will rise with low swells that will gently rush over the tiny pebbles which compose my perfect beach, leaving in their wake the undeniable smell of the fresh ocean—a mixture of salt, ozone, and the briny hint of fresh seafood not yet tasted. What more could you expect of the perfect beach beneath the perfect bluff?

I know. No need for you to say it. I will accuse myself. I am still being too poetic. I ascribe meaning where none belongs. Yet I harbor an untamed nostalgia for my past, my youth, my home, and all that it has represented over nearly seven decades. So why am I allowing scores of strangers to descend onto this seaside ranch? I am too old to change. Whatever am I thinking?

Damn, it is too fucking late to back out now.

Friday, 2:36 PM

In the heat of the mid-afternoon, I survey the bluff that will host the dinner. This coastline has been part of my family's ranch since 1885. My forefathers emigrated from Switzerland to America. They became dairy farmers along the barely populated coast between Santa Barbara and San Francisco. In winter they rejoiced in hills that became as vibrantly green as those of Switzerland—at least in those years when the unreliable rains appeared. The landscape was the embodiment of my ancestors' longing back to the old country scenes of their childhood. Dairy cows thrived; my great grandparents sent all the milk produced to the local creamery. The milk was transformed to butter, loaded on wagons, transported to the small wharf a dozen miles south, and shipped north to San Francisco to support the restaurants and homes of that cosmopolitan city.

After the great earthquake in 1906 and the full extension of the railroads that connected northern and southern California, the shipping of butter became less and less profitable. The dairy cows were replaced by beef cattle. On the coast, one couldn't dry farm orchards of walnuts and almonds as some did on the other side of the Santa Lucia Mountains. However, my grandfather was clever, and he turned his sights westward, away from the grasslands of the internal valleys of our sprawling ranch. He focused instead on the ranch's western border, where the land undulated toward the sea, ending in bluffs that were twenty or thirty feet higher than the water below. To Grandpa's milking forefathers, this shoreline had been an afterthought. Grandpa, on the other hand, felt the tug of the sea. In the ocean, he saw new possibilities.

The nearby ranchers called him a fool when he poured the concrete for the first long troughs on the bluff. Here, he proclaimed, he would raise abalone. No one had ever conceived of such an outlandish idea. Sure, their shells were beautiful, but the giant sea snails were practically a pest in those days. Anyone with any skill at holding their breath and diving beneath the waves could harvest a barrel of abalone in a morning or evening. Maybe Grandpa was just a dreamer, or, perhaps, he foresaw what the future could become as the wilderness died away. In any case, time proved him prescient. Others harvested the wild abalone into near extinction. But because Grandpa persevered, today fancy restaurants in the big cities still offer the delicacy. Today, despite the California Coastal Commission's concerns, our abalone farm is grandfathered into the economy—one of only a handful of such farms in the entire country. And abalone sells for $80 a pound.

This abalone farm, my beautiful bluff, and my thousand acres of ranchland with its herd of grass-fed cattle prompted a person from the Long Table Dinner organization to knock at my door some months ago.

"May we have a dinner here?" he asked.

Because I never learned to say no to the things that I thought mattered, I said, "Yes."

It probably was a mistake, but it's just one more added to a long list of things in life that I should never have done, but at least I have invited some friends to help me through the day ahead.

Friday, 3:07 PM

"You're so calm," my friend Frank says. He has quietly walked up behind as I watch the ocean and think about the day ahead. "You know the sea makes me nervous when it's so placid. You get lulled into not paying attention. Do you ever feel that way?"

Frank has consistently played a presence in my life—always around, always strong, always paternal, and always making me feel safe. Even now as he nears his eightieth birthday, it was a childhood reason that prompted me to invite him and his wife Jessica to the Long Table Dinner. To keep me calm I need both of them. Years ago, Jessica was my babysitter. At the time, she was a high school senior. Frank was a young officer at the nearby Air Force monitoring station, and he was besotted with her. Somehow he always dropped by our house when my parents were gone and had left Jessica to look after my younger sister and me. I never minded Frank's impromptu visits.

Frank is reminiscing. "Maybe it comes from sitting on that bare hilltop all those years hidden away in the radar station. You could never let your guard drop, the way you were always waiting for that blip of a Russian missile, knowing you were there protecting the American way of life. At least that's what they told us. You know, when they ran the tests. But what we always feared was that some day it wouldn't be a test, but the real thing, and those fallout shelters that some people built back then would really get used. Worrying about all those things changes you."

I turn to face him. The afternoon sun vibrantly lights his face. After all these years, he still looks so strong and resolute. I don't know what to make of his reflective mood.

"But they never came," I say.

"And now that base is closed," he replies. "From what I hear, pines grow in the concrete cracks. Just another ruin abandoned by our federal government. Not at all like your place here."

From the porch of my house high up the hill and overlooking the coastline, we enjoy quite a view. Frank gestures toward the cascading tiers of concrete abalone tanks that line the cove just below the bend. I smile. Some days, I wish those tanks were as empty and crackled as that old airbase a dozen miles up the road. But I'm not going to tell Frank that.

"It was nice of you to invite Jessica and me to this shindig," Frank says. "It's good to be back. At this place. With you. We miss all of it. The ocean's not at all the same in Santa Monica."

"What?" I joke. "You don't have a thousand acres of dying grasslands and disappearing pine forest around your beach house? You don't worry about a drought that won't end?"

I regret my words as soon as they are out. Somehow it seems as though I am cheapening my old ranch. The truth is that the place is priceless to me, and I don't care how much money Frank and Jessica have or how expensive their estate in the Santa Monica Mountains may be. I have roots here that no one can pull out.

"Seriously. We always love coming here. We should do it more often. Not wait for some fancy dinner. And Jessica really appreciates that you let us bring Otto with us. He's been a lost soul since his wife died. Jessica thinks he needs to get out more."

Of course, I appreciate his thanks, but what else could I do? When Jessica and Frank ask for something, no one can say no. There's a charm about them, always has been. It was obvious even to an eleven-year-old who jealously watched their ease as a young couple in love. Maybe knowing them warped me forever, because I never found that kind of love. Not that I didn't want it. I just didn't want to fight for it. As much as I love this ranch, there really should have been more to seventy years of existence than tending its grounds.

"So who are these clowns showing up with their long table?" Frank asks. "I've checked them out on the web. From their photos, they seem a rather free-spirited group of folks. What do they do? Just wander around the country, making heritage dinners? Whatever that means. I guess they seek out farms off the beaten path, but how did you get conned into letting them come here?"

"They wanted the abalone," I reply.

"Makes sense. But are you sure they didn't really want to use your bluff? Or that beach? I remember how you used to always go swimming there. And the way you would con me into being your lifeguard. We'd leave Jessica up at the house to take care of your little sister, and God you couldn't wait to get your clothes off and dive into that water. It was always so freaking cold."

"Still is," I say smiling. "But actually warmer this time of the year than during the summer."

Frank continues, "Well, I'm dating myself, I suppose, but seeing pictures of those Long Table kids and that bus they travel in reminds me of the beatniks in my day. Ken Kesey, Neal Cassady, the merry pranksters. It makes me think we're in for quite the event tomorrow."

Frank thinks he's joking, but truthfully it was that energy of free spirits, unbounded by societal expectations, that caused me in some momentary spree of giddiness to sign a contract to host the dinner. I wanted a little spark of freedom before all my embers died out. Maybe, I thought, my little bluff could become a wanton den of iniquity. Worse things could happen.

The same idea must be sneaking into Frank's head. "Maybe by tomorrow night that little beach will be filled with a bunch of cavorting, naked kids. And that should make you happy. You always were the skinny dipper."

The Previous Fall

About one year earlier, I stood in nearly this same location on my porch, staring westward, hoping to see the distant spray of a passing whale. I knew it was probably too late in the migration season to expect much. Still, you never knew.

That's when I heard the roar of an old engine, as though someone from my youth was coming off the main highway and motorcycling up the gravel road. It was one of those nearly still days, with a light wind coming from the southeast, a moment when sound skipped over the hills like it knew no boundaries. My house on the ridge is nearly two miles from the main road, and the intervening hills block the view. Then I saw the dust cloud. Like a minor storm of a dust devil hugging the curves of the road, it rose up over the hills. Someone was clearly driving too fast for a country path that is little more than a driveway. Normally only my ranch workers and the abalone tenders used it. For that reason, I never felt I needed to put much money into smoothing out its ruts and potholes. It wasn't a place built for speed.

But here was someone who looked a bit too big for his vintage Indian brand motorcycle. That cycle had the appearance of one dating from near the end of the company's run, maybe 1952 or even '53. The machine didn't look in perfect shape, but it managed to tackle the hills with more speed than needed.

Standing on my porch, I watched the approaching cyclist with dismay. I don't much like visitors. My house sits just below the crest of the hill. My Grandpa built it there so he could watch over the entire ranch and capture a view through the canyon of the ocean below. It did that well, framing a perfect scene of a small seasonal creek that cascades in a final rush to the Pacific each spring. The canyon, protected from the cold afternoon winds that often rise and just outside the reach of early morning fogs, connects the grazing lands of my ranch with the shoreline of the sea. Near the canyon and creek, on a slight rise above the abalone troughs, is a small grove of cedars. Grandpa planted this spot to be his picnic grounds.

The house was my grandfather's major folly, only possible because his wife, my grandmother, came to California at the turn of the last century with a large inheritance that was eventually spent to everyone's satisfaction. The two honeymooned at the San Diego Pan Pacific Exposition, a fair at which a flurry of romantically inventive Spanish-style architecture ignited the building imagination of the entire region. Grandma chose to travel to California after falling under the lure of the novel *Ramona* so it was only natural for her to be entranced by the Fair's buildings. Grandpa, more of an earthbound rancher, was not usually given to such fancy. However, even in his waning days he longed to live up to the mythology he created around his coastal ranch. I always thought it was how he distinguished himself from his parents and their emigration trip to America. His love for his wife gave him an excuse to also love this new phantasmagoria of decorated tiles, white stucco walls, red tile roofs, and wooden beams with heavy hints of a past that never truly existed. He willingly gave up the old wooden ranch house next to our traditional California barn so he could build a new house to match her vision of a coastal ranch.

So in the early Twenties, the construction began. His neighbors made fun of him, calling him Little Hearst, comparing him to the newspaper magnate further up the coast who at the time was building his own extravagant castle in the Spanish style. The neighbors' nickname was a rather unkind jest, both because locals held Mr. Hearst in low esteem and because Grandpa was noted for being on the short side. But a little name calling by the locals didn't stop Grandpa from pursuing his dream.

I have always been very glad that it didn't deter him. I love the old house with its spacious rooms and thick walls, the way the indoor space flows out onto porches and patios. In the nearly one hundred years that have passed since its construction, little has been done to modernize my house. The kitchen and baths still sport the bold colors of tiles popular at the time. The original steel-framed windows still open to catch the afternoon breeze. Between the climate and the house's focus on thick walls and good air circulation, there's never been a reason to add air conditioning.

But as much as I love this house, I'm not that fond of sharing it. That's why the unexpected presence of this fool on his Indian motorcycle was so unsettling. When he zipped by the leg of the road that actually leads to the house's entrance, I was secretly pleased. I figured he was heading on to the abalone farm. The interloper darted around the corner until he was hidden from the view. I could hear that the motor stopped, and I assumed he was heading into the office. Let Jake, my manager, deal with the intruder, I thought.

But the quiet didn't last. The unpleasant sound of the motor revved up. The rider came back around the corner, slower this time, as though looking for the road to the house. I could both see and hear how he slowed further and made the tight turn up my hill. He revved the motor again and headed straight toward where I stood.

He skidded a bit to stop at the edge of the steps. I said nothing, and I tried to show my disdain.

The man took off his helmet. He shook his head as though to loosen his long locks of bright red hair. Freckled, green-eyed, in his thirties, he was more than a few pounds overweight. Then he smiled, and I couldn't help but smile back, even though I wanted to order him off the ranch. I had no defense against his air of impishness.

"I'm guessing you're Teddy Mazzetti. You're a hard man to find. But I think we're both going to be happy that I found my way here.

"This is a beautiful piece of land you have here, Mr. Mazzetti. But, hey, I don't like being so formal. Can I call you Teddy? Or are you more of a Theodore?"

He didn't wait for my answer. Instead he started rummaging though his saddlebags with the ferocity of a badger.

"It's Teddy," I replied reluctantly, because even though I sensed this person was a likeable sort, at that moment I didn't want him around. "And what should I call you?"

"Aubrey."

He was still searching through the bags. He seemed to have an enormous collection of papers, flyers, and pamphlets stuck into the old leather satchel. "The name's the curse of my father. We're not even English, but Norwegian. I don't know what he was thinking."

Aubrey seemed in no hurry to inform me of the reason for his presence. Although I had no place to go—the abalone farm requires very little of my attention, and thanks to Jake, I pay no heed whatsoever to the care or breeding of the cattle—I still didn't like my time being wasted. After all, this incursion occurred without an appointment. A gentleman only has so much patience.

"Well, Aubrey, I don't really know why you drove up my private road and dropped in uninvited to my home, but let me assure you that there are no tours of the abalone farm, so you can be quite certain that you have wasted your time."

"Oh, I don't think so, though it is your abalone farm that lures me here. You can forget about a tour. If all I needed was a taste of your abalone, my buyers could get me that."

He was still scrounging through the bag. I wanted to grab it off the cycle and toss the contents onto the gravel road. Surely, whatever he was seeking couldn't be that hard to find.

Still my ears perked up when he used the word "buyer." The word seemed to explain so much. No doubt, he was some new-age chef from Los Angeles or San Francisco finagling to buy abalone directly from me instead of through my wholesaler. Occasionally the particularly zealous showed up with such intent. If the fellow hadn't been wearing a heavy leather motorcycle jacket, I could have seen his arms, which were undoubtedly covered in tattoos. That would have immediately led me to guess he was a chef.

I decided to cut him off. "I don't bother with direct sales. Everyone has to go through my sales agent."

"Aha, I found it!"

Aubrey lifted a tattered magazine into the air. I recognized it as an issue of *Sunset* magazine from some eighteen months earlier. They ran a story about various fish mongers, oyster farmers, and the like up and down the coast. Mazzetti Abalone had merited its own sidebar.

"This is what lures me here," he said triumphantly. "When I read it, I knew I needed your abalone and your beef. There's no place else in the country that would let me do what I need to do."

My patience was gone. Yet I still smiled. Sometimes it annoyed me that I liked certain people so instantly even though they have done nothing to deserve it.

"I just said I don't sell direct."

Aubrey smiled more broadly, his red hair glinted in the morning sun, and he shrugged off his leather jacket. He sported the very tattoos I had predicted, sort of an elaborate South Seas pattern up and down his arms. He reached out his hand. An old salesman's trick. You can't help but shake an extended hand. What could I do but grab it? His handshake generated such warmth and energy that I immediately regretted my automatic human reaction. Now I knew it was going to be impossible to get rid of this man.

"Teddy, I can see I need to explain myself. I'm not here to buy your food. I'm here to celebrate you. I'm here to invite a couple hundred special people to experience the beauty and quality of what you have. It's an opportunity that will cause them to envy you the rest of their days. I'm here to enable you to become the special genie who grants other people's wishes. Culinary wishes, just to be clear."

This wasn't explaining much.

"I got a brochure," he said and turned, ready to go back digging through his saddlebags.

"No, just tell me," I insisted.

"We call it the Long Table Dinner," he replied.

With those words my yearlong nightmare began.

Aubrey certainly grew animated as he explained the concept behind his company, really more of a traveling troupe of cooks, waiters, bartenders, and assorted ilk. For months on end, the group tramped like a traveling circus from one unique farm to another. On site, they created a pop-up restaurant for one night only, marked by a long table that would snake through the farm and feature a menu specific to the region and that specific purveyor.

It sounded a bit magical, a concoction seasoned with a touch of whimsy and a dash of romance. It wasn't exactly a one-ring circus under a big top, but it was an interesting open-air show. Whatever happened, the dinner would go on, rain or shine. Aubrey explained that originally guests brought both their own chair and plate. The individual plate (preferably ornate and unique) was still encouraged. Everyone sat down and food was served family style. There might be a hundred, two hundred, or more guests dining at a table pieced together until it ran the length of a football field. To the side, the Long Table cooking staff erected a temporary kitchen that would produce a gourmet meal.

As for the guests, well, first they had to discover that the Long Table Dinners existed by signing up to secret mailing lists. They also had to be willing to pay a couple of hundred dollars per seat. Apparently, the country is full of people willing to spend their money foolishly to feel special.

Even if I already knew that, Aubrey still felt compelled to explain it all.

He succeeded in describing a table snaking through my Grandpa's picnic grove on a warm autumn eve. This description seemed so real that I could hear the evening tide lapping against my beach. And I could imagine the wonders of a talented chef bringing out the flavor and texture of my abalone and knowing what to do with my beef. I acknowledged that it wouldn't be hard to convince local vintners to provide the perfect wines to such an event.

More importantly, in the euphoria of listening to Aubrey, I began to imagine how such an event would provide the perfect reason to convince Frank and Jessica to pay a visit and stay for dinner.

There was something about Aubrey that made me smile. I smiled when he decamped from his motorcycle. I smiled throughout his explanations even when they annoyed me. He was just so likeable. When Aubrey asked me to sign his contract, I didn't hesitate. I knew I had to do it. The ranch was meant for such an event. So I signed with a smile.

Only later did I begin to frown. Maybe if the dinner had taken place the next day, everything would have worked out perfectly. But it was scheduled for nearly a full year after that initial meeting. That gave me almost twelve months to worry about what I had done. Close to three hundred and sixty five days of thinking that I had made the worst mistake of my life.

Now today this dreaded dinner is only twenty-four hours away. I vow to be brave and live through it.

Friday, 5:37 PM

Here's something else you should know about me. I have trouble letting things go. I have even more trouble in accepting something new. Jessica and Frank are part of that condition. I'll acknowledge that Jessica was my babysitter for many years longer than I really needed one. Let me add that I never minded. I have true love and affection for Jessica, even if I have always been reluctant to tell her. I have never been much for speaking the truth to either Jessica or Frank.

I don't know what my parents were thinking when they kept hiring Jessica long after I was old enough to take care of my baby sister Gina. Mom and Dad did like to party and travel so they were gone more than usual for the era. That might have been it, or maybe they didn't trust me to look after my younger sister. In any case they ensured someone older was always on hand. Because Jessica liked both my sister and me, she was always eager to help out my parents. Mom and Dad were equally happy to please her. They never expressed any concern about how Frank, the Air Force boyfriend, showed up so frequently to keep her company.

None of it bothered me either. Now, from my vantage point decades later, I sometimes wonder why I didn't want to break free and be the one in charge. I guess I felt more comfortable being looked after. I never cared much for responsibility. When Jessica graduated from high school and headed south to study art history at UCLA, responsibility was thrust upon me. Accepting it made me angry and nervous. This was right after Frank was reassigned to the Air Force base in El Segundo and also just in time to experience my sister Gina's rebellious preteen years. My sister didn't care much for being under my control. Still doesn't.

Jessica was the local beauty. Everyone knew it. Her senior year, the town even elected her a Fourth of July princess for the Independence Day parade. In those days, she wore her long black hair tied back in a ponytail. She was also fond of poodle skirts and angora sweaters.

She may have been miles from any big city, but she watched the television programs on the station out of San Luis Obispo and always picked up the trends before her peers even noticed.

Now sixty years older, Jessica is standing in my kitchen with as much authority as though she never left. In many ways, I am still in awe of her. She could still tell me what to do, and I would happily comply. She is as stylish as ever. While her hair is now white, it is always perfectly in place. A string of pearls transforms her otherwise casual clothes into something almost too elegant for the ranch house.

I find her peering at the old Malibu tile counters. They're vintage stuff; I once saw the exact same pattern in the kitchen of the historic beach house of the family who first owned all of Malibu. Personally, I think my family's home is just as nice as that one, even though Grandpa ran out of inherited money before he could ever construct a pool. But who needs that? I have my little beach.

"You never change anything, do you?" she notes. It may be my imagination but to me, there's sadness to her smile. It is almost as though she has, somehow, in just the smallest of ways, misapplied her lipstick to create a shadow where none belonged.

"Why would I? It's all perfect."

She runs her hand along the tile toward the big farmhouse sink, original to the house. "I washed dishes here so often. It's a good thing I wasn't much of a cook in those days, or I would have fattened you up. You always hung around Frank and me when we were preparing supper, like you couldn't wait to eat."

"Maybe I just wanted to be with you."

"Was that what it was?" she asks. "Maybe so."

It is so good to see Jessica back in the kitchen. It's as though I am once more eleven going on twelve, feeling new stirrings and recognizing a world outside the boundaries of the family ranch. In those days when I felt protected by Jessica and Frank, I knew every hill and gully of this place. I recognized the ways the wetlands filled in with water after the winter storms and became a short-lived marsh. I understood the creek that flowed some of the year just beside the long driveway to the coast. I could count every stone in the small dam that anchored the ranch road. I knew the rocks where turtles liked to sun themselves, the stony coves where the waves made one type of sound as they slapped against the falling cliffs, and the sandy beaches where they made another. I even mastered the daring jump from one slippery rock to another, leaping over tide pools filled with crabs, anemones, and starfish.

Sometimes people tell me I love this place too much. Maybe I do, and I always did. I loved the way incredibly tall eucalyptus grew alongside the highway. When you peel off its bark in long strips, it leaves behind a medicinal waft. Solitary oaks dotted the grasslands where the cattle grazed. A fog-filled strip of pine on the northern border was the very edge of a last remaining stand of natural Monterey pine that inched along the coast northwards for only a few miles. On foggy days, I loved to stand just within the shadows of those tall spires and feel the shower of condensed fog as it dripped from their sheltering branches.

When I was a boy, the ranch teemed with life, at least enough life to keep me happy. Not just the cattle in the fields or the troughs near the cove filled with our abalone. There were bobcats, foxes, and ground squirrels. Quail would scurry in surprise out of clumps of grass. I could hear the otters that sheltered in the ocean kelp off shore as they tapped their rocks to break open shells.

This had been my life. I thought it was all I had ever wanted. Somehow having Jessica and Frank here now makes me aware that there probably should have been something more. Maybe I should have sought something beyond the ranch.

"Why have you never left this place?" Jessica asks.

"I've been all over the world," I reply.

"Only your body," she says. "Your heart and soul have never left the ranch. You've never opened up that part of you to anyone. Not once."

"That seems a bit unfair," I protest.

"Is it? Where have romances been? Why isn't there a significant other in your life? Or anyone who really matters?"

"You and Frank are here."

I feel unfairly attacked. I have many friends. In fact, I think of myself as quite social.

"And now you've invited how many people to invade this place for dinner? To sit at a single long table, like a plague of gophers infesting your precious ranch. Tell me. How many people are coming?"

"They sold at least 150 seats. Maybe it's up to 200 or even more." I state the facts firmly as though they don't terrify me.

"Oh, Teddy, what have you done?"

Friday, 6:32 PM

I don't have a lot of skills. I know my ranch, raising cattle and abalone, and a little bit about art. That might be why I stick close to home. When it comes to entertaining, I have mastered cooking one dish. It sits now in the center of my dinner table—a perfectly roasted chicken. You can judge its success by its crackling brown skin and the general looseness of the drumsticks. It is an ideal dish to serve Frank and Jessica—and Otto. There isn't much else I can cook well, certainly not beef or seafood. Not that I often put my culinary knowledge to the test. It has been months since I last entertained dinner guests. I truly can't remember when I allowed overnight guests.

But tonight, on the eve of the Long Table Dinner, there are three others around my much smaller table: Frank, Jessica and Otto. My plan never included Otto. Already this Long Table thing is going off the rails in an unexpected way.

I have my reasons for wanting to host Frank and Jessica again. But I am also a gentleman. What was I to do when both so persuasively requested to bring their old friend and neighbor, Otto, a man I had never even met? They told me he was lonely after his wife's death. Aren't we all lonely in one way or another?

Otto is one of those tall Dutchmen, much too tall for my taste. Jessica told me that he had recently turned ninety and she intimated that his past included some dark days in World War II. Well, he certainly seems thin enough to have survived a war. So far he hasn't stopped telling stories or joking about the old days. This began the moment he arrived. So much for still grieving the death of his wife.

Frank is obsequious in this man's presence, as though he is both a puppy rolling over to have Otto bless him with a tummy scratch of approval as well as his rival in winning Jessica's attentions. It is unseemly how both Otto and Frank cavort in their respective telling of stories. Jessica, of course, is amused by each and every tale they tell.

Put the four of us all together and it makes for an odd dinner—an old curmudgeon approaching seventy (I can admit that's me), a still beautiful prom queen who looks younger than her seventy-five years, a much too handsome former Air Force colonel in his eighth decade, and one old Dutchman who has outlived his life expectancy. We sit around a lovely crisp chicken on a platter in the center of the table. I fear it represents some sort of a trial run for the dinner tomorrow.

A part of me wants to bring up all the things that are on my mind concerning this impending dinner. There have never been this many people on this ranch at one time in its entire history—not even in the Sixties when my sister was married on that bluff. All those cars will be driving on my long dirt driveway, raising far too much dust because they won't be cautious enough to go slow and keep that dirt from blowing into my abalone troughs. What if I don't like the people who show up? It is most unlikely that I will care for Aubrey and his crew. God only knows what kind of people shell out $250 for a seven-course dinner on an unprotected cliff. No one even eats abalone anymore. No one will know what to expect. Somehow I fear that they will think that I, as the place's owner, should amuse them. But I am not one to amuse others.

Tonight, I keep these worries to myself. In fact, I say very little. Then again I don't have to speak. Between Frank and Otto, the conversation never lags.

"Let me tell you," Otto says, words that after only a few hours I already know are a sure sign that the man is about to launch into another tale. "Right after the war, when I was a young man I worked on the Netherlands Line as a cabin steward. Oh, I saw a lot. People could not fly here and there in those days. No, you had to take the slow boat, and believe me it was a slow boat. In those days all those old Dutch settlers wanted to return to Holland from Indonesia because they knew independence was coming to those islands and that they would no longer be welcome—and we carried those old folks home. Then we would turn back to Australia for the long run, transporting Brits wanting to escape the post-war conditions of England. You know they were just trying to get a new life Down Under.

"The ships of the Netherlands Line were always full, and such characters they were. Me and the boys would watch as the guests came on, especially those in third class because they were the most likely to involve some pretty young girls. Third class were the cheapest tickets, often three to a cabin, with a shared washroom down the hall, but they were the rooms that young women trying to make a new life could afford to book.

"I remember this one time. We saw these three young women, nurses I think, come aboard for a run to Sydney. Ah, we were impressed. One was a real beauty." Otto uses his hands to paint a picture of a curvaceous girl. "You know what I mean?"

We know what he means, and we all smile, but I feel Frank is already distracted, thinking ahead to tell his own story to top Otto's.

"A day out at sea, I was cleaning the women's shower room and I found this padded rubber bra still hanging there. Well, there weren't that many women, and I had a pretty good idea who this item belonged to, so I took it, marched straight down the hall to the stateroom of those three girls. I knocked. They opened the door. I got a nice breeze, because in those days, back before air conditioning, the portholes really worked, and theirs was open. Keep that in mind," Otto says it with a smile.

"I hold up the bra. Oh, you should've seen the look on those girls' faces. 'Does this belong to one of you,' I asked. I was so innocent. Of course they were quick to deny it. Red-faced, that's what they were, but we all knew what was what.

"But I, being a gentleman, didn't want to force anything on them. 'Well,' I said, 'I guess if it don't belong to anyone, then I better get rid of it.' And I did. I threw it right out the porthole before any one of them could say one thing."

I can't help but laugh. On one hand, I suppose it was a horrible thing for Otto to do, but the image he paints is so outlandish.

"Now," Otto continues, "here it comes. That night they walk into the third class dining room, and that voluptuous one . . . well, now she's flat as a board."

Otto leans back, a sly smile crosses his face, and his eyes twinkle.

We all laugh. Maybe Otto isn't such a bad fellow. The old man settles back in the chair with the satisfied look of a person who has told the same story a thousand times in his life and knows how people will react.

Frank jumps in. "That reminds me . . . " he begins.

Jessica taps his hand gently and smiles. You can tell she knows what's coming next.

So do I. There will be too many stories ahead. I can't think of one to tell myself. My long life has been rather sparse on fun. An optimist might think the day ahead could be a future story, but I lack the fortitude to feel so generous in my outlook.

After the first bottle of wine is drunk, I feel the evening is taking a turn. That is the moment Otto turns to us to say something unlike his initial tales.

"I like this evening," he says. "It feels good. In Holland, we have a word for the feeling I have right now. We call it *gezellig*."

He dips his head a bit and rubs his hands over one another almost as though they are hugging one another. He has a smile. "I don't know the English word for this feeling. I don't think you have one. It's when you're all together in the comfort and safety of friendship, with the confidence that you can depend on one another.

"That's what I feel in this room. You're so lucky to have one another."

Several Months Earlier

For several months after meeting Aubrey, I was able to avoid all thought of the impending Long Table Dinner. But then at the request of Aubrey, I traveled north to dine with him at Point Conception restaurant in San Francisco. The event only inflamed my early concerns.

At that dinner, Aubrey was sitting across from me. Next to him was the owner, Leon Fagatelle—one of the celebrity chefs du jour. Some said he was the brightest star in the Bay's culinary firmament. Others accused him of being an aggrandizing poseur. To me he was the grown-up son of a San Luis Obispo butcher who sold my farm's beef.

I hadn't seen Leon in years. When we last crossed paths, he was still a gawky, acne-faced teenager grinding the hamburger. There was a hint, even then, of the handsome man he could become; however, in those days he never seemed to pay attention to his father's suppliers, and there was no reason I should have paid attention to him. But small towns link everyone together, so I suppose it was no surprise that at this point each of us claimed to remember the other well. Although, I was a bit skeptical that Leon truly recalled me.

Aubrey, on the other hand, was over the moon. Until we sat down together at the chef's table, he hadn't realized that there was a preexisting connection between Leon and me. He had only wanted the chef for his dinner to meet the owner of the land. But when Leon said how happy he was to see me again and how he had always admired my family's abalone farm, Aubrey interpreted that as a celestial sign that the heavens were blessing his planned event. On the other hand, because I had taken the time to review my supplier's list of restaurants that bought my fresh abalone, I realized Point Conception restaurant was not on that list. Regional connection or not, I wasn't that excited about Leon.

I only half listened as Aubrey busily explained his vision. "This restaurant is famous for its imaginative take on surf and turf, you know, the way they add an unexpected twist on a classic. I thought, 'Who better to tackle Mazzetti beef and abalone?'"

"I can't imagine," I replied.

Leon seemed to take that as a compliment and he smiled broadly. It was as though he also thought we were long-lost blood brothers just because we both hailed from the Central Coast or perhaps because his parents did business with me.

It was so infantile that it put me in a bad mood. "It's not Mazzetti abalone," I corrected him. "We only use that term for the beef. The abalone is simply Pacific abalone. We don't try to brand it. Not everything needs branding."

I was being annoyingly precise. Most of our buyers did in fact call it Mazzetti abalone on their menus. I just didn't put that label on the shipping boxes.

The evening was a waste of my time. I didn't understand why Aubrey thought I needed to trek all the way north to meet his chef. He had required me to sign a contract that made clear I had no veto power over what chef he used or what dishes they served. I only agreed to sell as much abalone and beef as needed at a rather ridiculously low wholesale price. While Aubrey looked a bit like Santa Claus, I had discovered quickly I was usually the one handing out the presents.

But he asked me to dinner and I gave in—not because I had a curiosity in seeing Leon again, although I did—but because I had a yen to go to San Francisco. I don't know why but I find there's something I like about the city in the late spring.

As soon as I agreed to go, I knew that I wouldn't take the inland route to the road they once called the El Camino Real or worse yet drive all the way east to the interstate that went through empty barrens in the middle of the state. Instead, I determined to drive my little roadster all the way north along the coast. So I headed toward Monterey, driving slowly around hairpin turns that were perched hundreds of feet above the rushing sea below and speeding over the famous bridges of the Big Sur. When I felt the urge, I stopped here or there for a quick hike to check out some stunning waterfalls still swollen by the winter rains.

It had been a wet winter. The waterfalls were flowing freely, but for once there were no mudslides or rock spills that closed the highway. Driving north through all the little towns, past the Hearst Castle perched high in the Santa Lucia Mountains, glimpsing the breeding grounds of elephant seals, sailing by places called Gorda and Lucia, driving past turnoffs to some of America's most expensive resorts with the views to justify the rates, I zoomed through Carmel, Monterey and then turned inland. My mood soured as I hit an urban freeway, the 280, and headed north toward the city.

You see I live by the ocean. I hardly ever leave it. There's no explaining why a few extra hours perched on a precarious mountain road with the perspective to see migrating whales seemed so special. And maybe it wasn't. Sometimes I have trouble figuring out what really matters to me.

Aubrey was still talking. Once again I had lost track of what he was saying, something about how much he wanted each of his dinners to truly reflect the character and philosophy of the purveyor he featured.

"I really don't care what you serve," I stated. I was hoping a bottle of wine would appear soon. Conversations like this always were easier with a glass in one's hand. Finally, I asked, "Can't we get some wine?"

"Of course," replied Leon.

He motioned a waiter over. "Bring us a bottle of 712 and three glasses." He turned back to us. "This will be a very nice Albariño from your neck of the woods, Teddy. When you taste it, imagine it paired with an abalone tartare."

Aubrey smiled, "Leon is just toying with us. He's prepared an entire tasting menu for tonight of what he has proposed for your event. Every course, every wine. Multiple courses, so we can select the best of the best. I wanted the evening to surprise you Teddy. I even arranged to buy abalone through a third party, just so you wouldn't catch on. Of course, Leon's parents sent up the beef.

"Are you ready to go to heaven?"

I had set out from the ranch early that morning and driven all day. As lovely as the scenery had been, by now I was tired. I wasn't really interested in a big meal. A glass or two of wine and then a stroll back across the street to the hotel for a good night's sleep would have been far more my idea of paradise. I'm afraid my disappointment at the idea of a long night of eating flickered across my face. I never was good at poker.

Aubrey put on the hard sell. "Don't worry, you don't have to eat everything. Just a quick taste will be sufficient. Help us choose which dishes make it to the final menu and which ones we drop. Think of it as though we were doing the tasting for a wedding."

"One problem with that," I countered. "I never got married, and there's no universe in which I can imagine a groom and his friends making the wedding dinner selections."

Leon laughed. "If you're a chef, you do. Seriously, I just want to be sure that you're happy with what I'm planning. Artisanal food is what I do. And this will be like classic Pacific Coast Americana. I know some of my best customers are going to head down the coast just to do this dinner. They're going to love your abalone."

"Besides," Aubrey added, "tonight will give us the perfect chance to tease out your memories. I want to know your thoughts about the food you raise. After all, I have to find the perfect stories for you to tell at the dinner."

"What?!"

"Well, you know, you're the host. People expect certain things. They come to a special place like your farm and want to meet the people behind it. Of course, they're looking forward to Leon's food. His groupies come for that. Still, anyone can make a reservation to dine at Point Conception. But to graze on beautiful food in the place where it is raised with the man who makes it happen . . . now that's special.

That's what makes it so sought after. I see it with every Long Table Dinner."

"You never said I would have to talk."

"It goes without saying. Besides you're a charming man. I know you must have many stories to tell. Everyone will love you. The evening will be a great success. Ah, look here comes the waiter with the wine and the abalone tartare."

A plate was set in front of me. Another waiter whipped out a beautiful piece of stemware and poured a lovely wine showing just a hint of yellow-green.

Leon and Aubrey looked at me expectantly. "Taste it. Tell us what you think. Don't leave out a word."

I should have said "Fuck you" right then.

But I didn't.

Before I knew it, the evening was ending. There was only a puddle of wine left in my glass. A bit of sediment had dropped to the bottom. Although I was no expert on food, even I had to admit that the handsome Leon Fagatelle had done wonders with the short ribs. They went wonderfully with the wine. But no one asked for my opinion. Everyone at every table in Point Conception was more interested in their own tales.

Aubrey and Leon had already spent over two hours talking over one another, fueled by their passions, speeding along and completely ignoring me. It was understandable. Still their exclusion miffed me. Why had they invited me to give my opinion? It was my first inkling that the Long Table Dinner to come had nothing really to do with me.

I suppose I might have found more to say if either one had only chosen to ask me a question. Then too, I could have offered an opinion, but somehow I found it was more comfortable to settle back and watch the two of them engage in their orgy of food talk. Passion always eluded me. Once I longed to have it. At times I even actively sought it, but passion always kept its distance. Now enveloped by their animation, I felt a small spark of anticipation. Maybe something could catch hold within me. Perhaps I even deluded myself into believing that the Long Table Dinner would somehow become a personal moment of transformation.

You see how I can overstate things. Well, people can dream, can't they?

But in a flash of reality—as I surveyed the white linens and the polished silver, with the dirty dessert plates still waiting to be cleared—I made a decision. Tonight, between a full stomach and the loneliness of being politely overlooked, I vowed to invite Frank and Jessica to the special night ahead. I also decided I would not inform my sister Gina about this dinner. Reconciliation has its limits.

"Teddy. Teddy."

One of them was talking to me. Maybe I had drifted off. I had long since outgrown drinking quite so much wine.

"Aubrey tells me that Pedrag Miles is your next door neighbor. How in the world did that happen? Did you know that he and his wife eat here all the time? I had no idea they owned a place on the Central Coast. Pedrag is a financial genius."

Leon seemed such a promising young man back in those days when he unloaded the meat that I delivered to his parents' butcher shop. Smart, capable, friendly. That's how I thought of the young man. Why did becoming a celebrity chef make one so easily beguiled by other celebrities?

Pedrag, my next-door neighbor, might be a wizard of technology and the markets, but he caused my rift with Gina. I never understood what his technology company did, nor did I care, but he was richer than anyone had a right to be. It was his money that allowed him to extend his offer years ago to buy the best parts of the coastline that made up our family ranch.

Let me correct that. Pedrag was not a genius when it came to the coastline, because he didn't want the best parts, not that I would ever have sold him my perfect bluff and beach. He only wanted the things that intrigued him.

South of my house, the bluffs of our land rose higher over the ocean in formations that might justifiably be called cliffs. All beaches disappeared. Here the land was rocky and rugged. That's why it wasn't our best land. Cows could get too close to the edge of some crumbling rocks and tumble over. Admittedly, cows don't have much interest in looking out to sea. Still all it takes is one.

So it wasn't the best land. At least that was my opinion. Gina, on the other hand, loved to gaze toward the ocean horizon from high above. Naturally, she loved those cliffs. I had the beach. She had the cliffs.

When our parents died, they named me the executor and left me holding the majority share in the ranch. Dad did that on purpose. He thought clear majority ownership would keep the ranch from being broken up. He also thought that he had found a way at last to make his stay-close-to-home son a man who would take charge. Dad never was a practical man. He failed to foresee the expenses hovering over the horizon. Worse, he didn't understand the temptations that could confront children who were land rich and cash poor.

It was impractical of Gina, even unfair, to think that she could do all the things she chose to do—the schooling, the traveling, the wild life—and not have to pay some kind of price. Without acquiring a cache of money how could I buy at auction those paintings for which I longed? I blame Grandpa. He built a perfect house. It deserved to be graced with early California impressionist paintings. The walls were meant for moody watercolors of eucalyptus in the fog and bright oils of poppies among sun-dappled oaks. Back around 2000, the price for such art skyrocketed. If I wanted it, I had to find money.

So I found money.

Pedrag made it possible for both Gina and me to do what we sought. She should have thanked me. That's what I told myself. Pedrag wanted our land. We wanted his money.

On a whim, Pedrag once rented a helicopter and flew over a hundred miles of the coast checking out the shoreline. He fell in love with the very set of cliffs that entranced Gina. He offered more than Gina ever could.

What should I have done when he came to my door with an offer to buy so much of our ranch? I told myself we would still have the abalone. We would still have our small cattle herd. We would still have Grandpa's hacienda. In addition, we would deposit millions into our bank accounts.

Would anyone have said no? What did it matter if Gina loved those cliffs, now fenced off as the personal estate of a Silicon Valley billionaire? What did it matter if Pedrag's guards turned her away when she tried to walk the trails that defined her youth? We still had my beach. We still had our little strip of Monterey pine along the northern edge. We still had . . .

Oh, forget it. Maybe Gina was right to condemn me for taking what mattered to her without discussing it. But now it was done. It was in the past.

"Pedrag's estate is quite the place," Aubrey said.

I realized I missed a bit of the conversation while dwelling on the past. If I ever went to a dinner like this again, I really would have to drink less.

"How would you know?" I asked.

"His estate is where I first wanted to hold the Long Table event. The setting is so dramatic. Wouldn't you agree? I mean I would still have featured your abalone. But face it. Those cliffs. It would have been a stunning event up there."

I must have looked surprised.

"You don't seem convinced? Have you ever been to that bit of land? It's truly an amazing place. Don't get me wrong. Your place is gorgeous. But that bit of coastline. Man, oh, man."

Friday, 7:18 PM

Otto may have proclaimed that the four of us had entered into some special state of Dutch togetherness, but I wasn't feeling it. Jessica knows it.

"You don't seem very pleased with things, Teddy."

Jessica follows me into the kitchen; she is carrying the dirty dinner plates. I am heating up water to make some French press coffee to go with dessert.

"What do you mean? I'm very happy that I'm having dinner with Frank and you."

Jessica sets the dishes down with a thud. I want to remind her that she is handling my mother's Royal Doulton china. I took it out of the pantry just for the occasion. But I already know that she recognizes both the pattern and the importance of my using these plates.

"Oh, there's so many things wrong with that reply," she sighs. "First of all, you know I'm not talking about tonight's meal, but about what's going to happen tomorrow. And it seems as though you conveniently overlook that Otto is also your guest. That bothers me a great deal."

"You and Frank wanted him here. Of course, he's a welcome guest."

The truth is I am tiring of the man, but then, as most of my neighbors know, I tire of troublesome things quickly. There is no question that Otto's entertaining enough. Since he's already told a treasure trove of stories, he certainly has made me laugh, even when I want to be annoyed.

When I was a child and my mother scolded me over some unfair infraction, I always found a way to express my dissatisfaction with her. I saw no reason for my unhappiness to remain one sided. A particularly favorite technique was to sulk in my room until she felt guilty and came to apologize. As the years went on, it seemed to take longer and longer for my mother to reach that point, until one day she simply stopped. That didn't mean I stopped pouting. But now that I am a host in my own home, it seems rather impractical (even if tempting) to retreat to my bedroom, with its comfortable armchair, to sit quietly waiting for someone to notice. After all, I'm no longer thirteen.

"You're so transparent, Teddy. I could always tell when you were upset and I always knew the reasons why you were unhappy. I knew you better than your own mother. So don't tell me that you're not angry I invited Otto to join us. But why? He's a perfectly delightful man, plus he was lonely and hurting in his own way. Why begrudge him a little happiness?"

"I don't begrudge him anything."

"Oh, but you do. You know you do. And I think I know the reason why. You're jealous of him, aren't you? You always wanted my attention only to yourself. You didn't even like Frank coming by in the old days, did you? And you never liked my looking after your sister Gina because you wanted to be the center of attention. But you know what? Otto's a funny man. Frank's a funny man. And that's why we're going to dish up this apple cobbler, add a scoop or two of vanilla ice cream, and march back into that dining room, and you're going to smile at his stories, and you're going to let yourself have a good time."

"You still think you're my mother, don't you?" I proclaim.

"I try. Even after all these years."

Jessica likes to imagine that Gina and I thought of her as our mother. In truth, while I don't know what my sister may have felt, I only had one mother and one father. They really were quite enough for me. Dad was a bossy sort of fellow, prone to imagining big dreams. He was just like his father. Dad thought he could turn our seaside ranch into something far grander than it was. That's why he and Mom were always making those trips into San Luis Obispo or down to Los Angeles or up to San Francisco. They were always searching for another investor who could help fulfill Dad's dream of building a grand resort on our land. Mom went along with his fantasies for the alcohol, and, sometimes, maybe, for affairs she had behind Dad's back. Maybe he knew what she was up to. Who can say for sure? They had their dreams that never amounted to much, but they never stopped pursuing them. There's surely something to be said for that. Having dreams, I mean.

Even to this day, so many years after their deaths, I don't know why they never appreciated what they had. Who wouldn't have been happy with the golden rolling hills of our ranch? Why didn't they marvel at our craggy cliffs? Where else could they have seen otters, whales, and seals on their daily walks? What more did they need to make their lives worth living?

And what about Gina and me? Why weren't we part of their dreams? I don't know the answer. I only know that their hopes and dreams never involved either of us. They were quite eager to drop us into the caring hands of Jessica. She was barely older than us and, yet, somehow, they entrusted our lives to her for days at a time. Sure, she did have a large family in town, with aunts and uncles and cousins galore in the region to call in an emergency. She was only sixteen when they started hiring her. Maybe I did love her; maybe I still do. Quite certainly she loved Gina and me. But I never wanted her to be our mother. We already had a mother.

It wasn't wise how Jessica and Frank became our de facto foster parents. Did anyone in those carefree days in the Fifties really think that my parents' behavior was appropriate? Secluded among the ranchers and fishermen along the coast and buffered by the small hotel and inn owners, my father and mother always acted as though they were in another class. Certainly, they didn't have the kind of wealth that marked the Hearst family with its two hundred thousand acre ranch up the coast. Yet somehow the grandiose foolishness of the Spanish hacienda built by my Grandpa managed to confer on his descendants a special place in our coastal society. We had permission to do things that others couldn't, including having a teenage girl act as our mother.

"Tell me, Teddy, why did you invite Frank and me? After all these years? We haven't talked in forever. We would have, you know, but we felt you didn't want us in your lives anymore. After all this time, why invite us to this strange dinner and ask us to spend a few nights? Don't you think we wondered about that? Did you ever consider that we might have invited Otto as our own buffer?"

She pauses. "Maybe he's our way of protecting us from you? From hurting us again."

I look at Jessica in amazement. I wonder how she could ever imagine that I would want to hurt her or Frank? They certainly don't need some old Dutchman to protect them from me.

When I was a boy I lived for their approval. They defined my life as much as anyone or anything. Other boys in my grammar school probably envied me for having Jessica as a babysitter. After all, she was every bit as attractive and charming as a Hollywood star. As a high school girl she moved with a certain elegance that transported us beyond our small town views. I don't know where or how she learned such grace. Her parents were simple enough people, a local pharmacist and a stay-at-home mom renowned for her jam making skills. Jessica's other brothers and sisters were unremarkable, making Jessica all the more a rare rose in our little town's garden.

There was never a question that Jessica truly loved Gina and me. Jessica also tolerated all of my strange obsessions. She pretended great interest in whatever I prattled on about. She was always willing to play the games that I invented—and I was fond of designing elaborate board games that in retrospect involved mostly a serpentine path along which one moved solely as a result of chance determined by a throw of dice.

I suppose in some ways my games are a precursor to the way my life evolved. When I started college, I barely held a goal in mind. The subsequent stops along the nearly fifty years that followed were mostly based on the spin of a dial or an unexpected crush that made me hesitate in place for a moment too long. Far too many of those delays have been on squares that hurled me backward in my life-sized game of chutes and ladders. Looking back on my choices, it seems as though I never moved that far from square one.

Jessica was a high school cheerleader who knew her role well. She was always willing to raise a hearty cheer for me. It hurts me deeply to think that after all these years she wants someone to shield her from me.

And what about Frank? Strong Frank. Dad wasn't around my life enough to be a good male role model. In my adolescence Frank served that function. He was everything I wanted to be—or at least everything I thought a man should be. When I would lure him into swimming with me in the cold Pacific, I marveled at the breadth of his shoulders and the clean lines of his chest. He was the "after" picture from those Charles Atlas ads at the back of my comic books.

I am sure he liked me just as much as Jessica did.

Sometimes I think that both Gina and I shared the fantasy that Frank really came to our house to see us, not to spend time with Jessica. He was just a young Air Force officer, not really that much older than us, but he seemed the adult, the voice of the reason, the symbol of good government, and the man whose opinion meant something.

How could a person like that be afraid of me?

These two are my protection even to this day. I invited them to tomorrow's dinner to save me from my own foolishness. What will I do surrounded by scores of strangers?

But I can't say any of this to my lovely Jessica, can I? I try to wipe any emotion from my face before she has a chance to detect it.

(That's the way I lie to myself, imagining that I could somehow keep my feelings a secret from Jessica. She always knew what I was feeling before I even realized it myself.)

"We should get back to Otto and Frank," I say. "And you should know that without question I want you here . . . and Otto. Whatever happened in the past is history. Today is all about tomorrow."

I grimace as those words tumble out. I spoke without thinking. What in the world did that statement even mean? But I don't have time to worry. We're already stepping back into the dining room. Otto is full throttle into a new story.

I tell myself I will be a good listener. I need to prove to Jessica that I truly want all of them here.

Otto has Frank's attention. "It was such a rough crossing, even all the cabin stewards were falling ill. I was sturdy and felt nothing. So since I was the supervisor for the shift, I gave some of the boys time off. I wanted them to recover.

"In those days, we stewards would bring hot tea each afternoon to the first class cabins. One of those cabins had a very wealthy couple from Chicago traveling back to New York. Let me tell you. They were very rich.

"So I knocked on the door and asked if they would like tea. The gentleman came to the door. He seemed so surprised to see me—this tall, young, blonde Dutchman. I guess he was expecting his usual Indonesian lad. But I asked again, 'Do you and your wife want tea service?'

"He stuttered for a moment. 'No, no,' he replied. 'We want our usual.'

"'And what is that?' I asked. 'Well,' the man replied, 'our boy always brings us champagne and three glasses. Can you do that for us?'"

Jessica seats herself next to Frank, who seems to be smiling at where the story is going. I suspect this is not the first time that he has heard it.

Otto looks at me and winks. "Well, I thought to myself, this is odd. But I was there to serve, and the man had money. If he wanted champagne, we would bring him champagne and put it on his account. The ship was rocking that night, but that didn't keep me away for long. I was soon back with an ice bucket holding that bottle of champagne and three flutes just as he requested. I knocked on the door.

"Now here it comes, I'm telling you. That rich man, he opens the door. Not a stitch of clothing on him. And not a thing on his wife either. And he says, 'Come on in, young man, and open that bottle. Pour yourself a glass too.'"

Otto looks at each of us to be sure we envision the scene. "Well, I tell you, I got out of there as fast as can be. Millionaire or not, he could drink that champagne without me.

"Oh, I tell you, I have seen so many things."

The words are barely out of the old man's mouth when I notice that Frank is ready to speak. It's as though he caught the baton in some storytelling marathon. Jessica glances over at me with a look that instructs me to just sit back and enjoy the *gezellig*.

I try. I can see it is going to be a long night. And I vow to be a better host. After all, I remind myself that I wanted this visit to somehow transform me. Maybe it will take an old Dutchman to make that happen.

A Few Weeks Earlier

About a month ago, I had reason to go into our little town to shop at the hardware store. The Long Table dinner was rapidly approaching, and with some great difficulty, I had managed to keep from thinking about it. That day's errand had nothing to do with Aubrey or Leon or anything else associated with that night ahead. I was simply picking up some fencing supplies for my foreman, Jake.

It wasn't that I gave the dinner no thought. I had followed through on my pledge to invite Jessica and Frank. Of course, I had sat down with Jake to explain what I had committed all of us to do. We were well aware that for one evening in late September the Mazzetti ranch would be livelier than the norm. But foolishly I considered all that preparation my business only. There seemed no reason why anyone in our neighboring town should even know or care about the event.

I forgot where I lived.

When I went away to college to spend four years in New York City and attend Columbia I learned just how odd a little town might seem to the larger world. For me, it was a revelation slow in coming. While I had no great interest in leaving the ranch to attend school elsewhere and certainly not three thousand miles away, by that time Jessica had married Frank. She was a graduate student in art at Columbia University. She had chosen it because Frank was stationed in New Jersey, not far from Manhattan. By choosing Columbia's undergraduate school I thought I could recapture the past by being close to the two again.

It didn't turn out that way. Frank was far too busy to spend time with me. Jessica had grown so sophisticated that she frightened me a bit. Both seemed to think that I no longer needed their protection now that I was a college student. I knew they were right, but I found it hard to let them go. To deal with loss, I found another obsession. I grew homesick for the ranch.

By traveling so far for college, I lost even more than I expected. My fellow high school classmates weren't given to leaving our small town. If they did, it was to join the military or, for the more brilliant sort, to attend one of California's great public and inexpensive schools of the day. They considered me a bit of a snob for my decision to go east. That generally fit into their overall opinion of my character. For someone who would have been perfectly happy to have never left the Central Coast, I was never exactly one of the local boys. As long as there was enough of Grandma's money lingering in the accounts to pay my way, I did what I wanted, or what I thought I wanted.

Being in New York made me realize how odd I was. When you're odd in a little town, you don't get to be odd alone, because everyone knows a little bit about how strange one another is. In those days, the town up the main road from our family ranch was truly small. Yes, there was the Air Force monitoring base on the hill above it, and that bit of the federal government provided a link to a larger world. It brought in airmen and officers from around the country. Unlike Frank, the bulk of them largely stayed isolated. While Jessica's friends might have been just as eager as Jessica to date a boy in uniform, local parents tended to draw a line preventing that.

Aside from the base, the town's regulars were mostly small ranchers and owners of little seaside inns. The area was known for the beauty of the highway north along the Big Sur, but such an auto trip wasn't easy. You could only go north or south in those days. There wasn't even a highway over the mountains to Paso Robles. The route was just a rambling canyon road that was truly arduous. It resulted in our little town being a final island in a string of coastal destinations.

At the town center was a group of stores in a wooded glen. A couple of gas stations, a few motels along the shoreline, a general store, and the other usual requirements of small towns in those days: a hardware store, a drug store, a theater that was the farthest thing from a movie palace, and, of course, a few bars, We also had churches and a school . . . and naturally a cemetery on the hill.

It's not so very different today—except that there are more travelers along the coast who are eager to see the scenery or visit the Hearst

Castle. To the east, there are now world famous vineyards along a very modern highway that connects the coast to Paso Robles. There are many more hotels and restaurants, yet the place is still small and sleepy. Everyone still knows far too much about one another.

Despite that, I like to think the locals don't know about me because I prefer not to talk much to anyone in town. A reasonable man would understand that such behavior doesn't stop anyone from talking behind one's back. As I said, though, I wasn't the only odd one in town. There was also my one-time friend, Tiger Bixby.

I shouldn't have been surprised by what happened that day at the hardware store. I was just picking up some rebar and PVC pipes, the kind of purchase I would normally ask one of the ranch workers to make. But after extending my invitation to Jessica, I had become nostalgic. I wanted to drive by the house where she used to live. These days it was a quaint bed and breakfast, painted with one too many colors. I could still imagine it alive with the energy of Jessica's many brothers and sisters.

At any rate, I had the misfortune to stop at the hardware store on a day when Tiger was staffing the front counter. I should explain that his name isn't really Tiger; it's William. Ever since our high school days when he dressed up as the school mascot he became synonymous with his animal moniker. During our high school years, we were always at odds with other town folk because neither of us fit in. We liked each other though, and I don't think Tiger ever forgave me for leaving town. As a result, over the years, he has excelled in creative ways to show his disdain for me.

"Look who's here," he said as I walked into the store.

"Hi, Tiger," I said pleasantly. I hoped to make the purchase ahead quick and painless.

"What's this I hear about a fancy dinner out to your place?" he asked. Something in his tone made me certain that he already knew everything there was to know about the event.

"Well, you know," I answered, "some out-of-towners are renting the ranch to host a special dinner."

"I guess it's special all right. They say the price tag is two hundred and fifty bucks a person. What kind of fool would pay that for a single meal?" Tiger elbowed Mildred, the clerk who worked next to him at the counter. "Did you ever hear of such a thing? I guess you think those abalone of yours must be pretty special?"

"I'm not in charge. I'm just renting the place and they can charge whatever they want. It's their event. I think people who go to these dinners travel from places like Los Angeles just to participate. They don't worry about the cost. They make a weekend of it. Maybe the dinner will sell a few hotel rooms in town."

"So I guess it's too fancy for folks like me."

"Tiger, I didn't say that."

"I always wondered what that place of yours was like. Even though we were in the same class, you never had me out there. Did you know that? Now look at me . . . a sixty-eight-year-old man working in a hardware store and I never once got to see the famous Mazzetti ranch. Don't hardly seem right, now does it?"

"You never said you wanted to pay a visit."

Of course, I knew if he had asked, I might have ignored his request. I always told myself that it would be too unnerving to have him out to my cove.

"It don't seem right that one should invite oneself. What kind of person does that?"

I had enough of this. "Now you don't need to worry about an invitation, do you?" I said. "You can just buy yourself a ticket to this dinner, and I will have nothing to do with it. You can examine my place to your heart's content."

Tiger looked at me like he understood where I was going. The man was notoriously cheap. He would never spend that kind of money on a dinner. Even if he chose that route, his wife Elsbeth (also long renowned for being a skinflint) would never let him follow through. But

I saw a self-satisfied glint in his eye. It was as though he had been waiting for me to throw down exactly such a gauntlet.

"You're right. You're so right. The wife and I were just talking the other night and agreed that it was time to do the things we want to do. We ain't going to live forever. So we bought ourselves two tickets to your fancy event. What do you think about that?

"Teddy and Tiger. Back together for one night only. Two animals on the prowl, eh, Teddy? Just like in high school. Oh, I can't wait to taste your abalone."

I don't know why but hearing Tiger say that excited me more than it should have. And that scared me.

Friday, 8:31 PM

Frank is well into his story by the time we serve the apple cobbler. Jessica gives me a look that suggests everything we discussed in the kitchen is to remain unspoken at the dining table. She has nothing to worry about. There is no chance I will bring any of it up. I let Frank tell his story without interference.

"They always called him Happy," Frank says, "although he was anything but. He was actually kind of a sad fellow, the town drunk really. No one paid much attention to him. I'm not quite sure how he managed to get by. I guess people gave him odd jobs, and in those days you didn't need so much to survive. Anyway, Happy spent most of his waking hours in a well-pickled state, so perhaps he didn't much care what his clothes looked like or where he slept at night."

I can't help but watch Frank and note what a handsome fellow he still is. It is amazing how the strength of his younger years still shines through. The way he holds his body at the dinner table commands attention. There's nothing cloudy about his eyes or his mind. If he could have gazed into a crystal ball sixty years earlier, I'm sure he would have wanted to see the same thing he must see each morning in the mirror as he shaves. This man has aged well.

"So, Happy died," Frank continues with his story. He glances at Jessica as though he feels he needs her permission to continue. "Of course, he left behind no money or heirs. But the town was going to do right by him and everyone who mattered determined we would give him a proper burial. George Looper ran the cemetery in those days, but his normal right hand guy was out of town, so George asked me if I'd help out with the rites. No one expected anyone to show up for the service. Still George wanted things to go smooth. Naturally I agreed to be there, even though I was one of those guys from the base. I always liked to be part of the town."

I can sense that Jessica is looking at me as I watch Frank tell his story. She knows that I've heard this tale before. Hell, I probably first heard it the day after it happened, but it's still a favorite. Maybe that's why Frank chose to tell it tonight. Maybe he isn't competing with Otto about who can be most amusing. Maybe instead he is trying to give me strength for tomorrow. That's why I like Frank.

"It was this same time of the year when Happy died, a season when it's really too early to expect there to be any rain. But Happy's luck was about as good in death as in life, and the rain started coming down steady that morning and didn't give any appearance of wanting to let up. George and I went up the graveyard with Happy inside his coffin. It was all laid out in the back of George's hearse, and we were ready to do the interment.

"Of course, there was no money for this funeral. No one had placed a tent over the open grave. No chairs were set out for mourners. We knew as certain as the sun would come up in the east that it would just be the two of us that day. But then what should happen? Mrs. Scalpolini shows up all in black."

I feel myself smiling. I know what will come next. I think that maybe tomorrow won't be so bad. Whatever happens tomorrow could never compare to the disaster of poor Happy's burial.

Frank continues, "She must have been ninety by that point, and as far as I knew she hadn't once spoken a word to Happy in fifty years. But she liked to think of herself as a good Christian woman, and I'm sure she felt Happy shouldn't go on to the great beyond without an appropriate farewell. At any rate, with her black umbrella overhead and the rain dripping down, she slowly walked over the wet grass.

"It sort of threw a monkey wrench in our plans to make a quick job of the burial. With only the two of us, we never thought to be very formal about any of it, and the rain was coming down heavier. But now we had to consider how to put that coffin into the ground in some kind of dignified manner."

I look over at Otto who seems quite transfixed by this tale. Perhaps when everyone in the room is in the last third of one's life, stories of burial take on a new interest.

"We start moving the box down into the hole, but the soil is wet and slippery and we lose traction and suddenly the coffin is sliding. I try pulling back on it to steady it, but all I manage to do is tilt it and, well, the lid wasn't properly closed in the first place, and the whole kit and caboodle turns, opens, and the poor dead body tumbles out onto the wet earth."

Otto is shaking his head like he can picture what is likely to come next.

"There he was. Old Happy, lying in the wet dirt, outfitted in some second-hand suit that the undertaker scrounged up, with the rain coming down hard. And Mrs. Scalpolini walks right up to the edge of the grave, peers down, and says, 'Well, I'm pleased to see it really is Happy' and she turns and walks away."

Frank picks up his snifter and rolls around the cognac within and then takes a slow sip. "And that is the sad tale of Happy McMasters."

"How many times have you told that story?" I ask Frank.

"Too many times to remember or care if it's true or not," he replies.

At that, Otto roars with laughter and slaps his leg.

Yes, I decide, tomorrow will be okay. I will have friends with me. I will be in my favorite place. We will eat food that I raised. What can go wrong?

It's as though Jessica senses my thoughts. "Who else is coming to this thing tomorrow?" she asks. "I mean besides us. What folks might I know?"

The truth is I don't really have the slightest idea as to who might be there. I never requested the reservation list, nor do I know if it would have been given had I asked. There are only a handful of guests I can name for certain.

"Of course, there's the four of us. The chef is Leon Fagatelle. He owns a restaurant in San Francisco, but grew up nearby because his dad has a butcher shop in San Luis Obispo. Maybe you know them. They're good people.

"The only other person I know is coming is Tiger Bixby and, of course, his wife Elsbeth."

Jessica seems a bit surprised. "Tiger. Really? That's nice. You two used to be such good friends. I didn't know you stayed connected. You should have invited them tonight as well. I'm not sure you will get to talk to them tomorrow among all the other people."

Then she adds, "What about your sister? Surely, you invited her."

Why did she have to ask that? Something about the way she phrases the question makes me wonder if she thinks Gina will be at the dinner. The good mood from Frank's story is gone. Just thinking about the possibility of Gina at tomorrow's dinner convinces me it is bound to be a disaster.

Friday, 9:16 PM

Eventually, I manage to put aside any worry about Gina attending the Long Dinner. The rest of the supper with my guests is unremarkable. I laugh at the stories. They really are trying to cheer me up. Eventually, the men go out on the porch before heading to their bedrooms. Jessica and I wander into the living room.

Jessica peers intently at one of my watercolors. It is a California plein air landscape from early in the twentieth century. The subtle tones depict the hillside and shoreline of a small village just south of my ranch.

"It's by Albert DeRome," she says. "He did a lot of his work in the area."

"I know."

"It's a shame that he never achieved the recognition that I think he deserved. You know my parents have a very similar piece of his art. It always hung in our dining room. When we sold the family home, my siblings and I decided to leave it to the new owners. They turned the house into a bed and breakfast, and they wanted it so much. The house and the painting."

"They've taken very good care of the place," I tell her.

"Have they? That's nice. Maybe Frank and I will drive by tomorrow and take a look. It's very comforting to see this painting again. I always loved it. When I took care of you kids, I often stopped and looked at it. It made me realize how someone could capture the essence of a place and make an instant live forever. I think this painting might be why I became an art historian."

I am a little surprised to hear this. Jessica has quite a reputation in academic circles, and DeRome is at most a minor regional artist, but still I have to tell her, "It always spoke to me as well."

Jessica smiles in agreement. "I don't remember all of this other artwork. Did your family always have so many beautiful pieces? This is really an outstanding collection of early California impressionism."

I preen a bit at her observation. Every painting in this room speaks to me in a very direct way. Somehow, each one captures a bit of this place and explains why I won't leave the Central Coast.

She walks over to an oil painting of the moon over the dark sea. "This Granville Redmond is really quite extraordinary. I know he's better known for his mountain scenes, but in this painting he captures the light so perfectly. It's truly museum quality. Wherever did you get it?"

She has found the star of my collection. "I've spent more time than I should at auction houses. Especially Bonhams in San Francisco. They pull together a sale of California paintings each spring and fall."

"Even at auction, a piece like this must have gone for hundreds of thousands."

Again, Jessica shows her knowledge. The piece is definitely a big-ticket item. It's held its value nicely, although I can't say that about all the artwork in this room. I have tended to be an over-eager bidder at times.

"However could you have afforded such a piece?"

I bristle a bit. After all, Frank and Jessica have done quite well in life. Frank had a long career in the defense industry after leaving the Air Force. From what I've heard, their house in Southern California is worth millions, and, supposedly, she has her own art collection that is museum quality. Why would she question my financial ability to own this painting?

"Well, it's a hobby. After I sold part of the ranch, Gina and I had extra cash."

Immediately, I regret saying that. I don't want to discuss Gina with Jessica. She doesn't accept why my sister and I no longer get along, and I am afraid she will judge me harshly for not caring.

She ignores the opening. It seems Jessica has something else on her mind. "Seeing this room helps me understand why you don't leave the ranch. So much beauty."

"I leave occasionally."

"Then you should come down and visit us in Pacific Palisades some time. The door is always open."

I move toward the door. Maybe it's time for both of us to call it a night. But Jessica has more to say, "Frank and I really were pleased to get your invitation, and I'm sorry about what I said earlier about inviting Otto. We want you to know that we have always cared about you.

"We have also always loved your sister, and we know you weren't happy when we sided with her about the way you sold half the ranch. We recognize that the decision was yours to make, not ours. Certainly we never expected it to be a barrier between us."

"It hasn't been."

"Okay, but we haven't seen you since that happened. I just want to be clear that we accept your choices. It's none of our business. We just want what's best for you, even though at times we wished you would spread your wings more. To us it seems as though you're afraid to leave this place."

"Why should I leave? Everything I want is here."

Almost fifty years have passed since I left this ranch to attend college in New York City. I experimented then with big cities and crowds, with trying to love other people, and with spreading my wings. I once had hopes and dreams. They never seemed to amount to much.

When I graduated and came home, Dad welcomed my help in running the ranch. Mom was drinking a lot more by then, and they were more prone than ever to head off on their trips. Without thinking, I took over being boss. Gina had her own life. She left the place and didn't look back.

I stayed. I felt comfortable. I avoided the things I didn't want to see, and I wandered on my bluff and strolled on my beach. Sure, at times I dreamt of other things. I knew that time was slipping by, but there always seemed plenty of it ahead. Then one day, after decades have passed, a red-haired motorcycle rider shows up to make a proposition and for some reason I suddenly realized how old I had become, how few people remain in my life, and what little motivates me.

I made a decision to do something new. Months later, I remind myself silently that I need to stay positive about the day ahead. It can still turn out okay.

"I think it's time we went to bed," I say.

A New Day, Saturday, 1:57 AM

It's in the darkened hours when the moon has risen and the fog banks flee, when the frogs down in the creek bed croak out for love, and the evening breeze whispers through the dry leaves of the euca-lyptus. It's when the rising tide breaks on the rocky shoreline and sends the scent of the salt sea up the hills into my house. It should be a reminder of why I love this place; instead, it is in that quiet time of the night I feel panic. Despite everything I tell myself, I know I need to escape this day ahead.

Frank and Jessica are in the guest room where I made their bed with the stiff French linens my mother always preferred. Otto is given my sister's room. I like to imagine that placing him there is equivalent to burning sage in an ancient Indian ritual. Perhaps his presence will clear the walls of memories and obligations to Gina.

The house is as restless as I am. It breathes like an old man who can't sleep well after too many brandies. The massive beams in the living room creak as they release the heat of the day. The thick adobe walls that so pleased my father gather in the sound of the ocean down below but dampen it into the drone of a somnambulant dream. There's a clatter in the piping for no good reason.

I get up. Outside the moon is sinking toward the ocean. It carries with it a broadening ribbon of yellow light that shimmers over the swells of the sea. It casts shadow and light almost in syncopation with the dashing of the nighttime waves against eroding rock. From the small balcony off the master bedroom, I command a view through the "v" of the creek bed leading to my bluff and beach. I overlook the gravel road that connects my abalone beds to the highway that in turn connects us to the great cities of California. Along the side of the gravel driveway, just before it turns for its descent to the coast, three tall eucalyptus trees frame the ocean.

I hear the water. I smell the salt air. There's a squeak of a bat as it flies around the eaves feasting on small insects. I hear nothing from my guests within. Perhaps they are snoring; perhaps they are tossing and turning. I don't know. I don't care.

The tomorrow I feared has turned into today. Midnight has come and gone, and still I fret over what I have done. For a year, I have had an opportunity to avoid the event ahead. Yet now the brink is before me.

Somehow I have allowed myself to pull together too much of my life in one place. I wanted to keep all former actions and longings hidden by a veil of forgetfulness. I only wanted the burnished memories that were pleasant and nostalgic. Somehow I have done exactly the opposite. I have moved the past out from behind its veil and positioned it for a close up.

I have been lying to myself for so many years that I would no longer recognize truth if it came knocking at the door and sat down for dinner. What was it about Aubrey appearing and proposing this Long Table event that made me think I could change?

I hear the slightest of ruffling of wings. Perhaps an owl is flying over. Perhaps wisdom has appeared.

I only said yes to Aubrey because he embodied the energy and the vibrancy that I always wanted. Because Aubrey was here, on my land, I thought I could become like him. That's why I invited Frank. It wasn't to have Jessica here. It was to see Frank. Frank, the only man I ever really loved, even though he never knew it. No one ever knew it. No one should ever know it. After so many years, why does it even still matter?

I thought this dinner would give an excuse to reestablish contact. We could sit side by side and laugh over food and drink. In the dim light of a waning fall evening, I could look at him as much as I wanted and who would be the wiser? It might be my last chance to have such a view, the unfulfilled longing of a lifetime of longings. Just two old men. Nothing more.

But Aubrey. How did he manage to complicate things so much? Of all the chefs in the world, he selected Leon. I have tried to tell myself I didn't remember the boy. But that is so untrue. He is another fantasy of my past, from days when I was already too old to be having such fantasies. I always went out of my way to find reasons to deliver our beef to the Fagatelle butcher shop during those years Leon helped out. Anyone else from the ranch could have been on that delivery truck, but I wanted to see the young man who worked in the back. He wasn't anything special, but he reminded me of me. He too seemed caught within some curtain that constrained him to Central Coast norms.

I was mistaken. Leon knew what he wanted and he knew how to leave. Now for one single night, both Frank and Leon will be on my bluff above my beach at a dinner that celebrates my ranch.

This old man—who never admitted to one person that mattered that he was gay—will have to deal with both Frank and Leon at the same dinner. And then the thought whispers in my head, "Don't forget about Tiger."

How will I survive this new day?

PART TWO

THE GUESTS:
THE MORNING OF THE DINNER

Saturday, 7:04 AM

Sorry to surprise you, but there's more to the story than Teddy. It's time to step back. A reasonable reader might have thought this was just a story about Teddy. After all, he's been our only focus so far. But the man can be a bit tiresome, the way he's so tentative and worrisome. Some might want to tell him to have some balls.

So settle back, because actually this is also the story of the Long Table Dinner and one specific night. Of course, that also makes it Teddy's story, but it is not his alone. When a few hundred people dine along the ocean at a single table, there are many other tales. These tales aren't like the stars in the sky, in fixed and predictable paths. They are more like bits of flotsam floating in a strong current. If you understood physics well enough and employed a robust calculator to compute the trajectories, you might stand a good chance of understanding where each bit ends up. Then you would be like God, but none of us are God.

Still, it's time to consider these bits.

It is early on the morning of the Long Table. The sun has been up for well over an hour. There appears a low cloud of dust over the grass-covered hills. It hovers above the gravel road that connects the highway to the coast. Aubrey Amundsen and his team of Long Table employees are arriving en masse. The initial vehicle to appear is a 1940s-era passenger bus, perhaps one of the first of the Greyhound vehicles. There is nothing sleek about it. Once brightly painted in a swirl of colors, the lingering shades and designs suggest it might have been decorated during that fabled summer of love. However, time has muted it all.

As the bus turns off the highway, it stirs up the gravel road's reddish-brown powder. Its windows are all open and the dust swirls into the interior. That doesn't stop the five people inside from singing loudly. They, too, appear to have stepped out of the summer of love. Yet they were all certainly born long after the Sixties.

Each person on the team has been up since six. As with every Long Table event, there were last minute actions to clean up after the previous night's dinner. Only when all was in order did the entourage begin its one-hour drive to the Mazzetti ranch. The five consider themselves the best of friends. They have spent six months together—cooking dinners, entertaining folks, discovering new farms, and traveling to avoid a more settled life of responsibility. Each had their individual reason for signing on to this culinary circus. For now, they are here to serve dinner.

In the previous season, at an orchard set among blooming cherry trees perched above Lake Michigan, Annabelle was hired for a single night. She is a native born to that ridge of a peninsula jutting into the cold waters north of Green Bay. She never considered the old orchards home. The depleted fishing villages and expensive resorts of the area were just a place to escape. One year ago, she graduated from high school and knew she had no desire to spend any more time around her father. Lacking resources to head off to college and having no skills like juggling or acrobatics that might have permitted an escape to a real circus, she latched onto the Long Table.

A young man named Chase is altogether a very different sort. While this is already his second year with the team, it has never been quite clear how he was hired. One day he started following the group. In those early days he would jump in to handle different tasks. He proved adept at organizing and planning. He was always friendly and conveyed a certain fairy-like charm that seemed to please the female guests. Chase seldom talked about himself or why he chose this roving life. By now Aubrey can no longer run his business successfully without the young man's assistance.

Max's role is more clearly cut. He is both the driver and the mechanic. He looks and acts both roles. To him, this group of rovers is just a job. He's never been a person to form ties, but prefers to live up to his name—to the max. While the rest of the group might overindulge in the fancy food and fine wine that are the hallmarks of their company, Max tends to find the best burger at a local bar where he can drink a few too many beers. By morning he is always sober, if a bit surly. He is getting everything he wants out of life.

Then there are Cat and Hillary, the only couple in this traveling troupe. They stay in the group for each other, fearing that if they were to leave they would somehow lose one another forever. They never seem to realize that they could drop out along the way in any one of the many towns in America and continue to live and love as a couple. Perhaps they are too focused on one another to recognize their options.

So on this fine sunny morning in September, four are seated in the benches near the front of the bus (there are sleeping bunks in the rear). Max is in the driver's seat. The windows remain open, the dust streams in, and the morning sun flows in along with the ocean breezes. All are singing "California, Here I Come." They started a silly tradition two months earlier of welcoming a new site with a song relevant to the location. As the bus makes its final way toward the venue *du jour*, one in the group, usually Max, begins belting out the words of a song that they all know. Soon they all shout the words at the top of their lungs, joining their spirits together for the night ahead.

Ahead of the bus, Aubrey rides his roaring motorcycle. He is the person who makes all the decisions on what transportation to acquire. He carries a soft spot for vehicles that require frequent tinkering by Max. In his mind, it defines what the Long Table is all about—a celebration of everything that's disappearing in modern America: heirloom foods, family farms, conviviality, a spirit of anarchism, and a respect for the oddball.

Over the roar of his engine, Aubrey can hear his workers' song. He feels in his bones that this is going to be another great dinner. Admittedly, the previous night's event was a bit uneven. Max drank too much beer. Chase was in a strange mood. Sometimes the kid seemed to rev up his sexuality to see what he can get away with.

Still Aubrey feels good about the event ahead. The Abalone Dinner, as he likes to call it in his mind, is definitely a first. Never before has he featured a menu involving the giant sea slug. It is just as unusual for him to convince a man of Leon's prominence to serve as guest chef. Leon's presence alone has lured several guests from Northern California and is probably the key reason tonight's event is fully booked. In fact, due to the demand, Aubrey added fifty seats in the last week. The night ahead is definitely pushing the limits of what his team can pull off.

He glances in his rear view mirror to make certain Dixie, his final on-site employee, is bringing up the rear. In her trailer, she carries the bulk of the Long Table's key items, such as the folding tables, the chairs, the linens, the china, silverware, and glassware. Financially it doesn't make sense to rent those things in every town.

On the other hand, the pop-up kitchen is always a custom rental. It needs to vary with every site based on menu, what equipment might already be in place, and potential weather conditions. In some cases, locations are also used for weddings or other events and therefore already have an existing catering kitchen or pavilion. Tonight is a trickier spot. Nothing is available on-site other than electrical power and fresh water. In preparation, Leon and Aubrey spent hours going over the requirements. Just in case of rain, they planned a large pavilion tent to shelter the kitchen. Everything for this is being rented and trucked in. Soon the temporary stoves and prep tables, the refrigeration units, and steam tables will appear.

The original menu seemed so promising. Then, as Leon and he went through the specific equipment needed for the proposed dishes, Aubrey kept striking items. Selling tickets at $250 a pop might seem pricey, but there can be too many costs. He must minimize the rentals. He wants to avoid extra costs for laborers to set up and take down an elaborate kitchen—especially if it's merely to satisfy Leon's ego. At the back of Aubrey's mind is his fear that it was a mistake to hire an ambitious chef who is gunning for his first Michelin star.

Aubrey glances forward and then into his rear view mirror. Where is the truck with the kitchen equipment? It should already be here. The team needs time to set up the main tent and then install the cooking equipment.

The kids on the bus are still singing, with no concern for the schedule. The long gravel road crests the hill and then heads down toward the abalone tanks. Aubrey sees the turnoff toward the house of Teddy Mazzetti. He considers that guy kind of a prick, but to date Aubrey has restrained from stating this aloud. He mourns once more that he didn't talk Pedrag into hosting the dinner on the billionaire's bluff. That site would have been a coup.

Everyone knows it's one thing to eat on a ranch that seldom welcomes visitors, but it is surely an entirely different opportunity to promote dinner at the home of a technology mastermind. Aubrey knows he could have sold at least three hundred tickets for a night like that.

Saturday, 7:37 AM

Some twenty miles away from the coast is the small college town called San Luis Obispo. On its outskirts is the warehouse of a local supplier of rental gear. Leon Fagatelle is inside.

The situation is a mess, an absolute mess. Awake and active since five, Leon feels exhausted, yet it is still hours until he will serve the first dishes of his dinner. Already, he is cursing the day that Aubrey appeared in his restaurant to talk about a "once in a lifetime" opportunity.

He never expected to be roaming a rental warehouse in San Luis Obispo at seven in the morning and scrounging up whatever he could muster in support of tonight's preparation. He planned to have been on site thirty minutes ago and already prepping the veggies. If there is anything Leon is good at, beyond the creativity of the food itself, it is organizing a kitchen timeline. He never calculated on hiring an incompetent supplier of prep pans.

Luckily, he knows all his ingredients are already on their way to the Mazzetti ranch. At least he planned right on that. Earlier in the morning, he securely placed them in a refrigerated truck that he sent on toward the site. Because he had worried so much about what could be purchased locally, he spent the previous day at San Francisco markets to ensure the best and freshest produce. The night before, he sat next to the driver, as they traveled south and parked the truck at his father's home overnight. First thing this morning Leon and his father opened the butcher shop cooler and added to the truck all the Mazzetti meat that his father had precut and aged. That included the abalone that Leon's supplier had pre-delivered to the butcher shop's coolers. After a few minutes of loading, Leon was able to send Becca, his sous chef, and the driver on their way. For that brief moment, Leon felt in control.

But pristine ingredients will mean nothing without a kitchen. Leon thought and planned out every item he would want or need. Aubrey was equally maniacal. By the time the two mutually agreed on their menu and what was needed to execute it at a remote site, both men thought everything would be eminently doable. Now Leon realizes his hubris.

This morning when he stopped by the rental place he felt good. The first truck was already on its way. He would need only a moment to confirm the dispatch of the cooking tent and the pre-ordered equipment. Then he walked into a scene of chaos where no one knew what ladle was going where. This vendor supplied conventions in the area and the large catered weddings at picturesque wineries. Nothing Leon requested was out of the ordinary, yet confusion reigned.

It took him fifteen minutes just to find the person in charge, then another ten to locate his original pre-order list, and even more precious minutes were wasted in getting everyone organized. Luckily everything required for the main tent including the mobile ovens and burners are now in one place. He is able to send that truck quickly on its way. Aubrey's team will have to direct the arriving crew on the details of the kitchen set up because Leon can't leave yet. His only comfort is that his sous chef will already be on site with a truck filled with the best of meat, abalone, and produce. Becca understands what he wants done. She will at least start some dishes on time.

Simple things are his undoing. All the standard rental items had been laid out: the number of roasting pans and sauce pans, the platters and special dishes, and the extra linens. How could they now not be boxed and in place? His father assured him that the owner of Triple Coast Rentals was the best in the county, so Leon hadn't worried.

He sighs, takes a deep breath, and searches out his triple espresso. He needs the jolt of caffeine, even though his final truck is nearly loaded.

"Hey, Leon," he hears. His father is walking through the warehouse. "Everything okay, son?"

"Dad, what are you doing here?" he asks. Leon doesn't like help, a trait he shares with his dad.

"David, the owner, called me. He's thinks you're about to go ballistic."

"Nothing's ready."

"But now?"

"Well, now, I've got everything organized, found everything I need, and the truck is about to head out."

"So all is good."

"Well . . . "

"Don't say 'well,' Leon. Just look around, do a final check, and get in your car to head to the coast. There's still a twenty-minute drive ahead, but much of it is along the shore. Take a moment to enjoy the ocean. Just remember. Everything will turn out okay."

"But the incompetence."

Michael Fagatelle holds up his hand. "You aren't being tested. It's just a dinner. Remember Teddy Mazzetti has been a friend of this family for decades. Whatever you do he will be happy with. He always had a soft spot for you."

"Dad, the dinner's not for Mr. Mazzetti."

"I know, I know, it's for those 250 paying guests and that Aubrey character. Nevertheless just enjoy the day. You don't owe them anything other than doing your best. After tonight you'll never see them again. Have some fun."

"You don't get it Dad."

"What don't I get?"

"The dinner's not for any of those people."

"Then who's it for?"

"It's for Pedrag Miles. He's going to be there."

"So? He's just another rich man."

"Yeah, so rich. Yet I still owe him over a million dollars for Point Conception. It's money he wants back. I have to please him tonight, or I might lose my restaurant and everything I care about."

Michael would like to tell his son to just focus on his dinner, but he doesn't. He knows all too well what it's like to owe someone money.

Saturday, 8:16 AM

Except for some physicists, most think of time as moving forward in a linear way with everything in its own place. No one expects Leon's worries to act like some astrophysical quark particle that impacts actions at the abalone farm. After all, everyone there knows what to do. That includes Chase.

In the young man's mind, the morning is going quite smoothly. For nearly a year now, he's been in charge of pre-event logistics. After that amount of time, Aubrey barely pays attention to Chase's work. Chase likes it that way.

Some might think Chase's job is easy because everyone on the Long Table team likes him. That always makes it a snap for him to get activities quickly in place. When he hands out directions, no one ever has a chip on their shoulder or acts all puffed up or eager to say no. From the very beginning with the troupe, he commanded respect. In fact most of the team no longer remember how the Long Table ran before Chase's arrival. The nearly three years before he attached himself to the group seems like ancient and challenging times. Now, whenever he is around, things work as planned and everyone has more fun. And after all that's why this team does what it does.

None of the crew would likely admit it, but they place Chase in a special part of their affections. If they ever talked to one another in detail (which they are too complacent to ever do) they would be astonished to realize that each of them sees a different virtue in the man. But in the end, none of that really matters. At the conclusion of a dinner, they all sleep in their bunks on the bus and say goodnight to one another like in some long-canceled television show. They get along, and whenever they don't, it is usually Chase who brings them back together.

In short, Chase is their man.

Aubrey and Chase visited the abalone farm together a couple of months earlier. At that time, Chase scouted everything he needed to know for the actual day of the planned event. He took a few photos, wrote quite a number of notes, and filed away even more details in his astonishing memory. As soon as the caravan pulls into the ranch that morning, he has his mapped-out plan of action.

He directs each vehicle exactly where it needs to go. He releases Max, Cat, and Hillary to pre-stage the items that need unloading: the chairs, the tables, and the special event dishes. He asks Annabelle to mark the parking lot dimensions with a spray can of paint. Unlike many event locales they use, this place is blessed with a sufficiently large level flat space perfect for handling over a hundred cars. Next he directs Annabelle to place the standard signs along the driveway and onto the highway.

For each event, the most ticklish part is always the same. Chase needs to make sure Aubrey reviews the night's events with the site's owners. While Aubrey might claim everything has been pre-arranged, Chase is frequently surprised by how easily things fall part. That usually begins with the owners not realizing what lies ahead. In Chase's mind it is always Aubrey's fault; the man dominates conversations and pushes ideas without waiting for agreement. A part of Chase always feels a little sorry for the poor landowner who suddenly realizes just what it means to have hundreds of strangers descend. But he never extends more than a small of amount of sympathy because he doesn't have much patience for that particular kind of dismay. People should know what they are agreeing to before they agree to it. Chase is a person who always knows what he is doing.

He finds it easy to set his sights on where he wants to go. He seldom allows much to get in his way. When he first encountered Aubrey's little band of traveling foodies, he simply decided to hitch a ride. No one could have explained how Chase ended up on the bus that first night. Everyone assumed someone else had invited him. Frankly, Aubrey assumed the boy was a one-night stand for one of his other workers, but he couldn't decide which one of them. But sex had nothing to do with the boy's presence. He simply curled up beneath one of the bench seats and fell asleep within minutes, long before any one could ask him who invited him, or what he was doing.

No one felt a need to ask the question in the morning as the bus prepared to leave. Somehow it seemed right that Chase should stay on board. When they arrived at that day's destination, things were chaotic as they always were; yet somehow Chase always appeared in the right spot with the right tool. As a result that day went a little smoother than the ones before. No one thought to challenge Chase when he stayed on the bus again the second night. Each of them felt he could be a worthwhile addition. That's exactly what he proved to be.

Since the arrival of Chase, Aubrey has enjoyed his business more. For Aubrey, all of the fun is in chasing down some new locale or highlighting an unusual ingredient. Actually he has no interest in the details involved in making a dinner work, such as selling the tickets or serving the food. He also enjoys sparring with the hosts. Chase, on the other hand, would prefer to do nothing with humoring the landowner. To-do lists are more Chase's thing.

Chase watches as the group's vehicles are put into place for the event ahead. He notices that Aubrey is strolling back from the main house up the drive, and Chase suspects the older man walking with Aubrey is the owner. Owners always amble with a certain arrogance and diffidence. They think they are in control, yet they soon begin to realize they have relinquished responsibility to a group of misfits in tie-dyed t-shirts.

As though a throwback to the eighties, Chase is quite fond of wearing very short shorts. He knows his legs are his best feature—strong and at the same time delicate and lithesome. On his legs the faint blonde hair shimmers in strong sunlight. Chase has always been overly fond of watching how the owners or their wives react to his legs. Most men pay no attention; most wives do. Eventually, some men notice, but only after they jealously realize their wives are paying too much attention.

Sometimes there are male owners who directly favor Chase's boyish looks. Even from a distance, Chase suspects this owner fits into that latter camp. The man should be paying attention to both the road he walks and Aubrey's words. Instead he is pointedly staring in Chase's direction. Chase, knowing what that means, decides to have some fun.

"Aubrey," he yells out. He begins a quick run up the gravel. His long blonde hair flops a bit and grows just a touch disheveled. An element of chaos and a slight sheen of sweat make him look younger and more vulnerable, or so he thinks. "We have a problem. The chef hasn't arrived."

It's true. Normally the absence of the chef would be a major concern, but Chase received a phone call twenty minutes earlier. He knows Leon is on the road and has a good reason for the delay. Besides Chase also is fully aware that the important elements—the cooking tent and equipment—are in place. Max is already working with that team. There's time aplenty.

No issue exists, but Chase likes to keep Aubrey a little jittery. It helps to reinforce just how valuable Chase is when the boss isn't quite certain everything is going his way.

"There were some problems down in San Luis Obispo," Chase explains. "Leon had trouble getting everything he needed for tonight, but he's called in and said that the details are in place and the truck is en route. Still, it's cutting things close."

All the while he speaks, Chase looks directly at this owner. The man's eyes skitter away, like a lizard on a hot boardwalk who hears approaching footsteps. Chase finds that amusing.

"Then there's no problem," Aubrey says. "There's plenty of time to get everything set up, and Leon's the best."

"Yes, he is," the owner interjects. "I've known him since he was a kid."

Chase is surprised by this affirmation. He takes a more careful look at the man. He seems to be about seventy, just under six feet and just over weight. He still has most of his hair, but it is definitely thinning. All in all, Chase judges him an acceptable old man.

"I'm Chase," he says and thrusts out his hand.

"I'm Teddy. I own the place."

Aubrey jumps in, "Ah, my two essential sidekicks. Chase and Teddy. Together you're going to make this night one to remember."

Chase laughs. He can tell Teddy smiles at hearing him laugh. He likes that.

"Not if I don't get back to work."

Chase turns and walks down the hill.

He doesn't need to look back to know that Teddy's eyes are following him all the way down the hill.

He guesses he knows what kind of owner this one is.

But even Chase doesn't know how much Teddy is thinking about the spark of electricity he felt upon shaking the hand of this young man, and Teddy makes a vow to himself. He will avoid Chase for the rest of the day.

Saturday, 10:03 AM

In the small village, just north of the Mazzetti ranch, a tall redwood dwarfs a story-and-a-half house. Behind that house built at the turn of the last century is another more modern structure. While designed to resemble an old carriage house, it is clearly much larger than the original house facing the main street. Together they comprise the Old Redwood Bed and Breakfast.

This inn is just far enough down the main street to avoid being part of the downtown area. People like it that way. On the other hand, the commercial district is only a few blocks long so it doesn't take much to be outside of it. Still the house conveys a character that suggests it was an important home even in the early days. A passer-by might think that it had been home to the doctor or the hotelier or some equally important personage of the nineteenth century.

In the present, it is freshly painted with a palette of colors, and all of its plantings are carefully tended. Roses bloom along the white picket fence and well-pruned shrubs nestle against the house. Everything suggests a precious interior filled with antiques and graced by afternoon wine tastings and morning scones with strawberry jam.

Two of its guests, Henry and Sylvia Metternich, sit down to a late breakfast that features those very scones and jam. Henry would prefer a meal with fried eggs and a rasher of bacon, but he isn't certain that the inn even offers anything more substantial than a continental breakfast. There are no signs that one can ask for heartier fare. Even if such items were available, he knows that Sylvia would frown if he requested eggs or breakfast meats. If he argued, she would claim that it is because she prefers to enjoy a more substantial lunch in just a few hours. Henry knows the disapproval is really her way to keep cholesterol and calories out of his diet. Since Henry is slathering the scones with the offered whipped cream and jam, clearly she isn't having much success at her goals.

Still, Henry is being careful. And for good reason. He does not intend to cross his wife on this weekend. He booked the holiday as a surprise for her. She relishes treks into the hinterlands of California with stops in old buildings with even older beds. The evening before when they arrived, there was a small hiccup; he realized the room he booked was not part of the original historic structure. Instead they were offered a spacious suite in the more recently built carriage house. Sylvia sighed with disappointment as they were escorted to the rear building, but she put on a brave face to show her understanding. Truthfully, the room turned out to be the much better accommodation. From the second story, it overlooks a small creek. There is even a balcony.

He tried to convince Sylvia to ask for breakfast to be served in their private space, but when she awoke, she was intent on eating in the main house's communal space. He isn't certain whether it was because she hopes to meet other guests or because she wants to breathe in the spirit of a living space more than a hundred years old.

Henry has never fully understood his wife's fascination with sleeping in old buildings. Their home in the Valley in Los Angeles is old enough in Henry's view. It was built in the 1980s, but Sylvia frequently complains that it lacks character. She wants roots. He tries to accept that.

Unfortunately, their only roots are entwined in the Valley house. They purchased it when it was newly constructed. Their only son spent his teenage years growing up in that two-story, stucco, pseudo-Mediterranean. Now it has become a memorial of sorts to Matthew. The shock of his death during the first Gulf War nearly destroyed their marriage. Keeping the house and finding ways to surprise Sylvia with small tricks remains Henry's price to pay for keeping their lives intact. Retirement looms on the horizon, and he often worries about how they will maneuver through the emptiness without jobs to mask their loss.

That's why he knows these weekends are so important. This one is more so than the others. September marks the anniversary of Matthew's death and he needs something truly major to soften the past. Booking two tickets to the Long Table Dinner at the Mazzetti Ranch is meant to be that grand diversion.

Sylvia is a great user of Facebook. Over the past months she often showed him posts featuring elaborate dinners around the country. They all portrayed the same long tables laden with food in bucolic settings. Those photos prompted Henry into some sleuthing; he discovered the event's web site and signed up for advance announcements. When he learned that the group would be hosting a dinner near Sylvia's favorite seaside retreat, he pounced on the chance to surprise her—even though the price of tickets gave him a start. With two nights at the inn and other expenses, this weekend will cost him well north of a thousand dollars. He is hopeful that it will prove worth it.

Now the dilemma is when to surprise Sylvia with unveiling the details of the evening ahead. He can't put it off much longer. If he doesn't let her know about the evening's plans, she will force him into a long lunch and an afternoon of wine tasting. That would be completely wrong. They would wind up with no appetite, or worse come back to the room after a few too many sips of wine, fall asleep on the comfortable king-size bed, and slumber right through the event. No, he needs to tell her now. He can't risk letting her work herself into planning the afternoon ahead.

Already, Sylvia is on the prowl around the dining room, studying the old photos and the one small watercolor that line its walls. Henry hasn't really looked at them. Breakfast rooms in places like this are fond of faded old photos of streetscapes from a hundred years ago, always labeled with tiny plaques beneath overly ornate frames. This place looks to be the same. However, Sylvia is intent on inspecting each one.

The innkeeper walks in with a fresh pot of coffee and another tray of scones. Perhaps, Henry realizes, they aren't the last to get up. Even though it is already after ten, she is refreshing her buffet table.

"Aren't those old photos marvelous?" the woman says to her guests. "I don't know if you read the details in the pamphlet, but this house is just redolent with history. It was one of the very first homes in the town built after the great fire in 1888 that burned almost everything. And the same family lived here from the day the house was built until the day we bought it sixteen years ago. It's a rare thing to have such continuity, even in a little town like this."

She walks over to where Sylvia is standing. "That is the drug store that belonged to the next to last owner of this house. The druggist died in the 1970s, I think, and left the house to his son who still lives in town. That's the man we bought this house from."

"Oh, come over here, there's a picture of the whole family, as well as some shots of the other children. You know one of those children became a famous art historian, well if art historians can be considered famous. But in a little place like this, we like to claim whatever fame we can."

Henry finds the innkeeper annoying. She acts as though she were a native daughter of this village, even though he knows that she spent her entire working life in Bakersfield and only moved to the coast to open this inn when she and her husband retired. He pays attention to such details in the pamphlets at these inns.

"Look at this. This picture is of Jessica Venturi, the art historian I mentioned. Well, Venturi is her maiden name. She's Jessica Mueller now. That's the name people know her by. She and her husband Frank visited us when we opened the inn. They came just for our opening.

"See, there they are. He was in the Air Force. I think he retired as a general. Their story is so romantic. They met here in this town. You wouldn't know this, but there once was a small Air Force base just up the hill. It monitored the Pacific for missiles or some such thing . . ."

Something significant has occurred. Henry is no longer listening to the innkeeper. He rushes to his wife's side. She is visibly shaken. They know the name of Frank Mueller all too well. Henry looks at the photograph while holding tightly to his wife's hand. There is no mistaking the look of this man.

It is indeed the same General Franklin Mueller—the General Mueller who commanded his son's squadron—the very man they blame for ruining their lives.

Henry curses to every god he could think of or know. He can only pray that the Long Table Dinner later that night will somehow erase this most horrific of coincidences. As he looks at Sylvia, completely lost in her thoughts and despair, unguarded as she is in that moment, he knows only that he must make things right. He can't let this day be ruined.

Saturday, 11:00 AM

Nearby, in another house in the same village, a cuckoo clock is on its eleventh and final tweet. Tiger Bixby hates this clock almost as much as he hates all of his wife Elsbeth's various German trinkets and mementos. Most were inherited from his in-laws. He was never fond of them either.

Tiger is feeling restless. It is his day off, and he never knows what to do around the house when he isn't working or embarked on a major project. He doesn't dare start any major project today. Today is his wife's special day. She is going to get all dressed up, force Tiger into some kind of monkey suit as well, and they will head down the coast highway to the Mazzetti Ranch. Oh, she is beside herself with glee at the thought of the evening ahead. It is all she has talked about for the last week and a half.

Not that Tiger begrudges her any bit of her joy. He understands why this evening is so important to the woman, even though he doesn't think she understands one iota about her own motivation. The two of them have been together nearly fifty years, raised three kids, and celebrated the birth of five grandchildren. Admittedly, they have been through a lot. At her heart, Elsbeth is still the giddy high school girl he married right after graduation. She lives in her dreams, and tonight she anticipates one of them might come true.

Oh, he knows that she could never actually verbalize her dream. He suspects she doesn't even realize how she has embedded a fantasy deep in her soul. Funny that after all this time together, he has learned to truly love and know Elsbeth. Maybe she only views him as a roommate of chance, a provider who barely ekes out a living for them such as it is, and a somewhat reliable companion for watching the nightly news and "Dancing with the Stars"—but for him their relationship is another story.

Tiger is okay with that. He never expected a lot out of life, and so it never disappoints him. He realizes that he can be an ass at times. In particular, he regrets how he recently tried to embarrass Teddy Mazzetti in the hardware store. He really bears the man no ill will. Sometimes he just wants others to be as uncomfortable as he is, and Teddy can be such an easy mark.

Tiger just hopes his words and actions won't come back to haunt him later in the evening.

He recalls when Elsbeth showed him the printout of the Long Table Dinner with such enthusiasm. There was a spark in her eyes that he hasn't seen in years. Another fellow might have been jealous or upset. Tiger's initial reaction was laser focused on the price.

"Two hundred and fifty dollars!" he practically shouted. Half a grand for a dinner for two. He thought her loony for the mere suggestion.

"But look where it is," Elsbeth proclaimed.

Seeing the location sealed his fate: the Mazzetti Ranch. That told Tiger everything he needed to know about why this dinner was so important to his wife. Back in his high school years (and maybe just like all his years), Tiger didn't fit in. He never understood why. He'd look in the mirror and think to himself that he was a decent looking fellow. Even to this day, he keeps his weight in check, and he remains tall and reasonably groomed. He judges that he has a reasonably handsome face. But everyone always looks right through him. Maybe he isn't really very talented at anything. He never did connect with writing or arithmetic. Sports eluded him. He was a bit too slow or a bit too fast for whatever was going on. The only thing he ever excelled in was dressing as the school mascot. As a result he's still called Tiger.

He figures being a loner was why Teddy started to hang out with him back in high school. There was no other good explanation. Teddy was smart, always at the top of his class, didn't give a damn about any of the town's sports, and usually paid little attention to his fellow students, and, in turn, most high school kids ignored Teddy. Tiger didn't mind any of that baggage. The two of them started to do things together, not that much really, but enough that the other kids began to think of the two weirdoes as friends.

That's what attracted Elsbeth. She loved reading and she loved smart talk, plus she always wanted in on things other people didn't get to do. She only started talking to Tiger because she hoped being nice to him would let her become friends with Teddy. The recluse rancher kid was her true target.

Tiger knew that then. He knows it now, but he isn't certain Elsbeth ever knew it, so when she showed him the flyer for the dinner all he said was, "Where are we going to get five hundred bucks?"

"I've been saving up money for our fiftieth wedding anniversary," she replied. "I didn't want to tell you because I know you don't like parties, but really the kids expect one. I haven't gotten all that far in the planning or the saving. Your job just don't pay that much, and I can't get any more hours at the bakery. But still I got a little put by."

"How much?" he wanted to know.

"Enough," she replied.

"And what about the party?" he pressed.

"The party's really for the kids," she replied. "If they want us to have a golden anniversary they can throw us a do at the Vets Hall and pay for it themselves. There's enough of them. We should do something we want with my money. And I want to go to this dinner."

"You think I want to do this?"

Elsbeth sighed. Decades ago, Tiger already learned that this particular sigh meant that there would be no way to win any argument ahead.

"Think of it," she said. "We can have dinner at the Mazzetti place. Teddy was your best friend in high school. You know I always wanted to go out there and see that famous ranch house. You never invited me, because you always wanted to keep Teddy as your friend and not mine. But I still want to visit the place. Besides we deserve a fine meal. It's been nearly fifty years," she said, then stopped and blushed.

Their marriage had been odd, Tiger reasoned, but one thing was true: they had always been there for one another. By now, they knew what each other was thinking, and he knew exactly which memories coursed through her mind.

It was all about a dinner before the spring dance, when Teddy and Tiger had agreed to go on a double date that would start with a fancy meal at the town's best restaurant. Tiger and Elsbeth were to meet Teddy and his date at this spot overlooking the Pacific, dine, and then attend the dance at the high school gym. As Tiger recalled, it was decorated to the theme of "Springtime in Paris."

When he never heard Teddy mention a name for the date, he should have been suspicious about the likelihood of this plan's successful conclusion. When it became clear the only reason Elsbeth agreed to be his date was because she found out Teddy would be part of the evening, his alarms should have gone off. But he didn't think like that.

That long ago night, Tiger and Elsbeth sat in the restaurant a long time. No Teddy showed up. The two ate their lobster dinner at a table for four. Tiger couldn't afford lobster in those days anymore than he could now, but he paid the bill and pretended to enjoy it. When they left the restaurant with still no Teddy in sight, the sun had already set. Elsbeth wanted to go home. But Tiger, having secured wine for the evening, convinced her to park on the bluffs north of town, open a bottle, drink away their disappointment, and finally decide what to do about the dance.

Neither was accustomed to drinking. The bottle was soon gone. Freed from inhibition, they started kissing which soon progressed beyond that. Even in the scramble of removing clothes as they made out in the back seat of the old Ford, Tiger somehow knew that in Elsbeth's mind his naked body was a substitute for Teddy. But he was a virgin. He didn't care. He went for it.

He became a man. She became a woman. As such things go, mistakes happen. When Elsbeth showed up many weeks later, long after graduation, to tell him she was pregnant, he did what a man should do. He offered to marry her. She agreed as girls in small towns (and large) sometimes do. Fifty years passed.

Maybe those years weren't all that great, but the two of them had shared some good moments. They bore kids that they loved. They stuck together. Tiger knew he could refuse to go to the dinner. He understood how a part of Elsbeth was still hoping to experience her springtime evening and the attention of Teddy Mazzetti.

Tiger figures he knows enough about Teddy to know that Elsbeth would never have lit that spark. He fears that no matter what happens at the Long Table Dinner, she will be disappointed.

Still, when he looked at her in the light of that morning months ago, with her enthusiasm freeing her of all pretense, he saw Elsbeth as she really was. He knew that however things commenced so many years before, he loved this woman. Yes, he loved this woman and he would do what she wanted.

"Okay, we'll go to the dinner," he said.

Because of that promise, later this evening, he will get dressed in fancy clothes and drive his wife to a dinner they cannot afford. And he will have a good time.

Saturday, 11:21 AM

Back in his store, Michael Fagatelle is exhausted. After spending the early morning with his son, he supposes he could ask his staff to run things for one day. After all today is special. There won't be another time when his son cooks a gourmet dinner on the very day that is his father's fifty-second birthday. But he doesn't really have a staff anymore on most days. Money problems.

The shop should have opened at ten. He walks over to the front door, unlocks it, switches the sign to read "open," and turns on the full lights. To his eyes, the rows of fluorescent lights always seem to flicker on in waves, with the ones illuminating the meat counters coming on last. It has to be an optical illusion. They are all on a master switch.

Sometimes lately he thinks all of life is an illusion. That includes birthdays. He isn't looking forward to this one. Maybe it's for the best that he's celebrating the day with hundreds of strangers on the bluffs of the Mazzetti Ranch. Personally, he would prefer staying at home, watching television, and eating a steak grilled on the back patio. Leon is the one who insists he join this fancy dinner. He says he wants his Dad to experience his full cooking skills. That statement is nonsense. Michael has eaten many times at Point Conception. Besides he's enjoyed dishes at Leon's place that were almost certainly a whole level above whatever his son is going to produce this evening in a pop-up kitchen.

His real motivation for extending an invitation in a way that allows no turndown is exactly the same reason Leon's two sisters persistently badger their father about this night. Not one of them wants him alone on his birthday. They're all afraid that his life's biggest loss will wash him out.

They would never utter anything so blatant. They always tiptoe around the death of their mother. But it's been over a year since Linda finally gave in to the ravages of her breast cancer. She suffered a long and slow decline. There had been no surprise about what was coming and Michael had been prepared. Linda made him promise to seek joy once she was gone.

Despite his pledge, he really wasn't ready then and still isn't. Maybe he never could be. He never expected the pain of coming home to an empty house, the cool emptiness of a wedding bed, and the slow movement of every little thing. Milk, toothpaste, soap, every item lasts twice as long. It is as though time has slowed down without his wife. What he wants is for time to speed up. What he needs is a whirlwind of emotions that would let him fall asleep exhausted.

But he never feels exhausted. He just feels empty.

The kids see that. He knows that they do. They want things to be different. That's why they say the stupid things:

"Dad, you should go on a cruise and meet someone."

"Did you ever think of asking Mrs. Sampson out? She's very pretty, don't you think?"

"You should get out of the house more. Mom would have wanted it."

It no longer matters what Mom would have wanted. She is gone. They all know that. Her memory won't be less vibrant by bringing strangers into their lives. He understands that, but he suspects his children do not. They are the ones who try to keep her glow alive in their minds. His loneliness, he senses, somehow keeps memories from going dark in their lives. And he doesn't want that blindness for them, so he plays the role they ask of him.

Tonight's dinner seems a safe compromise. It will honor Leon's skills. It will be festive and hectic and emit the aura of fun. People will surround him in their very best clothes. The illusion of happiness will hover about. Leon truly wants him to be there and, in turn, Michael wants to taste Leon's food. He also wants to attend out of respect to Teddy Mazzetti. For decades, there have been close ties between his store and the Mazzetti ranch. He knows—even though it is planned as a surprise—that his two daughters will be on hand, no doubt accompanied by their millennial boyfriends. It will be a private family affair in a quite public setting.

He will go. There is no way he could ever say no. In the back of his mind there lingers the one good reason to stay away. His account with Mazzetti is several thousand dollars in arrears. Business has been tough lately and hospital bills linger. He hasn't paid attention to the things he should have. Especially after hearing Leon bemoan about the money he owed Pedrag Miles, he could have used his own debts as an excuse. Of course, Leon might have seen through such an excuse from his dad. Teddy has always been a gentleman. Even if Teddy were afraid that Michael might never catch up with the overdue account, he would never hold a grudge or bring it up at a public affair.

Something more important is bothering Michael. He understands how his plans for this night will test his children, but he is confident they will pass with flying colors.

He has met someone—Naomi. Just like him, she lost her spouse, who died in a car accident. For her, there was no time to prepare, no opportunity to hear from a dying husband on how he might want her to carry on. Michael met her two months ago at a counseling session at the local Catholic Church. So far he hasn't said a word about Naomi to his three kids.

He doesn't know why he holds back. Maybe he fears things will suddenly fall apart with Naomi. She is such a lovely soul. Part of him worries that his kids will think Naomi is too young. A dozen years separate them, but when one is middle aged, what are a dozen years? Time flies by like that. In a flash, one decade segues into another, and suddenly tomorrow is today.

Then there is the fact that Naomi isn't a bit like Linda. She is prettier, livelier, and wittier. He knows Linda would have loved Naomi. She is exactly the kind of woman Linda always wanted as friends. The truth is Linda had a great many friends who are a lot like Naomi. That's one of the reasons it was so easy for Michael to talk to Naomi. It was as though Linda introduced them, even though he first suggested having dinner together. In those early conversations, he imagined Linda at his side. But Linda's spirit has left. Now it is just Naomi and him.

Tonight his children will finally learn of Naomi. A part of him recognizes how unfair he is being. There were many earlier opportunities to bring Naomi into their weekly conversations. He could have asked Leon for two tickets for the dinner. That would have been a clue.

He chose not to do that. Instead, he went onto the web site for Long Table and bought a single additional ticket for Naomi. He excuses his behavior by saying that there was no reason to feel beholden to his son for an additional ticket. There is more to it than that. He wants to be certain he sees true first reactions when his children meet this new woman. This person is not their mother, but she could—if things work out right—be the person at Michael's side for the rest of his life.

Saturday, 11:51 AM

Back in the cooking tent, some unexpected ingredients are interacting.

"How can I help?" Annabelle asks Leon. "What do you need done?"

It is nearly noon. Leon finally feels that things are going his way. He and Becca have confirmed that everything needed is on site. Together, they have organized all the ingredients. Cooking stations are in place. In the distance, just beyond his eyesight, he hears the roar of the ocean's waves breaking on the beach below the bluff. He calculates it is nearly high tide and there seems a long swell offshore. He welcomes the breeze. Cool air would be appreciated for the hot work ahead.

"We have it under control," Leon responds. He has never liked strangers in his kitchen, even if that space is a tent on a coastal hillside. He didn't sign up for an episode of reality television, and he doesn't need assistance from someone who probably knows nothing.

"Aubrey likes me to make the offer to our chefs," Annabelle responds. "Especially when things are running behind."

"Everything is on schedule."

"Is it?"

Annabelle chooses not to say anything more. By now, she has participated in a year's worth of dinners. She recognizes when a chef has everything under control and when he doesn't. This one doesn't. Tonight, as always, there will be a lot of guests and many courses. During the cocktail hour, only five hours away, three different canapés must be passed among over two hundred people. Then the dinner itself will feature five major courses: an abalone appetizer, a soup, a composed salad featuring abalone, the main course involving Mazzetti beef, and finally the dessert. Leon has also planned an intermezzo involving a tomato and basil ice, but Annabelle just checked the printed menu and saw that the sorbet isn't listed. Based on the disarray around her, she is worried the ice will never be served.

Just a month earlier, Annabelle celebrated her twentieth birthday while on the road with the Long Table crew. From her vantage point, she judges Leon as an older man in his thirties. She knows her friends would think he was far too old for her, but there is something about him that she finds alluring. He is kind of rugged and soft at the same time. After meeting many chefs, experience suggests to her that this one is right at that cusp of turning to the fat side. But he has nice eyes and a funny way of biting at his lip as he works through his menu. Aubrey really does want her to offer help; he considers it part of Annabelle's job to assist the chefs. She would have done it anyway. She thinks this man needs another set of hands, plus she wants to hang around.

When she joined the team in Wisconsin a year earlier, she saw it as a way to escape a bad family situation. Her family life was what it was, and although she knew she was strong enough to keep things under control, she thought, "Why bother with all that?" Life was too short to always be on the defensive. There were places to see, things to learn, and people to meet. She saw the Long Table as a heaven-sent opportunity to put her minimal skills at waitressing and kitchen tasks to work. In the months since, she never regretted joining the caravan.

Her work mates aren't all to her taste. Truth be told, pretty much none of them are people she really wants to hang out with. But it doesn't matter. After a year together, she has visited thirty-seven different states and eaten some of the most remarkable food in the world. She has met people from all walks of life, and there are some she actually follows on social media.

Aubrey is okay, although Annabelle can't understand how he manages to keep the business going. He seems to live in his dreams and flits about on his motorcycle to scout future locations and vendors. Sometimes he isn't even on hand for the actual event.

In some ways, when he's absent, the days go smoother. That's thanks to Chase who Annabelle considers a human computer. She wonders if he isn't on the autism spectrum, given his incredible skill at laying out plans. He never forgets a detail. There is something a bit off with his social skills; he doesn't react to other people like a normal guy would. She can't explain it, but sometimes she thinks Chase views personal interactions as a chess game that he's trying to learn. He makes moves with other people just to see how the other responds, and he can plan out a board several steps ahead. Sometimes he seems just plain mean. Other times, he is remarkably gentle.

Leon isn't that kind of person. You can read on his face exactly what he is thinking. Right at the moment, she knows he wants her out of the kitchen, but he's too polite to say it. Maybe another part of him recognizes that he needs some help. She decides to stay even if he doesn't ask.

"Are you sure you don't want an extra set of hands?" she asks. "It looks like your beef still needs trimming. None of the greens are washed for the salad course. And I would think you would want to get the *mire poix* into the kettles for that abalone chowder. But of course you know best."

She turns as though she is going to walk away. Inside she has a bet with herself on which task he will ask her to do.

"You think you're pretty clever, don't you?"

She turns around smiling, knowing what she will see, and she does. The man smiles broadly. It makes him look younger. She's not certain if that makes her like him more or less.

"You identified one of my weak points," he says.

"This isn't my first dinner," she replies.

"In that case, where do you think I should put you to work?"

"I could do the final trim on those filets, wrap them in bacon and get them back into the coolers."

"You could," he agrees, "but I want Becca to handle all the proteins. Tell you what. I could really use help on the planned ice.

Otherwise I'm afraid it won't make it to the table. Could you take over peeling and deseeding all those tomatoes? I need to get them juiced and well chilled before I can use the ice cream machines this afternoon. Can you do that?"

She gives him a big thumbs up.

Inside she is secretly pleased. He asked her to do a task that she hadn't even mentioned. It also means he is fully committed to the intermezzo course which seemed at risk to her. She likes a man with ambition who bats for the culinary bleachers. It says something positive about him. Perhaps, it also suggests something about the evening ahead.

Saturday, 12:33 PM

Pedrag closes the window on his video conference call. He pushes the top of his laptop closed. Things just don't work as they should when you aren't there in person. Today's discussion is such a matter. The two young men in Boise are pikers with no understanding of the potential value of the software they've programmed. It shouldn't take so much effort to close what is only a third-rate deal. Yet he's wasted half his lunch hour trying to do just that.

It isn't that the young men, right out of Brigham Young, don't place a great value on their translation algorithms. Youth always seem to overvalue their innovations, Pedrag thinks, but they also tend to be greedy and unaware of where the real money is. All too often they think a million dollars is a fortune when of course it isn't at all. No, it isn't the fault of these fervent young Mormon missionaries that they're angling for a big payday. They just don't know what they have available to barter. The concept of the company itself is silly and has no legs. On the other hand, they do possess a truly unique software concept. It could be patented as the basis for a great many applications, which is exactly what Pedrag intends to do when he acquires the company. If he destroys these boys' faith in their juvenile business plan, then he can pick up the whole company at a modest price. There's no reason to overpay for anything, not even a great software idea.

He blames his wife for today's slow pace. If all of the players had been in the same room together, this would be a done deal. Instead, he finds himself moping in the office of his ranch retreat frustrated with a deal still undone . . . just because Helena, his wife, doesn't like the view of the abalone troughs from the top of their highest hill. For God's sake, she doesn't have to ride up to that spot and look north. She has two thousand feet of ocean frontage and a thousand acres plus of land in which to wander. What does it matter what can be seen next door from one hill? He never even wanted to buy this place. It was always her idea. She said it reminded her of being young and growing up in South Africa, but without the baboons.

Now, because of Helena, he is foundering in an unrealized deal while needing to attend some silly dinner at that detested abalone place. Pedrag doesn't even understand why Helena wants to make an appearance. Of course, the business issue is partly his fault. In retrospect he should have held this meeting in Provo, flown back to Northern California, and taken a helicopter down to the coast. There was time. Of course, Helena would not have approved. She doesn't like making a scene, and locals don't like it when a helicopter flies over the area. That concern is yet another thing he doesn't understand about her. She's the one who wanted the helicopter pad, even though he had to fight with both the county board and the California Coastal Commission to win permission. It wasn't an easy battle. Now that the pad is in place, she refuses to let him use it.

It isn't like she ventures out to these little towns to go shopping. She never faces the angry stares of the old retirees who hate anything that is different. She doesn't read their angry tirades in the local papers. Still, she curries their good favor.

There's also her unexplainable fetish about forcing the abalone farm to close because she finds it annoying to look at. What does she think the town would think about that? The damn place has been on the coast for decades. It is a veritable landmark of the seacoast.

But it's no use getting worked up over the matter. Pedrag loves his wife. He will do what she wants.

In the meantime he thinks through how to handle this negotiation for the Provo firm. He tried to resolve every detail in the conference call, but several issues remain open. Of course, his lawyers' job is to think through the alternatives, but he prefers keeping one step ahead. He considers taking a horseback ride to give himself some time to think. Maybe he could head up to that hill and take in the view that so incenses his wife.

In any case, it might be comforting just to take a look over the Mazzetti Ranch, or what's left of it. He doesn't hold Teddy Mazzetti in much regard. The man and his lawyer were easy pickings when Pedrag negotiated buying half of the original ranch. Afterwards he heard Teddy's sister was outraged about the deal. She hadn't even known an offer was in the works or that Pedrag intended to complete- ly seal off his newly purchased acres. For some reason, Pedrag enjoyed reports of how his staff kept turning Gina Mazzetti away when she first tried to wander back onto her old place. Perhaps it was a bit vindictive of him, but he doesn't really care. To the victor belong the spoils. That's what they always say.

Pedrag is not looking forward to the dinner tonight. First of all he doesn't really care that much about hanging around people he doesn't know, and he doubts very much that an event like this will attract any- one who interests him. Helena tried to sell him on the fact that the dinner featured the cuisine of Leon Fagatelle. That only reminded him of their less-than-stellar investment in Leon's Point Conception res- taurant. He tells himself that those investments are his wife's thing. He prefers not to pay any attention to them, as long as she doesn't lose too much money. Besides, he rather enjoys being fawned over when- ever he and his wife dine at a place supported by their money. Success has some advantages.

The problem with tonight is that his wife has some crazy idea that she will uncover something during the evening that could be used as ammunition in a future battle. She has spent months conferring with people who knew the ins and outs of coastal regulations. She was cer- tain she could find a reason to force the closure of the abalone farm, even though every one confirmed that it was grandfathered in. There's no chance in hell of success. Everyone has been consistently proven right, but to this day she remains convinced that somehow the place is a public nuisance. She wants to believe that their hosting this event breaks some covenant. All of it is nonsense.

He suspects something else is going on with Helena. For their first twenty years together, they had virtually nothing. Then success struck. In general she adapted well to great wealth. She seldom displays greed or condescension. But there are moments when some long ago slight blooms into craziness. Today seems to be one of those times. Hell, the abalone place doesn't emit any smell or sound. You can't see it from their house or almost any point on their ranch. Only a few workers and almost no traffic go in and out of the place. Abalone doesn't even pollute the water in any way—or so he's told. In short, his wife's obsession is without merit. And it's interfering with his real business.

But still. She is his wife.

They will go to the Long Table Dinner.

And, by God, he will find some way to make the evening worthwhile. He doesn't know how, but he will not throw away a whole evening of his life simply to please a crazy wife. Even one he loves.

Saturday, 1:09 PM

In a car on the interstate heading north from Los Angeles, Gina, Teddy's little sister, appears determined. The other passenger finds this determination concerning.

"Slow down."

Clem is incensed. Just because Gina and she are driving on the interstate through the empty flat lands of the Central Valley, she sees no reason for her friend to be speeding ninety miles an hour.

"We still have to go another hundred and fifty miles," snaps Gina. "Besides there's almost no traffic."

"It's also hours until this dinner. What will you do if we get there early? March in on your brother and start shouting?"

"I'd like to," replies Gina, before she starts to laugh. "What I'd really like to do is box him around the ears, like I used to do as a little kid. You know he deserves it."

"I know."

Clem reaches out and touches Gina's leg lightly, an action she has used before to get what she desires. Gina acknowledges the touch by lessening the pressure on the accelerator. The car slows to just above seventy. Soon the traffic around them, even the heavy rigs, is streaming by. No one sticks to the speed limit on this dreary stretch of freeway. As far as the eye can see, there are only empty fields of tumbleweeds or vast pomegranate orchards. But still Clem values sanity, and Gina values Clem.

The occasional billboard on a parked truck bed along the freeway reminds those rushing by that without water there would be no food. As a rancher's daughter, Gina knows the value of water. But she also remembers that when her grandparents first came to California, this dustbowl of a valley was best known for its giant freshwater lake called Tule Lake, which once was large and deep enough to support steamboat traffic. Now there remain only scattered wetlands, and those appear only after wet winters. Gina realizes there's more to the California story than is told on billboards.

Because Gina respects the old California and never wants it all to disappear, she will never forgive her brother for dividing up their family ranch. He allowed the best part of it to become the personal playground of a technological plutocrat who has no respect for the land's history. Maybe Pedrag Miles owns half of the family place now, but Teddy never had a right to sell it to him without first getting her permission.

Clem senses Gina's thoughts. "Forgive your brother. It's been over five years. What's done is done. Why live in the past?"

"Why shouldn't I live in the past? He does. He's never grown up, and he's never faced up to anything that's true. He needs to man up and look in the mirror."

"Boy, you're butch today," Clem jokes. "I think I like that. Maybe you should get incensed more often."

Gina doesn't respond. The truth is that this long drive from West Hollywood to the family home provides too much time to think. She hasn't set foot in the old house since the year Teddy sold the land out from under her. When she walked out that final day, furious with her brother, she determined she would never return. He destroyed the ranch just to get them a little money. There was no way for him to plead ignorance. He knew she would have fought him tooth and nail if he had asked, so he used his majority control of the family trust to make it happen without her consent. Her father had been an idiot at estate planning. The man should never have placed so much trust in his son's judgment.

No, she was wise that day to simply walk out. She had her own life to put in order. And she has—even if there were a few times she tried to sneak back on to some of her favorite old trails, only to be turned back by Pedrag's goons. Maybe it was all for the best. Once free of ties to her childhood home, she took new stock of her life's priorities. She divorced her husband in Boston. She moved to Los Angeles to be near her two children and return to a climate without cold winters. She started a new life, took up pottery, and met Clementine.

She supposes people label her a lesbian because of Clementine. Maybe she is, but she thinks it's more like she and Clem feel right together. In every way. Her two boys still don't quite know what to make of their new mom—the kiln in the garage, the girlfriend in the bedroom, the cottage in West Hollywood, and their need to set out extra plates at family gatherings. But she doesn't live her life for them, as important as they are.

The truth is that she has never known what motivates her life. In some ways, her only anchor ever has been the Central Coast. Maybe she was a strange child, but she was truly alive when she took those long walks along the bluffs and shores. That's why she often longed to go back.

There were never a lot of chores on the ranch, and she wasn't always given that much guidance. Her parents liked to travel, and for a while it had only been Jessica looking after Teddy and her. Then Frank showed up. He was wooing Jessica in that long ago world, and the two of them were just kids themselves. Neither of them placed a lot of restrictions on Gina. She could sit on her favorite rock and stare out to sea for hours. No one worried about what she was doing. She had the time to imagine whole worlds, notice the colors of the rock, watch the swirls of waves and froth, and let the wind sweep over her. To this day, that's what she seeks to recreate in the glazing and shapes of her pottery—she wants to control in her hands the world she knew as a small girl.

But how is she to succeed at that when Pedrag Miles owns the most important parts of her childhood landscape? To make matters worse, she has allowed herself to voluntarily abandon even the parts that he didn't buy. She had been impetuous to walk out on her brother in anger. But once done, how could she ever turn around and make peace?

And then she learned about the Long Table Dinner. It isn't the kind of event that either Clem or she would normally consider. They aren't much for eating fancy food or drinking expensive wines. They never frequent trendy restaurants. Over the years, she has increasingly opted for simple vegetarian choices when she eats out. She knows what to do with tofu. She has no desire to eat her brother's grass-fed beef or rare abalone.

But still life works in funny ways. After returning to Los Angeles three years ago, she looked up her old babysitter Jessica. She and Frank live in a beautiful spot in Pacific Palisades with a stunning ocean view. Gina likes visiting for the occasional morning coffee and sitting on their terrace, sipping a freshly brewed cup of Kona coffee, and feeling secure in the attention of a woman who might as well as have been her mother.

It was during exactly such a moment last week that Jessica asked Gina if she would be at Teddy's for the big gala. Of course, she had no idea what Jessica was talking about. But Jessica went into the house, carried out her laptop and fired up Google. Before long they were scanning the website of the Long Table Diner and looking at the description of the night planned for the Mazzetti Abalone Farm.

"So Teddy didn't ask you to come up for the event? He sent an invitation to Frank and me weeks ago. He even suggested we spend two nights and be his guests for the dinner. I just assumed he would have asked you as well."

"No, he didn't," Gina mumbled back. She was in a bit of shock from looking at the picture of the old abalone farm and trying to imagine it outfitted with a long table and hundreds of guests. She was even more baffled by the idea that Teddy would allow such a thing to happen. "Teddy and I haven't spoken since he sold half our place to that tech guy."

"I knew you were on the outs, but I never guessed it was that serious. I just assumed you had made up. That's what you used to do as kids. But I guess I should have known. You never talk about him, and he surely is reclusive. I have to admit we were quite stunned to get this invitation. We haven't seen your brother in years—not since your falling out."

"So are you going?"

"Of course. We accepted right away. Frank thought it would be fun, and I still have family there. It would be good to see them, so we said yes. We also wanted to mend some bridges. We're not getting any younger, you know."

"Maybe Clem and I should go." As Gina said those words, the possibility coalesced into reality. It was suddenly so clear that it was time to return.

"But you said Teddy didn't invite you."

"It's a public event, right? There's no reason I can't purchase a pair of tickets. If we just go up for the dinner, I don't need any invitation from Teddy for a stay in the family house."

And that was that. As soon as she arrived home, Gina went online, found the website, and purchased two dinner tickets. She nailed down a deal for a hotel night in nearby San Luis Obispo. Only once all non-refundable reservations were made did she walk into the living room and tell Clem that they would be making a small road trip. Clem took one look at Gina's face. She decided not to comment or question.

Now they are on their way.

"Turn off the fans," Clem suddenly says.

"Why?"

"The big cattle holding pens are up ahead. You know how they smell."

"I grew up on a cattle ranch. The smell of a little shit doesn't bother me."

Clem laughs, "First of all, there's nothing little about the odor from these pens. And second, your cows were free range and I am quite certain you weren't surrounded by the overwhelming smell of manure. Because if your ranch smells like these pens, then I can't imagine anyone will be very happy tonight about spending two hundred and fifty dollars to eat in that field. I don't think crap wafting in the air is the aroma that makes you hungry."

"Well, you're right about that point."

Clem looks directly at Gina. They are still within the speed limit. "So how are you feeling about this evening? Ready to go back home?"

Gina pauses before answering. "You know what Thomas Wolfe said. 'You can't go home again.'"

And yet she wants to try. How much she wants to try.

Saturday, 2:32 PM

Leon has two younger sisters sisters, Lucy and Leanne. They are twins who live together, and both plan to attend this dinner. They are in their apartment in a house just down the street from their father's butcher shop. Tensions are a bit frayed.

"Did you tell Leon?" Lucy demands of Leanne.

"Yes," her sister replies. "He knows tonight is Dad's birthday. He'll have a special cake sent over to wherever Dad sits."

"That's not what I mean. You were supposed to let him know what your pal Dennis and his friends are planning for us."

"He doesn't need to know about that."

Lucy gives her twin sister one of her famed dismissive looks. They are fraternal twins, born nearly ten years after their brother Leon. Lucy, much like her father, is the practical and planning one. Leanne bears such a remarkable resemblance to her mother Linda that sometimes Michael finds it difficult to look at her. Neither girl knows this fact. They ascribe their father's tendency to look away as part of a general depression that began with their mother's breast cancer. While he has never mentioned feeling depressed, that doesn't keep them from being certain that it's true.

"Leon doesn't like surprises," Lucy says in the voice she uses when she expects her sister to acknowledge how right she is.

"Well neither does Dad, and that isn't stopping us. Dad can't go on moping, staying around the house, and not living life. We need to give him some joy."

"Still, Leon won't like it, and it's really his night. Do we know what we're doing?"

The girls are planning to hijack the Long Table Dinner and turn it into an impromptu birthday celebration—their father's first birthday since the death of their mother. They deem it as a perfect opportunity to prompt change. As the practical one, Lucy knows there is seldom an opportunity for the three children and the father to be together around Leon's food. Plus Dad has always thought of Teddy Mazzetti as a family friend, so surely the landowner won't mind a little surprise. Lucy feels no need to check in with Teddy, just as she dismissed the need to inform Leon or their father about their elaborate plans.

Leanne, always the more impetuous and romantic one, imagines the evening ahead as a cinematic fancy. A third-year film student at Cal Poly, she visualizes the night in detail: how the ocean will crash on the rocks, the sun will set in clouds on the horizon, and diners from throughout the area will sit at a long table. Many of them will be patrons of Dad's meat market. All of them will be so pleasantly pleased to play a role in a surprise birthday event. Leanne has quite a vivid imagination.

It's hard to explain what the two girls have devised. Perhaps that's the reason they are so reluctant to share the vision. It isn't exactly a flash mob to surprise their father, but that description is close enough. Leanne spent an entire afternoon brainstorming the idea with Dennis, her gay best friend from high school who is now a drama student at Pacific Coast Repertory in Santa Maria. Perhaps she was inspired by the wedding scene early in *Love, Actually* when surprise singers and musicians suddenly appear in the church chapel to serenade the newly wed couple.

In any event, the opportunity appeared when Leon offered Dad tickets to the dinner. That's when Leanne realized the event coincided with the birthday, so she asked Leon if he could get the girls tickets too—and their boyfriends. Before she dared discuss her brainstorm with Lucy, Leanne planned out the whole escapade with Dennis. Fearful that her sister would find all sorts of reasons the surprise was a bad idea, Leanne chose to unveil a fully planned approach. It increased the odds that Lucy would agree.

It worked.

The whole surprise was rather complicated. She needed to get Leon to agree to present a small birthday cake to their Dad. Leon resisted. He reminded her that the event's concept was for everyone to share the same menu served family style. Leanne, long practiced at talking her big brother into one of her productions, pointed out that by dessert everyone around Dad would already know that he was the chef's father. If Leon was really concerned about guests' reactions, all he had to do was step out during any course and mention it was his father's birthday. That action would remove any objections to the presentation of the cake.

Of course, Leon also had to agree not to mention anything to Dad. Leanne always harbored a small concern that their father might suddenly decide not to attend the dinner. He could be stubborn about social events. Luckily, in the end, he seemed to be quite looking forward to the evening. Days ago, she stopped worrying about his not appearing.

She continued to fret about the second element of her plan. It would be a bit more challenging to pull off. Leanne knew Lucy wanted to share details with Leon, but that was quite impossible. Leanne was certain Leon would absolutely forbid doing what she wanted to accomplish. She had this idea for a variation on a flash mob, really a flash song. It was complicated, but it would work.

Dennis, being theatrical, recruited several of his friends to help. Dennis and his best friend would join them as Lucy and Leanne's dates. Another four friends, supposedly just two other couples on a date, would also buy tickets and be present. After the cake is delivered, wishes made, and candles blown out, the plan is that Dennis will stand unexpectedly and start singing. Everyone agreed that the usual happy birthday song would be too easy and forgettable. Instead they wrote a simplified and shortened version of "The Best of Times" from *La Cage Aux Folles*. Leanne considers Dennis's reworked words a perfect reminder for Dad to live in the moment.

First Dennis will stand, begin singing, and then Lucy and Leanne will rise and join in. This will be followed by Lucy's supposed date. Finally, with enthusiasm, the other two couples are to jump in.

Leanne also plans to secrete a little concertina in her tote bag. Dennis will drag it out and start playing, thus encouraging other guests to join in the singing of the rather simple verse. Leanne foresees it all, and it is perfect. She is positive that the long table of guests will join in the fun. Some might know Dad, others will not, but surely all will enjoy shouting this gloriously loud song against the sea and wind. Dad will know that this moment really is the best of times.

Dad needs this. He needs to live again.

She is determined to give it to him. What could go wrong?

Nothing, because she isn't going to let a skittish brother know anything about the party. That simply wouldn't be fair to Dad. Dad's happiness is the most important thing.

Saturday, 3:01 PM

By now, the sun is high in the sky and the shadow of the eucalyptus tree is starting to edge back toward the house. The time for the big night is drawing close.

Frank and Otto are sitting in the coolness of the covered porch. A small table with a pitcher of iced tea sits between them. Neither is drinking. Jessica is upstairs in the bedroom, resting before the festivities begin. Teddy left earlier to meet up with the staff from the Long Table team. He has yet to reappear.

Both men are silent, in the way that older people can sometimes be, in the midst of their own reflections. Although the two of them have been neighbors for years, they don't really know each other well. Their wives were the real friends. When Otto's wife was still alive, Jessica was the one who planned events for the two couples. More recently, she was the one who noticed how Otto had grown withdrawn and therefore chose to invite Otto along.

"I don't know if I should have come," Otto says. "I know your wife meant the best by inviting me, but I'm too old for these extravaganzas. Sometimes I think it's just time to move along."

Frank doesn't want to acknowledge the sentiment. It makes him uncomfortable, and he would much prefer to return to the good cheer of last night's dinner. There is something wonderful about the moments when Otto entertains them with stories accumulated over a lifetime. Knowing his wife wants this trip to be restorative for Otto, Frank decides to steer both conversation and memories to better places.

"Did you know I served in the U.S. Air Force?" he finally asks, figuring it might be best to recount his own life. He asks the question because he means to talk about how he first met Jessica while serving in this very area. Even as he begins talking he wonders if he's taken the wrong tack. The topic seems all too likely to remind Otto of his loss.

Otto nods. "Of course. We've been neighbors for years. I even know that you were once stationed here and that's how you met Jessica. Is it nice to be back?"

Frank acknowledges the question and sentiment with a nod and a barely audible murmur. He wondered how soon Jessica plans to join them. He tries to think of a funny story to occupy the silence.

Otto doesn't give him an opportunity. "Did I ever tell you about the first time I encountered your American Air Force?" he asks.

Frank shakes his head no, but Otto wasn't waiting for an answer. He, too, wants a story to break the silence. "It was during the war. World War Two, of course. I was just a boy. Already a young man I guess. Maybe in those harsh days in Holland, I was really an old man. Americans don't know how bad so many of us had it. But that's why I love Americans. They saved us. You know that, don't you?"

This isn't going to a place where Frank had hoped to move, but he isn't quite certain how to change the subject. He knows from their years of being neighbors that once Otto starts a story, it's hard to avoid the full telling.

"It was nearly the end of the war, although we didn't know that at the time. I had biked out into the fields outside of town seeking to scavenge whatever I could find. And that's when I saw them overhead, the low-flying American planes. They were circling above and pushing out bundles, each with its own parachute, which I watched slowly falling to the ground. The Americans knew how desperate we were. It was hope that you were sending with those packages. Yep, that's what it was. Hope. Food, sure, but really it was the reminder that we weren't alone. That we could survive. We needed that then, you know.

"I could see how one bundle was floating in the breeze and would land in the field directly ahead of me. I scrambled to reach that field. I wanted to claim it before anyone else. I had no idea what the American might have sent, but I had faith in Americans that it could only be good. So I rushed."

Frank is watching Otto's face. There is an aura quite different from the night before when he was recounting his farcical tales. An almost boyish innocence seems to come over the old man's wrinkled face. Maybe it reflects his wonder at the goodness of life. Whatever it is, his expression makes Frank long for some of that same peace.

"I got it. No one else was around, so I sat in the field and opened it. Such wonders. There was a pack of American cigarettes. It was like gold to me. And some chocolate candies too. I hadn't seen those in years. There was also potted meat and things that would really matter to my family. In that moment, I felt such a joy, because I could imagine how happy everyone would be when I got home and showed everyone what the Americans sent.

"I wasn't even watching what was around me. I just hurried back to the road and my bike. That's when the soldier stepped out. A German soldier who must have been hiding in a bombed-out barn. Maybe he wasn't hiding; maybe he had been assigned there. Things were quite confusing at that time of the occupation. But one thing was for certain. He was a German and he had a gun. And I think he was just as hungry as me.

"He made me stop. I could see that he was just a boy. Like me. Not much older. Both of us were blond and tall. Both of us were too thin. But he had a gun, and I figured he had orders.

"But I had the box. Contraband really. It was forbidden to collect such dropped rations. But we were both boys. And I think we were both scared and just wanted to go home.

"He could have shot me. I knew that then. He was probably supposed to shoot me. I don't know. An idea just came to me. I took out the pack of cigarettes and handed them to him. An offering of sorts. He looked at me with a look of wonderment or fear. Who knows what was going in his head?

"But he reached out and he took the pack. Then he turned to go back in the bombed-out barn. He let me go. I got on the bike and cycled home as fast as I could. I never looked back. I was afraid he would change his mind, and a bullet would suddenly drop me dead.

"Yet here I am. Still living. Over ninety now. Alone now, living only with my memories. Some are good. I like Americans for their chocolate. And I love that German boy for my life."

Frank doesn't know what to say. He can see that there is a tear in Otto's eye, but he pretends not to notice. He thinks of his own life in the military, wondering what he might have said if he had been that young soldier in the fields of Holland, wondering what he might have done to that German boy if he had been the officer who discovered what he failed to do. He wondered about all the orders he had given over the years.

What is right? What is wrong? He doesn't know. The moment of stillness is broken by the clamor of tinware down in the recently erected cooking tent. There is a string of cursing. Frank figures it has to be the chef, who has no idea how his cursing can skip up the hill with the wind.

The sounds break the mood. Otto smiles.

"And here it comes," he said, "we ate that canned meat that night. It was called Spam, and I love it to this day. Don't suppose they will be serving it tonight at this fancy dinner?"

Saturday, 3:31 PM

Preparing for the dinner ahead is like an intricate dance on the Mazzetti ranch. It's not a waltz or tango, perhaps more of a bewitched quadrille in which the moves are formal and beautiful in their patterns especially when viewed from a distance, but maybe not that clear to all in the moment of execution.

On the ranch, Teddy is doing his best to keep his emotions in check. He is feeling far too busy, especially considering nothing requires his attention. If he were to stand still for more than an instant he would be reminded of all his second thoughts about the evening ahead. He doesn't want that. In roving around his place he keeps encountering the same young man. Every time he sees Chase, he feels a slight start and a strange tingle. He wants to stare at the young man, especially his legs. He doesn't know why. He can hardly remember the last time that someone seemed so attractive to him. He tells himself it is only a case of admiring the beauty of youth. To make sure it stays that way, whenever he catches a glimpse of Chase's long legs, he abruptly changes his course as though some urgent mission has suddenly occurred to him.

Teddy doesn't realize that the young man is perfectly aware of the landowner's fascination. Chase finds it amusing to change his own path and make up reasons to talk to Teddy. He likes seeing how befuddled he makes the man. Still Chase knows there is a dinner to put on. Aubrey's success depends on Chase's due diligence, so there is only so much time he can spend playing with the frightened oldster.

Aubrey, for his part, is trying to keep chef Leon focused on the evening ahead. He has done these dinners often enough that he can tell when someone's game is off. Something is definitely going on with Leon, and it's more than the earlier problems with the equipment. Everything is running slightly behind schedule and Leon doesn't seem to recognize how he is on the precipice of a disaster. Fortunately, Annabelle has stepped in to help with the prep work. Like Chase, she is quietly competent. Aubrey feels lucky that they both fell into his life. Sometimes Aubrey likes to imagine that Chase and Annabelle will fall in love. One day he imagines throwing a surprise wedding as part of a Long Table event. Aubrey enjoys these big thoughts that blind him into missing the tiny indicators, such as how Leon currently has an unnecessary interest in how the salad greens are being cleaned.

Back at the ranch house, Frank joins his wife Jessica. He is planning to suggest they drive to town for a swing by the old family home. He'd like to see how the place is doing as a bed and breakfast. At least that's what he plans to tell Jessica. The reality is different. His conversation with Otto has left him troubled. He doesn't like thinking about war. He supposes that in reality he is lucky that there were no major conflicts during his career. Even during the first Gulf War, his involvement was rather minimal. There were tough decisions, but thinking of Otto as a young boy facing the German soldier in the field is very distant from his own experience.

Many people are preparing for the dinner ahead. The Metternichs, on their weekend escape, try to forget the memories stirred by seeing an unexpected photo on the wall.

Tiger thinks of his checkbook and suffers second thoughts about the wisdom of letting his wife play out her fantasy. He is sure tonight will not be anything at all like what she wants or expects of Teddy. If he were a braver man, he would find some reason to cancel their plans and head to a movie. No one ever calls Tiger brave.

Gina is back to exceeding the speed limit as she draws closer to the coast. Clem holds her tongue because she wants to believe that when they turn off the interstate, Gina will slow down. She hopes that fast driving might calm Gina down before she meets up with her brother.

Meanwhile, Michael Fagatelle is growing more nervous as he thinks about introducing Naomi to his children. At the same time, his daughters Lucy and Leanne are bubbling with the excitement as they all complete a quick run-through of their pop-up musical birthday surprise. Back at the ranch, their brother Leon checks yet again on the state of the greens.

There is so much activity, so much anticipation. Not just among these people, but also across the region. Over two hundred people are preparing for their night out. For some it is a special once-in-a-lifetime event. For others, it is just another fancy dinner.

All feel blessed by a beautiful fall day. There is no chance for an unexpected early shower to dampen the field or a late afternoon fog to roll in and chill everyone. No winds will tip over the flower vases on the table. If ever there were a chance to see the green flash of light as the sun sets in the western sky, tonight is certainly that kind of night.

The Long Table Dinner at the Mazzetti ranch holds every promise of being a most spectacular evening.

Even Teddy Mazzetti must surely feel that.

PART THREE

TEDDY:
THE COCKTAIL PARTY

Saturday, 4:03 PM

One summer, when I was a youngster, my mother shipped me off to northern Minnesota for a few weeks to stay at her aunt's cabin on some mosquito-laden lake. I don't know why I'm thinking about that long ago summer instead of the dinner ahead.

Even though nearly sixty years have gone by, those two weeks still seem vividly alive for me. Maybe I'm recalling this because at that time a part of me always wanted to huddle inside the safety of my great aunt's screened-in porch. I had a reason. She claimed that certain people held a sweetness in their blood that acted as a siren call to the female mosquito. Imagine your body sending an alarm in the night, ringing bells loudly to invite the voracious insect to feast on your blood. She claimed I was one of those blessed people. Just a moment outside, at evening or dawn, and I was instantly the center of a swarm of the buzzing beasts. I was pricked left and right. In moments my extremely healthy antibodies would kick in and swell my skin into a pinprick map.

There's not one bit of me that wants to experience that summer again. I'm certainly no longer that sweet boy, but something about that summer once again lurks about me.

Okay. Okay. I am being overly dramatic once more. But that summer truly was a horrible time. When I returned to the safety of the Central Coast, I begged my mother to never again send me to the land of ten thousand lakes. Now on this late afternoon slipping into the Long Table Dinner ahead, I feel I am back in a Midwest twilight. There aren't mosquitoes buzzing about, but there is a human sort of vermin around. At least it seems that way to me as I look out across the milling folk below. I know they're here under my own imprimatur. But it still annoys me the way they move about the place. They constantly seek my opinion and ask questions to which they should already know the answers. None is worse than this young man named Chase. Aubrey may hold him in high esteem, perhaps because the lad is young and attractive, but I swear that the boy is deliberately trying to provoke me. And I don't need the aggravation.

But, before I forget, back to Minnesota, I must acknowledge that there was something wonderful about those sunny Midwest days. It was quite unlike anything I ever experienced in California. I still remember the skies. So blue and so immense. The clouds were enormous fluffy confections of white that slowly floated across the afternoon sky like fantastic dirigibles of the gods, dragging shadows across the lake, turning water from blue to black. I would lay back on the dock staring up at that sky in motion, imagining whole worlds in the movement of white. There were horses and mountain lions, even whales from the ocean that I missed so much. Castles and countries, people too.

My great aunt left me alone in my fantasies. She probably wasn't very happy that my mother saddled her with a prepubescent for two weeks. She even tried to send me off to visit neighboring cabins where younger families from the Twin Cities were up for a week's getaway.

I always resisted. As a moody and solitary child, I liked to stick to my dock and the sky above.

You may find it hard to believe that there is something about all the activity on the ranch below that reminds me of those Minnesotan skies. But there is. I want to find Jessica to tell her about it, just the way I remember once telling her about those Midwestern clouds. But Jessica would think me silly.

Still, the ingredients for imagination are there. Having retreated to the verandah of the ranch house, I get the bird's eye view. If you squint and think about it, the big marquee tent for the kitchen is a cloud set against the dusty browns of the fall grasslands. It seems ready to billow across the horizon if challenged with a strong gust of wind. Thirty rectangular tables are laid end to end in what looks like an almost endless row. Together, they create a gentle curve through my Grandpa's picnic grove, matching the shoreline below the cliff. The tables are covered with white linens, all safely anchored with clips, although the fabric still flaps. It isn't stretching this imagination to picture them as billowy clouds.

Off to the side I see that Annabelle is working with Chase. They are adding white ribbon of some sort to further outline the parking areas. From my height, it's as though they're sketching a cloud. All we need are cars to appear to fill it in, just like a pencil sketch before the wash of watercolor. My own ranch might as well be one of those early California impressionist's work that line my living room walls.

Further off, back toward the main road, dust is rising. It reminds me that the initial guests are driving in. Soon the parking lot will be filled in. I can no longer pretend this dinner isn't happening. I might continue to think of it as a torment from a myriad of biting insects, or I suppose I could buck up and see it as an opportunity to imagine new worlds. I know myself; I will choose the insects.

My ranch is ready for the onslaught. No fears about that. Yesterday Jake moved all our cattle to the northeast corner of the grasslands. No sense in risking a tipsy driver running into an errant cow later. I wouldn't care about the driver, but the cattle are important to me.

Jake and I also worried about what inebriated guests might do to our abalone. We couldn't imagine any real problems. It isn't likely that sea snails will be bothered by laughter and revelry. Maybe the people and cars will raise clouds of dust that settles into the water troughs, although the water is always flowing. It gets pulled up from the sea on one end and heads down hill through the concrete formation, from tank to tank, until it returns to the ocean. Any dust will find its destiny back in the Pacific.

I should locate Jessica, Frank, and Otto. It's time for us to head down to the cocktail party. I look again at my imagined clouds. I try to think of them as a lovely country I am about to explore—one filled with rare and wondrous beasts. Like any sky of clouds, it will no doubt move throughout the evening and remain always shifting, always changing. Why can't I anticipate a night that will continually surprise me with things I never thought possible?

Well, I can't.

I turn to go in and round up my houseguests. The afternoon wind off the ocean reaches us for the first time that day. It presents a sudden chill and then it's gone, as though the breeze only wanted to remind me of its presence. It does something else. It evokes yet another memory from my Minnesota visit. I recall how bountiful cumulus clouds could rapidly transform into a summer thunderstorm.

I push that thought aside and hurry in. The party awaits.

Saturday, 4:31 PM

A loud knock at the front door. I wonder who's bothering me now? Maybe if I ignore the sound, pretend as though I haven't heard it, Jessica or Frank will answer it and deal with the intrusion.

Another rap. Louder this time. I hear sounds from the kitchen, and I realize that my guests are in that room. It is up to me to deal with this. I flip my untied bow tie onto the bed. I judge the polka-dotted thing pretentious. Why do I even need to wear a tie?

A third round of loud sounds. What an obnoxious lout. I certainly have better things to do on this day that deal with unwelcomed visitors. I stride to the door and fling it open.

It's him, the kid they call Chase. He wears a smile as though he is happy to see me. He is also still wearing those unnecessarily short shorts. I thought he was in some kind of management role with Aubrey. Shouldn't he be in more formal attire by now? After all, the evening is about to begin. There must be guests already on hand. I look down the hill and see that waiters are starting to pass the wine and appetizers.

The kid speaks. "Aubrey wants you down at the plaza."

I smile at the thought that he calls the lawn in front of our small office building a plaza. Still, it is the location where they set up the tents to protect the bartenders. From my walkabout earlier in the day, I know they are planning to serve three kinds of wine: a sparkling, a white, and a red—all sourced from a nearby vineyard. With the hot afternoon sun beating down on the area, I think it won't be a very pleasant spot for the drinkers. Maybe the sea breeze is strong enough to keep them cool.

"Well, are you ready?" the kid says.

His impudent tone makes me stop and really listen. I realize I have no idea what he is talking about. He's behaving as though I'm late for some appointment. His right foot is lightly tapping in some kind of countdown. Frankly, it annoys me.

"Ready for what?" It's all I can manage.

Now he looks annoyed. Behind me, I hear Otto, Jessica, and Frank enter the room. Their presence gives me a strategic advantage. I press the point. "I have no place to be."

Behind me, Jessica laughs. "Of course you do. You're the host. You have to join your party."

Chase adopts a smug look. He recognizes his ally, but I feel betrayed.

"I am not the host. They're just renting the property. I don't even have to go if I don't want to."

I want to laugh at the look that crosses the boy's face. For some reason, it makes him more endearing, and I momentarily think I will forgive him for being under my skin all day.

"Mr. Mazzetti . . . " he begins. Well, at least he is polite. My three guests draw closer as though they expect some grand proclamation to come out of the boy's mouth.

I feel magnanimous. I want Frank to see that I know how to be a good fellow. The same with Jessica, maybe even Otto. I invited them to this event. I want them to be glad that they accepted. "Chase, call me Teddy," I say.

"Mr. Mazzetti," he continues. The imp. "You most certainly do have some place you need to be. Aubrey is expecting you at the cocktail party. Just like this lady said, you're the official host. That's the way it is with every Long Table Dinner. The farmer or the rancher is always the special guest host. You have to be there. You have to do the welcome."

"You're expecting me to speak?"

I am appalled. I know for a fact that this was never stated. I don't do public speaking.

"Of course. Aubrey explained this to you. He's always very careful with every host so that the person knows what is planned. He must have prepared you. I'm sure he gave you an outline for the tour."

"The tour!"

"Of course, the tour. People want to see how abalones are raised. Between cocktails and dinner, you have to lead us through the place. You just have to explain how their dinner came to be. You also have to talk about your grass-fed beef."

There's a peculiar look on Chase's face. It's clear to me that he's just tried to perform some tricky sleight of hand and failed. I am certain he knows that Aubrey never mentioned any of this to me. Well, maybe the man said something about being one of the hosts. But I would have remembered an expectation of a tour because I would have assigned it to someone else. I recognize guilt on a face when I see it, and that's exactly what I spot on this boy's face. Plus, the boy is sporting some type of self-satisfied smirk.

Stop thinking of him as a boy I say to myself. He's probably in his mid-twenties. Just because he's so slight doesn't make him a kid. He knows what he's doing. I don't know why, but he's up to something.

Jessica starts talking. "Teddy, you're not going to get like you did in high school, are you? The way you would obsess over certain assignments or commitments and never follow through. Surely you realized you were expected to speak. Why, I even think it said something to that effect on the invitation. You know, that email message that promoted the dinner. Frank, you remember reading that, don't you?"

I shot Frank a warning look. I am in no mood to let a few facts interrupt my righteous indignation.

Otto, clearly not comprehending my body language, starts one of his tales. I've only known him for a day, but already I can spot the signs of a budding Otto story.

"Teddy, just relax and enjoy the moment. This reminds me of a time when I was just starting out, and our ship was docked in Sydney, down by that Circular Quay, and I convinced the boys that we should have a little fun before we got back on the ship."

Good Lord, where was this going? I need to settle my role for the night, and it will have nothing to do with a bunch of boys Down Under.

"Your boss did not discuss any of this with me, and I am quite certain it was not a requirement listed on any of the paperwork I signed. I have absolutely no intention of becoming some kind of talking monkey for the evening. Even if I knew what to say, this is not the kind of thing that I like to do or am prepared to do."

"Teddy," Jessica begins.

Otto is paying no attention to any of this. He's just off on a roll. "So I convince the boys that we should all get our hair dyed. We're all Dutch boys, blonde as can be, and I don't know what went wrong, but then . . . "

Chase seems about to laugh. Surely it's not at Otto's silly story. Frank watches me. I wonder why he isn't coming to my defense. I always thought of him as my protector. Don't they understand why I invited them to this dinner? They're supposed to be soothing my nerves. Instead Jessica is egging on Chase's request, and Frank is idly standing by. How is that taking care of me?

"So we show up back to the ship. The captain had already loosened the ropes and was about to leave so we had to dive into the water and climb up a rope ladder." When was Otto going to realize no one was paying attention to his inanities?

Now Jessica is trying to reason with me. At least I think that's what she has in mind. "Teddy, I don't know why you find this upsetting. You know everything there is to know about this ranch, about the abalone, and about the cattle. You could talk for hours without running out of things to say. Just talk about how you love the place. People just want a sense of meeting the owner. You only need to connect. Just for an instant. How hard is that?"

I thought Jessica understood me better than that.

"We boys all end up on deck facing the captain, who is not happy with how we delayed the ship. And then he sees our hair. And here it comes. The dye turned all our hair bright green. Well, he sent us right up to the barber to have our heads shaved and he docked our pay . . . "

Chase makes a move toward the door. "We don't have time to argue, Mr. Mazzetti. I was afraid Aubrey might not have fully briefed you, so I approached your foreman Jake to talk about abalone processing and to ask him to help lead the tour. Plus I've jotted a few notes for you. You can use them after you get introduced. But we really need to go. People are beginning to arrive.

"Don't worry though. I'll be here whenever you need me."

The young man reaches out his hand to take mine, as though I am a little boy who needs to be safely guided across traffic to school. And I let him be my guide.

Saturday, 4:41 PM

Chase releases my hand as soon as we're out of the house, or maybe it just slips away. I feel I am sweating a copious amount—nothing to do with Chase, just my anxiety over the event ahead.

Like a little group of ducklings, we follow Chase down the hill toward the reception area. I am directly behind him. Closely behind me, Jessica, Frank, and Otto follow. I swear that Otto is still telling his story.

Below us, cars continue to fill the large flat field that borders the main processing shed for the abalone. There're at least a dozen by now. One of Aubrey's young women is standing near the entrance to direct the newly arrived. I realize we should have left the house sooner, because there's no way to get to where we need to be except to walk along the main driveway. Arriving cars may not be paying proper attention as they go around the curves and along the rolling road. One could hit us. It would serve Aubrey right if his host were to be catapulted into the dry grass with a broken leg. How dare the man not tell me about my need to speak this evening?

What would my parents have made of an evening like this? Probably they would have been quite pleased. Although it is unlikely that the two would have stuck around. They were always so eager to rush off to their parties and their weekend trips. Gina and I must have been quite the burden.

On the other hand, if it hadn't been for my parents' aversion to the domestic life, Jessica and Frank would never have been a part of my teenage transition. Having Frank around toughened me up. After all, I learned to swim in the cold Pacific just as a way to lure Frank to a place where I would have him all to myself.

I look back at Jessica guiltily. I know she thinks I always favored her, but it was really Frank that I liked having around. He represented what I wanted to be.

Jessica sees me look her way. "Teddy, everything will work out fine. As this young man has pointed out, he has everything planned for you. You've always been so good at following directions."

Frank smiles, and I wonder why. We're nearly down to the flat field. An arriving car passes us carefully. Perhaps Jessica is right. I do worry a lot.

Chase speaks, "Did you ever imagine that so many people would want to come to this dinner? We had to close out sales. We couldn't accept one more reservation. We just didn't have the capacity."

That would have made Dad happy. Maybe he and Mom would have stayed on the ranch for an evening like this one because they liked large crowds and being the center of attention. I remember, especially when Gina and I were younger, how my parents threw lavish parties at the old ranch house. At those big events, some of the guests parked in this very same field. I can remember how they would cackle from the free-flowing booze as they tottered down the hill at the end of the evening. Didn't the school principal's wife once lose her footing and roll down? She wasn't hurt, as I recall. I should ask Gina if she remembers.

I wince a little at the thought of Gina. Of course, there's no way I can ask her. We haven't spoken in years. It's all her fault. She's the one who walked out on me. It was for no good reason. I negotiated a great deal with Pedrag. His money is what freed us to live the lives we wanted.

At that moment, Jessica brings up Gina's name. It is almost as though this woman can read my mind. Maybe that's what happens after taking care of a kid for so many years.

"What do you think Gina will think of tonight?" she asks.

I shudder at the thought. My sister would be outraged at having all these strangers on her ranch. She always thought this place belonged just to her. She wanted it to remain suspended in time like a private link to her childhood. That simply wasn't realistic. Everyone knew it. She should too. The past is one thing, but the present is another. Both can't exist at the same time. Anyone who thinks they can is delusional.

"I prefer not to think about that," I reply.

"You didn't ask her to come?" Frank adds.

"Who is this Gina?" Otto wants to know.

"She's my sister. And, no, I did not ask her to attend. Didn't we already have this discussion? Gina and I don't talk to one another. Was no one listening? I guess you were all too busy telling your stories." I immediately regret my harshness. It's my anxiety at play.

"Is your sister named Mazzetti too?" Chase asks. Jessica, Frank, and I were in a personal conversation. Why was Chase listening?

"I really don't know," I reply. It's true; I don't know. Obviously, her maiden name was Mazzetti, but she got married and then divorced. I don't have the slightest idea what surname she may or may not be using.

"Because there's a Gina Mazzetti on the guest list," Chase continues. "Could that be your sister?"

I stop. I turn to face the row of ducklings. Suddenly, the undercurrent of tension makes sense. I felt Jessica knew something that she didn't want to discuss. Foolishly, I attributed it to her worries over how I would deal with this evening.

I accuse. "You knew, didn't you?"

"Your sister's always been very independent. I have nothing to do with her decisions."

"But how do you know?" I am demanding.

Frank doesn't notice the volcano bubbling up. "We see Gina all the time. She lives in Los Angeles, you know."

Jessica is non-plussed, as though this is some small boo-boo she can bandage. "We just assumed you had invited her, or at the very least told her about it. After all, you reached out to us. How long has it been since we got together? Why would we think you wouldn't tell your sister"

"And you're only now telling me now."

"I was afraid you would react just this way. I thought it would be better if you ran into her at the cocktail party without time to think. You know, it's just silly the way you two still fight over the ranch. Grow up!"

I know I should listen to Jessica. She has always made sense, but I am feeling too stubborn to accept her reasoning.

Chase grabs my hand again. "We have to keep going. Lots of people are about to arrive and I need to help sign them in. But first, I've got to get you to Aubrey. He'll take over." He stops to look at me.

"You're okay, aren't you?" he asks. He seems genuinely concerned.

I don't know how to answer.

Saturday, 4:50 PM

Aubrey is in the kitchen tent, so that's where we head. I am a little excited to see Leon again. For a moment, out of the corner of my eye, I think I glimpse that ancient Ford Tiger drives. Surely the old fool isn't actually showing up with his wife. They couldn't possible afford the price of two tickets. On the other hand, I can't imagine that anyone else attending has so little taste or money as to drive an old beater like Tiger's. Imagine both Gina and Tiger at this dinner. That would be my worst nightmare.

I don't have time to think about it. The kitchen is chaos—not that I would know what a professional kitchen should look like. Still, I have certain expectations, and the mood in this kitchen definitely does not meet them.

My three houseguests dutifully walk behind as Chase leads us down to the semi-secluded catering tent. Only now does he notice that he's heading a small procession. He turns with some surprise to say, "Shoo!" He tries to make it sound playful, but he clearly doesn't want them there. From the looks on the faces of Aubrey, Chef Leon, and the others, no one wants one more person in this constricted space.

Chase quickly tries to make nice, "I only need Teddy here. Why don't the rest of you go directly to the cocktail hour. They're already serving canapés and a lovely sauvignon blanc."

I take advantage of the break to grab another look at the parking lot. Tiger is definitely the person getting out of the old jalopy. I'd recognize his lanky look anywhere, as well as that stringy hair on his wife Elsbeth. I don't know how the two ever got hooked together. While Tiger may have been a bit dim and socially inept, he had been a good-looking boy. He should have done better.

Tiger looks over toward the catering tent. I quickly turn in hopes of escaping his glance, and I nearly run into Leon. I quickly think of something to say, "You going to treat my meat good tonight?" I ask.

I cringe at my own words. What in the hell did I even mean? My support team is already heading toward the main party. At that moment I would prefer listening to garrulous Otto launch into a story.

Leon smiles at me. He always did have a nice smile. "Of course, Mr. Mazzetti," he replies. "We're going to do you proud tonight. I've spent a lifetime handling your beef and abalone. I think you're going to like what we serve. Besides . . . " and now his voices drops to a whisper . . . "tonight's Dad's birthday. He's going to be here and I have to be certain he has a wonderful time. So I've got to live up to the expectations of two of the men in my life."

I feel a little thrill. Who would have thought that Leon placed me on a level similar to his father's? True, I always looked out for the boy because I saw something special in him. I'd have liked a son like him myself, someone good looking, talented, and polite. That's what the boy always was. Too bad that his father now owes me all that money. I probably shouldn't mention it but, now that I think of it, I'm not even certain I've been paid for tonight's steaks. The meat better be cooked to perfection.

"Aubrey, Aubrey."

Chase is shouting and trying to get his boss's attention. At the same time, a young woman from Aubrey's bunch is calling out Leon's name. He seems to turn to her eagerly. For a moment it's just me.

For the first time, it dawns on me just how complicated it must be to serve over two hundred people five or six courses. A lot of people are working under this canvas roof. Off to the side, a big generator provides power to the various coolers, stoves, processors, mixers, and what have you assembled on rows of stainless steel tables. None of it makes any sense to me. I am not certain what everyone is doing or even when everyone and everything arrived on the ranch. Only five or six people were in that strange bus this morning. Now there are clearly many more workers.

I take advantage of the moment to scan the parking lot once more. I want to be certain that Tiger and Elsbeth have moved on. In my mind, I make plans to avoid them the rest of the evening. The woman has never forgiven me for not showing up to dinner before that high school dance decades earlier. But how could I? There was no way I was going to explain to those two that I didn't even have a date for the evening. I had some stupid idea that Tiger wouldn't be able to get a date either, and then we could go swimming at my favorite beach. When he asked out Elsbeth, I couldn't figure a way out. I just kept adding complications to the situation, pretending I had asked this girl from San Luis Obispo (when I don't think I even knew a single high school girl in that town). Before you knew it, my only solution was to not show up. Who could ever explain that? Nevertheless, to this day, I don't understand why Elsbeth holds it against me. She got what she wanted. She shagged Tiger. Wasn't that all that mattered to her?

Traffic into the parking lot is picking up. Aubrey's people are directing a couple dozen cars into specific spots and pointing their passengers in the direction of cocktail party. Aubrey chose a good spot for the car park. It is sheltered a bit from the sea on days with strong breezes. Due to a small line of eucalyptus trees, it also provides some natural shade on sunny days. Today is a perfect day, not too hot, and the view out over the water is beautiful.

Was that a Tesla that just pulled in? No one nearby owns a Tesla except for Pedrag Miles. He's the kind of arrogant Silicon Valley tycoon who makes sure people know he has both money and high tech taste. Surely he wouldn't attend this event, although a small part of me hopes he might appear. His presence would be a kind of insurance policy when Gina shows up. She would be so outraged at encountering him that she'd have no time to lambaste me. The thought makes me chuckle.

"I guess somebody is feeling pretty good about the day," says Aubrey. Chase has finally managed to bring his boss over.

"No, I am not," I snap. "Your assistant tells me that you expect me to speak or some such thing at this event. That was never part of the deal."

Aubrey laughs. "Oh, of course it was. You're just suffering a little stage fright. Perfectly understandable. I know you're not a natural showman, but we'll just let your ranch speak for itself. The food will tell its own story. Won't it Leon?"

He shouts out the last statement. Leon looks up from his prep table, and gives a big thumbs up. I am certain he has no idea what Aubrey is talking about. When Aubrey appears to be walking away, I grab his arm.

"Seriously, you never mentioned this and I have not prepared anything. I have no idea what you want me to say."

That is the moment I realize I have lost. Maybe there was never even a battle. This man played me throughout our previous negotiations. For months, I have been afraid that when this day arrives it will be hell. It is. Now I just have to endure it.

"Hey, just follow the kid's lead. Chase has it all under control. Don't you, kid? He always does. He's your guy."

The man is off. He hasn't told me a thing. But it seems to have satisfied Chase. He dragged me down here and now acts as though I am his employee.

"I have it all outlined. There's nothing to worry about. I'll be at your side the entire time. I'll tell you when to speak and I'll nudge you if you need to shut up. I got your back, man."

He gives me such a look that I know that he's playing me, just as I know that he knows. The thing is, he's got gorgeous eyes and a great smile. I think I just need to calm down. The kid knows what he's doing. I just have to get through the night. Besides who else do I have to rely on? My former babysitters walked off into the afternoon heat to get a drink. When my little sister appears, she'll torment me as always.

Chase may be all I've got.

Saturday, 4:58 PM

Chase pulls me along toward the main office. We pass the lawn where the tables are set for the cocktail party. He's talking the whole time, going through everything Aubrey expects me to cover. I'm barely paying attention. Other things are on my mind.

Let me just admit it. The guy is drop dead gorgeous. I knew it the first time I saw him. All day long, I've been trying to deny it. Sometimes I think I've spent my entire life trying to avoid facing up to a very simple fact. I find men attractive.

I'm sure my father and mother knew it. Maybe that's why they created so many excuses to stay away from the ranch. I am equally certain that my sister Gina knows it. That probably accounts for her ongoing dismissal of me. She thinks everything should be perfect, and a man-loving brother can't possibly be that.

I have tried. For example, all day I attempted to ignore Chase, even when he poked his beautiful long legs in front of me. If I didn't know better, I'd say he's flirting with me. But of course I know it's just his job. Everyone is trying to help Aubrey put on the perfect dinner.

Still, there's something about the downy light hair on his legs.

Stop it.

I am being ridiculous. I have never acknowledged these urges to my family, and I never will. Maybe in these modern times, homosexuality is nothing to be ashamed of. Practically half the world finds a reason to celebrate it. I'm not one of them. That's why I stay on this ranch. It keeps me out of trouble.

"Are you paying attention to what I am saying, Mr. Mazzetti?"

Chase finally notices my mind is drifting. Of course, I nod at him like a rapt student. I even look him in the eye. His eyes are a lovely shade of grey, not a hue I ever recall seeing before. He doesn't look away. I find that odd and strangely unsettling. I quickly break free to scan the grounds instead.

"Your team has done a good job," I say to cover my awkwardness. I have had a lot of years to perfect the phrases meant to bridge the difficult. Chase gives no sign that he is aware of my discomfort. Maybe he simply gives my compliment its due.

In reality, I made a true statement. Sometime during the day everything has been straightened and groomed. There must have been some mowing of grass, but I can't imagine how I missed that sound. The parking lot is quite clearly marked. At some point, a set of portable toilets has appeared. I hadn't even thought about the facilities people would need. I never asked Aubrey even the most basic of questions. Thank God Gina isn't aware of what's going on. Then I remember. Gina is attending tonight.

To the west, the line of tables stretches for two hundred feet or more in a slightly undulating row. Its long cloths are billowing in the wind. It makes me think of a cloth-draped centipede emerging from the sea. Maybe if I knew exactly where to jump on that table, I could give the magnificent beast a poke. It could magically trundle me off into the sunset.

"Mr. Mazzetti, please pay attention."

I face him. His commanding tone annoys me, but he is so good to look at. Over the years, too many men who I liked to look at have stood on these cliffs. Where did it ever get me? Did even one of them know what I wanted? As a youth, a young man, or even a middle-aged man? Let's face it, now, I'm too old. My time has passed. It doesn't matter who I look at any more.

"Mr. Mazzetti. I am not kidding. In five minutes, we're going to walk into all those guests circulating with their wine glasses and nibbling on the abalone ceviche. You are going to greet them. With me at your side, we will walk up to each group, and you are going to say, 'Welcome to my ranch. I am Teddy Mazzetti and I am so happy that you can join us tonight. I hope you enjoy my beef and my abalone at this beautiful place on the ocean.' And you will smile at whatever they say, and you will be nice, and you will try to answer their questions.

When appropriate, I will find a way to break us free and let you move on.

"You don't even have to think. I am here. All you have to do is make them feel like they have talked to the owner.

"Can you do that Mr. Mazzetti?"

How ironic! For all these years, I have lain in bed at night and thought about men I have met and how they might tell me what to do, to use their hands to push me along as they desire, and to make me their puppet. How limited is my imagination. I never quite foresaw someone dragging me through what I currently consider the ninth circle of hell.

"Of course, I can do it," I snap. "Do you think I am some kind of senile invalid?"

There's a scuffle off to the side, and a familiar face breaks through the small crowd. I must move in an odd way, because Chase darts a quick glance of concern.

"Teddy!" my sister screeches. Gina rushes toward me, towing along some heavy-set woman, who seems to be trying to hold Gina back, but, unfortunately, she's not successful.

"Hello, Sis. So good to see you," I say with fake sincerity, "but I am really quite busy and young Chase here needs me to work the crowd." Isn't that what a politician calls the process? Working the crowd.

"How could you?" she snaps. "How could you desecrate our family land with something like this? Isn't it bad enough that you sold the best parts of the coast to that high tech scumbag? Now you open it up to anyone with a few bucks to spend?"

The light goes on in Chase's eyes. He realizes it is Gina. He's smart. He knows I need to get away from this.

"Excuse me, Gina," he says smoothly, "but I need to have Teddy for a few minutes. But I believe you know Jessica and Frank. They're guests tonight as well. They are right over there by the bar. I promise I'll bring Teddy back as soon as we're done."

With that, he smoothly guides me into a group of six people that I have never met before. Gina is left behind, mouth agape, the other woman seemingly consoling her. Who is that woman I wonder? She behaves as though she were Gina's lover. I start to laugh to myself at the ludicrous idea, but stop and look again. Could it be? But I have no time to think. Chase has started the introductions.

"This is Teddy Mazzetti," he says. "This is his family's ranch."

Off we go. Everyone proclaims the beauty of the spot and how they anticipate the meal ahead. I am having trouble concentrating. The idea that my sister might be a lesbian suddenly seems overwhelming. Certainly, it can't be true. How would I not know?

Then I hear her loud voice scream out again. Only this time it's not my name that she screams out.

"Pedrag Miles! What the fuck are you doing here? How dare you show your face on my land!"

Maybe the heat is off.

Saturday, 5:03 PM

There's no time to waste. It's a fiasco in the making, and Chase dashes away to control it. That leaves me adrift in unsettled currents. For once I am happy to be taller than most because I can see above the crowd and can attempt to seek out Otto and Frank. Two old codgers like them should be easy to see in this crowd. The general age of the attendees surprises me. I thought the hefty price tag would limit participants to people more my age. I guess our type is more prone to early bird specials. There are a surprising number of millennial types mixing about and far too many tattoos and piercings for my taste.

"Mr. Mazzetti," a voice calls out. I can tell I am about to be trapped. I could pretend as though I didn't hear my name or, perhaps, act as though I am somebody else, but there's no longer any way to pretend I am anyone other than who I am. This is my fate.

I turn. A pleasant enough couple, slightly younger than me, pushes through a crowd of twenty-somethings who seem focused on someone else. I think I recognize the person, but I only catch a glimpse of him before this couple snares me.

I smile. Remembering my coaching from Chase, I extend my hand. "Yes, I'm Teddy Mazzetti, the owner of this ranch. Welcome to my home."

"Oh, Mr. Mazzetti," the woman coos. There really is no other word to describe the way she says it. She has a bit of a look of a pigeon. A touch heavy in the posterior, she waddles slightly as she heads toward me. Her eyes bulge a bit too. Maybe a thyroid problem, I think. Her husband hangs back. I can guess who wears the pants in this family. But he might have been handsome once. There's an air of melancholy over them. I think I will need to have Chase rescue me quickly—or else connect up with Jessica and Frank. Even Otto will be better than these two.

"You can call me Teddy. I do hope you enjoy both my beef and my abalone tonight. I've known the chef since he was a young man, and he can do wonders with both."

That should hold the two of them and allow me to move on. They can't expect more than that from me. Over the din, I think I hear Gina's voice raised and the calming tone of Chase. I would turn and check it out if I weren't afraid it might cause Gina to head my way.

"Of course. Teddy. So nice to meet you. So wonderful to actually get a chance to visit this historic place. Why I've known of your abalone farm for years. My husband and I just love coming to the village for special occasions. We do it all the time, and whenever we drive by the entrance, I tell Henry . . ."

She pauses and nods her head toward her husband as though I wouldn't be able to figure out by any other means that she was talking about her companion. "Anyway I tell Henry, 'Did you know that they raise abalone down this road?' I just think it's so amazing that you can raise something like that in captivity. I always thought it was a wild fish or something. And I haven't had it in years, because it so expensive, and you hardly ever see it anymore in a menu, and I don't really remember what it tastes like, to be honest, but we do so love being in this area and by this coastline."

She is determined. Her husband looks embarrassed by her long stream of consciousness. I throw him a look begging for his intervention. I stand a bit straighter too, like a lizard on a sandy path doing push-ups to show who's boss. I have to remind myself that I am a very important person at this event. I think Chase said that, and if he didn't, he should have.

She still prattles on. "It's our wedding anniversary, and Henry surprised me by driving up for the weekend, without saying a single word about what he had planned. He's not the type to normally spring surprises, so when I was trying to get him moving this morning at breakfast, I didn't understand why he wasn't eager to go wine tasting. That's what we usually do when we're here, you see."

"Sylvia, I'm sure Mr. Mazzetti has other things he needs to attend to," the man says. So he can read my signals.

"Don't try to shut me up!" I hear the scream from a hundred feet away. The voice belongs to Gina. I have to look around. I see the heavyset woman who came with Gina pulling her away. At the same time, Chase is trying to steer Pedrag and his wife in another direction. I consider how to escape.

"That sounds heated," says Henry. "Unless it's part of a floor show," he jokes.

Sylvia laughs with pleasure. I think she really loves this man and actually thinks his lame remark is clever.

"Teddy," someone calls out. "We wondered where you had gotten to."

Frank is coming to my rescue, and not a minute too soon.

Sylvia suddenly stops talking. She pales. The laughter goes out of Henry's face, and they seem ready to flee. How strange.

Jessica, Frank, and Otto arrive at my side. Maybe I can pawn Sylvia and Henry off on them and go on my way. How would Chase do it?

I begin, "Let me introduce my friends Jessica, Frank, and Otto. This couple is named Sylvia and Henry. They like to spend weekends in the area. At least I think they do. You know Jessica and Frank used to live in the village."

"Where are you staying?" Jessica asks. It seems a natural enough question, but the man is clearly uncomfortable.

The wife answers, "The Old Redwood B&B."

"How extraordinary," Jessica replies. "That was my childhood home. It's such a beautiful place. Of course they added on, but I do love the breakfast area. It's where my mother used to feed me oatmeal. Frank, can you believe that these folks are staying in the old family homestead?"

Personally, I like to say I love coincidences. If this had just happened to me, if I had just encountered the person who grew up in the building where I was spending the night, I would want to pepper that person with a million questions. But Sylvia retreats to the background. She is clearly staring at Frank in a horrified manner.

Her husband mutters something along the lines of "We should mingle," and then guides her away. Well, whom do they know, I wonder. But who cares? I can stick with my friends. I am not that intent on playing the host. I had been bulldozed into the role.

"Did anyone else find that a bit odd?" Otto asks.

"Maybe there's a story there," I figure my comment is a sentiment that Otto should appreciate, but I move on. "Are you having a good time?"

All three are holding wine glasses filled with a rather hefty pour. Otto's charm must have been put into overdrive with the server. If everyone is getting this much to drink, the place will be overrun with drunks before dessert. Quite a buzz is already floating about. I realized I had stopped hearing the wind through the trees a while ago. Even the sound of the ocean no longer rises above the din. In fact, I can't hear the arriving cars. At least one hundred vehicles are in the area by now.

"It will be a marvelous event," Jessica replies.

For a moment I don't know what she is talking about, and then I recall I just asked a question. I am truly distracted. It must be time to conduct the tour and I wonder where to find Jake. I hope they weren't lying when they said my foreman has been briefed and will lead the tour.

"Have a glass of wine," Otto said as he hands me his glass. "You're looking a bit drawn. A little alcohol will do you good."

I take a sip. A lovely sauvignon blanc. Then I gulp the whole glass.

Chase reappears. "There you are. Why are you standing around with your friends? Didn't I tell you what to do? Remember, you're the host."

Maybe it's already the wine talking, but I really think he's cute. Where was he forty years ago when I was still in my twenties? Why didn't I ever find someone like him?

"What happened with Gina?" I ask.

"Don't worry. It's all taken care of. Gina won't be a problem."

I see the way Frank and Jessica exchange a smiling glance. They know better than Chase. Gina is never taken care of.

Saturday, 5:21 PM

I am back under Chase's control. The glass of wine has gone straight to my head, but that doesn't stop me from grabbing another serving as a waiter walks by with a tray. Chase notices, but he doesn't say anything. He's scouting the lay of the land ahead. Quite a crowd is gathering at the cocktail tables. The noise is a little horrific, but all the commotion only serves to hide me from Gina. I can't help but smile to myself.

A hand reaches out to touch my shoulder. Instinctively I pause. Chase immediately notices and whispers, "We can't stop, Mr. Mazzetti, I need to get you to the front of the space."

Another voice behind me calls out my name with even more fervor than that voiced by Chase. I am beginning to like this evening. I have not had so much attention in years, maybe never. My wine glass is already empty, and I motion to another waiter passing by, but I think Chase shoos him away. Meanwhile the voice behind me calls out again and touches my shoulder once more. Naturally, I turn around.

It's two young women. Their faces seem familiar in a pleasant sort of way. They were part of that group of young people I noticed earlier. Their skirts are too short, and the young men have their pants cuffs rolled up and are wearing no socks. I don't understand these choices.

"It's Lucy. Don't you recognize me? And my sister Leanne. You always said 'hi' when you dropped by Dad's butcher shop."

Memory kicks in. Of course, the Fagatelle girls, Leon's younger sisters. Seeing them reminds me of that unpaid bill in my office awaiting payment from their father. "Is your Dad here?" I ask. I wonder if my words are starting to slur.

"Oh, he's right over there. Should I get him?"

One of the young men is already poised to go in the direction the young woman pointed. (Was that Leanne or Lucy? They don't look at all alike, but who can remember which one is which?) Who are all these young people, walking around with their little plates and glasses, acting as though they are adults?

"No, don't bother. I was just asking. I need to get to some place, and I'm late." I can feel the tug of Chase's hand on my other sleeve. "It was so nice to see you. And welcome to my ranch. You know my family owns this place?"

What am I saying? Of course they know. Their father has been doing business with me for decades, probably from before these girls were born. I turn to Chase.

"Where next?" I demand. I am certain there must be something important to do.

But the girl won't let me go so easily. She leans in close and whispers something. I can't hear in the general hubbub. I hope this isn't an indicator that I need hearing aids. Glasses have been bad enough.

"What?" I ask.

She gets in even closer, which I don't like at all. Now she talks directly into my good ear. I don't like admitting that I am going deaf in the other. "We're surprising Dad tonight. It's his birthday."

With that, she pulls away, all smiling and coquettish. Her friends are all laughing, and she put a sole finger to her lips in warning. I see her father coming through the crush of people nibbling on appetizers. He seems excited to see me, so I do the natural thing and look elsewhere.

There goes that strange couple who were so eager to scurry away from my friends. Oh, God, there runs Gina down the hill heading toward the shore. I can see her prey. It is Pedrag and his wife who are perched on the edge of the lawn where they can admire my perfect bluff and beach. I hope they're not plotting to buy the rest of this ranch. It's mine.

New people are with Chase. I recognize them from earlier in the day. They were involved with setting up the kitchen and this party area.

"Cat and Hillary, this is Teddy Mazzetti," Chase is saying. He's mumbling something about needing to take care of another matter and how these two will make certain that I meet up with Jake because it is almost time to take the group on the tour of the abalone farm.

"Wait," I say, but he's gone.

My new guardians seem unhappy with their role or maybe just displeased with me. I can't tell. Older than Chase, the duo emit the vibe of an entrenched couple. They seem to know what each other is thinking without speaking, so strongly in fact that I feel I am picking up that they would far rather be working with the kitchen team.

"So more meet and greet?" I ask.

My faithful trio is off in the distance. Jessica gives a little wave. Otto raises his plate of abalone ceviche and gives me a thumbs up, as though I had anything to do with the food. When we tested the various dishes at Leon's restaurant in San Francisco, I told Leon that I didn't think the ceviche was a very good dish. My opinion was that people would find it too crunchy. Yet here he is serving it anyway. I know I'm not a world-renowned chef, but why did they bother asking for my opinion. Who cares? I want another glass of wine.

"We don't have time for that," says the woman. Is that Cat or is that Hillary . . . and did I express my wish for wine aloud? I didn't really pay attention to the names of these two earlier. Neither name is good for a man or a woman, I think to myself. I stop for a moment to make certain that I didn't utter that thought out loud as well.

They have nametags. The woman is Cat. That must mean the man is Hillary, like that mountain climber when I was a boy. But wait, his name was Edmund Hillary. Not the same at all. Either I am getting drunk, or I am unduly nervous. I really don't know which. I wish Chase were back.

"We have to get you to Aubrey and Jake. No more time for chit-chatting. We need to start the tour or the dinner won't start on time."

"Well, not really," I counter, "because Jake's agreed to give the tour and he knows everything that has to be said. I don't even know why you want me there. I'll just be in the way."

"No, Mr. Mazzetti. That's not how it works. Jack and Aubrey will do the general overview and welcome, you know, to pull the group together and to get everyone set up for the general walk ahead. But there are too many people to do the tour as a single group.

"Hillary and I will divide the group into two segments and then help you and Jake walk them through the process. Jake will be the docent for the first hundred, and you will do the second. We'll stagger the starts and end up back at the main dining area in twenty-eight minutes for the start of the dinner. It's all carefully choreographed. You got it?"

"But no one's given me the plan," I counter.

"You were talking to Aubrey earlier this afternoon. He said he explained it all to you then. Besides you've owned this place for years. You must know everything there is to know. You probably give tours all the time."

How little they know. They have, however, been good at ferrying me through the crowd. They accomplished it without starting a pied piper effect. I have reached the clearing behind the main office. Aubrey and Jake are standing there. Jake has a bemused look. I think he's enjoying this. I am not certain if I mean the evening itself or my discomfort. He's been my right hand for a long time. He knows I don't speak to groups. I also have never been quite certain if he actually likes me.

"Well, boss," he asks. "You ready?"

Have I ever been ready for anything?

Saturday, 5:32 PM

The call has gone out. I see the results. The crowd draws closer. In front of the office shed's main door, there's a small porch. Aubrey drags Jake and me up the two steps to stand beneath its slanting roof.

Servers have set down their trays at some hidden station. The serving of the abalone ceviche and the steak tartare on toast points is done. Under the pitched tents, the bartenders appear to be slowing down their pours. The staff focuses on gathering the flock and moving them toward the office, toward the official start of the evening, toward Jake and me.

The office is on a slight rise. Standing on its wooden planks, I have been given another foot or so of height. As a result, I see over the heads of the more than two hundred people who have gathered. Beyond them stretches the long table along the coast. The staff has set out the plates. The chairs help anchor the linens. Beyond that table is the edge of the bluff and beyond that the blue of the ocean and beyond that the lighter blue of the far horizon. I think I see the tip of a sail from a pleasure boat. How rare to see a yacht this far north. The decent harbors are all well to the south. Maybe those on board are on an overnight trip to the Bay area.

I want to be on that boat. I want to escape the crowd below. I'd like to be transformed into a gull and take off. No, that would be the wrong bird. Gulls operate as a flock. Everyone below me, looking toward me, would see me alight, and take wing as well. Like a nervous cloud of birds, we would flitter over the water and then turn in the wind to descend once more on shore as though nothing had happened. Better to transform into a pelican. Maybe Otto, Jessica and Frank would do the same, and we could set off in a line to beat our way low across the water, like the prehistoric vestige of the past that we are, seeking in the water below something to connect us back to the dreams we once held.

Of course, it might be better to just be alone and leave the melodrama behind.

What I really want is another glass of wine. I look for Cat or Hillary. They seem to have disappeared into the crowd, ready to move their groups along.

My mouth is dry, almost cottony. I feel slightly sick. I should go back to the house. Why can't I have another glass of wine?

"Welcome," Aubrey shouts out. He holds up his hand, and silences the crowd. He holds some power over this group. He can bring their chatter to an end and amplify these people's anticipation with the energy of a great evening. He knows what he is doing. I realize the man isn't shouting. He has a microphone and amplifier. That's why everyone hears him.

Where is Chase? Why can't he be here beside me? If Aubrey expects me to guide half this group, I need a spiritual assist, something to distract me and give me support.

"Welcome," Aubrey continues. His long red hair is vibrant in the sunlight. In this setting, his weight gives him authority "This is the famed Mazzetti Ranch and Abalone Farm, and you are its welcomed guests."

He turns to me as though he expects me to say something, so I croak out, "Thank you for coming."

"As you probably have already met him, you know this is our host for tonight, Teddy Mazzetti. His family has owned this marvelous place for generations."

Aubrey turns toward me. "In a moment you can tell us more about the cattle raised here and the marvelous abalone which will highlight tonight's dinner. But first . . ."

Aubrey is off into the details of how the evening will work. I should pay attention, because I realize I don't recall the slightest idea about timing or sequence. But I don't really care. The Long Table people rented my farm, not me. I should just enjoy the night. To do that, I really need a glass of wine. I scan the crowd. I want to find and catch the eye of Chase.

Aubrey drones on. The sea of faces before me comes into focus. It should make me more frightened of what is about to come, but it doesn't. When I have attended a concert or play, I have noticed how performers manage to look out over the audience, without making eye contact with any single person. I could do that, I suppose.

There are also those who say that to calm one's nerves you should try to imagine your audience naked. How can you do that unless you have specific people in mind? I target individuals and I find myself being calmed. I actually imagine some of these people naked—not as they appear today but as they once existed in the past.

The voice changes. My foreman, Jake Driscoll, begins his overview on raising abalone. I have no worries about what he will say. He knows the process far better than me.

"Abalone has been a favorite food along this coast for centuries," Jake says. "The Chumash once lived on these shores. They would dive for it and other shellfish. There's evidence in the middens, or waste piles, that dot these shores. But in the twentieth century, we nearly harvested the native abalone to extinction. That is when Antonio Mazzetti, Teddy Mazzetti's grandfather, began his great experiment in farming abalone."

Who knew that Jake could be so eloquent? But I am still focused on finding Chase. I only feign paying attention to Jake. Very near the front of the group, I see all three of my houseguests in a row. They seem the perfect audience. Each of them also holds a full wine glass. How did they manage that? Would it be rude of me to step off the porch and grab one from Jessica? She doesn't seem interested in drinking.

I get distracted in thinking about how Frank would look naked. An eighty-year-old man probably wouldn't be that attractive. I have never have seen him completely nude. All those times that he accompanied on my skinny-dipping excursions, he always kept his white boxers on. They were quite transparent when wet.

"In the early stages of spawning," Jake explains. It sounds like he will go through the whole life cycle of abalone and how they are moved from concrete trough to concrete trough as they increase in size and age. His drone calms me. I realize the key information is being given in this intro. Maybe it really doesn't matter what I say when we divide into small groups.

Gina is in the crowd. She glowers at me in a way that I find unfair. She made the decision to be here, not me. I never thought she would want to come. Even if I had considered that possibility, I wouldn't have invited her. I wonder again about the woman with Gina. Should I try to talk to them?

On the opposite side of the group are Pedrag and his wife Helena. I never thought his wife cared at all for this place, yet tonight she is listening intently, almost enraptured, to Jake. Who would have thought she'd show such interest?

"When they reach the size of a quarter," Jake continues, "we move them to another trough."

For some reason, I notice the middle-aged couple who are staying at the inn. They appear uncomfortable, even angry. They focus their gaze on Jessica and Frank. Maybe they're bored. They probably just came for the dinner and weren't expecting a biology lesson on a giant snail.

The sun is lowering and getting into my eyes. I am having trouble picking out faces in the group. I notice the Fagatelle family group around Michael. The younger ones aren't paying attention either.

"While abalone are growing, they do nothing to pollute the water. In fact, the water leaves the entire process as clean as when it entered."

Why is Pedrag Miles' wife scowling at that? And then I notice Tiger and Elspeth next to Pedrag and Helena. There is a disturbing self-satisfied smirk on Elsbeth's face. For a moment, I imagine Tiger without clothes, but tell myself quickly that I am over that.

So many people, so many faces. At the edge I see Chase. He's holding a full glass of white wine as he moves toward the stage. He's bringing it to me. He read my mind.

And I can't help it, but I imagine him naked.

Quite delightfully naked.

Saturday, 5:41 PM

The tour is underway. Although divided in half, the groups are still unwieldy. Portable amplifiers are attached to Jake and me so that our voices can be heard. Even so, I'm not certain anyone is listening. Chase is constantly prompting me to say the next thing and to speak slowly and clearly. Admittedly, he is very good at moving the group along.

Here's the odd thing. I am enjoying the experience. There's something profoundly uplifting about having dozens of people you don't know trying to hear your every word. I find I am a funny fellow. At least, most of the guests laugh at my jokes.

Chase whispers in my ear, "Now, this needs to take at least twenty minutes so the culinary team has time to get the initial courses prepared. Don't go too fast."

But there's no fear of that. I forego all pretense of trying to explain anything about the raising of abalone. If they wanted the facts, people should have gone with Jake. He's far more conscientious. I have stories to tell.

In all these faces, I sense an innocence, I suppose, and an eagerness to learn. There's also a trust. After all, they were told that I am the expert. They know nothing about my tribulations over the years, nor would they care why I remain linked to this piece of Californian coastline. It's liberating.

Frank and Jessica linger near the edges. The worry that lined their faces begins to abate as we move along. I am glad they get to see me do this.

"So let's start with the basics," I say. "The abalone is really just a giant sea snail. You might say it's the escargot of the sea. When we get to the end of the tour, I will let you run your fingers along their foot. It's a most intriguing texture."

I find such details boring. I want to impart a little bit about what makes this place so special.

"My grandmother never understood why her husband would embark on this silly adventure of abalone raising. 'You're the son of a Swiss dairy man,' she would say as though that somehow should keep my Grandpa from anything to do with the sea. It certainly didn't stop him from raising cattle, and there were the cow pies all over the ranch to prove it.

"Don't step in those," I warn.

People seem to think that statement hilarious, although I meant it to be a legitimate warning. There aren't strong fences on this ranch, and sometimes the cattle wander down to the edges of the abalone area. An unexpected splotch is a real risk.

As we stop at the first tank, I look for Jake and his group. They are at the far end working backwards. Currently positioned in front of a giant pile of discarded abalone shells, Jake is asking some of the guests to touch the shells. They're a little oily before polishing, but even so their iridescent colors truly are beautiful. I get distracted for a moment and think we should create a namesake line of jewelry.

"Your grandmother," Chase prompts.

I take a sip of the wine and I wonder if there's enough to keep me going for the rest of this tour.

"So what's in this water?" someone shouts out.

"Well, I'm glad you asked," I reply. "We pump water up from the cove directly below here. The water is brought straight from the ocean, unfiltered and untouched, and then it runs down hill from concrete holding pan to concrete holding pan, all the way down the incline until it flows back into the ocean."

"Isn't that polluting?" someone says. Who said that? It's a preposterous idea. Jake already explained how clean these creatures are. Wasn't that person listening? Then I notice that halfway back in my group is Gina. She perked up when she heard that question and is looking for the person who asked it. But I just have to wonder how she ended up in my group.

"No, it isn't at all polluting." I try to put on a schoolteacher voice. I look to Jessica for some sign of praise for being so calm and professional. "Abalone are among the cleanest creatures. In fact, you could say they are an indicator species for the cleanliness of the water. They won't do well with almost any kind of pollution or roiling of water. During our entire process of raising them, they don't pollute the water. They feed on our special kelp shakes," I joke.

Somehow, I mumble on, but my mind is taken back to when I was a small boy. I used to walk with my Dad and Grandpa through this very nursery. I decide to tell the crowd about it.

"Many of the original holding pens remain from my Grandpa's day. Over time, Grandpa learned to make the bins shallower which in turn made it easier to pull up the screens on which the abalone attached themselves as they fed and grew. The whole secret of managing the process was to move the abalone from one tank to another as they reached a certain size. That way you could control the inventory as they slowly grew to a marketable size, about seven inches across. The process takes about eight years.

"While Dad and Grandpa didn't agree often over the cattle, the abalone pens were a place of peace. I would walk as a little boy between them, sometimes holding hands with each of them. I remember once they both simultaneously raised me up and swung me back and forth as I faced my favorite bluff. It was a beautiful day."

I think I'm losing my crowd. I try to get back on subject.

"Let's move down to the next set of stations and look at the size of the abalone there, and I will tell you more about why abalone have become so rare in the wild."

Hearing my words, Chase naturally falls into his sheep dog role. He ensures that no stragglers are left behind. I am happy to see that Jessica is helping, while Otto and Frank are engrossed in some whispered conversation.

From the corner of my eye, I see Gina inching forward. So far I have avoided her. There really isn't anything to say. I would prefer to keep it that way, but the woman with Gina seems to be egging her on.

"Back in the Seventies, California created a Coastal Commission and because of their rules and regulations, it would be pretty much impossible for anyone new to start such a business today," I point out. There's a woman nodding her head as though that is particularly meaningful. I realize it's Helena Miles. She acts as though she's an expert on this topic.

"Hi, Teddy."

Elsbeth and Tiger are standing directly in front of me. They are interrupting my train of thought and my presentation. This isn't a social hour.

"I see you know how to show up for this dinner," snaps Elsbeth. I don't understand why she looks so mad.

"Well, this is my home," I reply.

"You know I always wanted to see your place."

"Now, honey," Tiger says with little enthusiasm.

"It's so nice to finally get a chance to peek at the inner sanctum of the great Teddy Mazzetti," Elsbeth proclaims this insult with what I am sure is a fake smile.

Jessica, breaking from her volunteer herding duties, seeks to rescue me yet again. "I can't believe it. How nice to see both of you. It's been years. Do you still live in the village?"

My personal amplifier device is on, and I think the whole crowd heard the exchange. Many of them look at me expectantly.

"Old friends," I say in explanation.

Chase is coming up with the last stragglers and motioning me to continue with the talk. I look down at my watch. It's been more than fifteen minutes. It should be mostly downhill from here. I chuckle at the thought because that is literally true. We are on a gentle hillside and the rest of the tour is downhill.

"So, as I was saying," and I am on to discussing the peculiar nature of abalone sexuality. "Did you know that I've been told that some snails can be a male at one point in life and a female at another point in life? I wonder what that means to them."

The whole sexual world has always been a bit of a mystery to me. I wonder what lessons my parents failed to teach me about the birds and the bees.

"Hi brother," a voice whispers. It's Gina. She sidled up when I wasn't paying attention. "Have you met my girlfriend Clem?"

Gina has a wicked smile. I am sure she said that to confuse me, just as I was about to finish up the whole tour. And I was doing such a good job. On the opposite side of the tanks, Jake and his group are walking up hill to the beginning of the cycle. I can hear him carefully explaining the whole process of pumping the water.

"I want to talk," Gina whispers.

"Not now," I whisper back. "You know I'm in the middle of something."

Then Gina grabs the little microphone away from me and takes over my tour.

"Hello, everyone, I am Gina Mazzetti, Teddy's sister and the other owner of this ranch." She glares at me as she says that. "I thought I would add a few things that my brother forgot to mention."

Saturday, 5:56 PM

Before Gina can say anything embarrassing, Chase grabs the mike and moves us all along. Gina hangs back, tapping her foot. Her companion is whispering in her ear. One can only hope that she's convincing Gina to leave the event. At one point, I thought I would enjoy seeing Gina lash into Pedrag and his wife, but now I'm not so certain. I am still thinking about Pedrag's wife who asked the question about abalone pollution. Why would she ask such a thing? For that matter, why are they even here?

As the groups move toward the long table, Jake's and my groups of diners are beginning to merge together, the old with the young, the well-dressed with the scruffy, the excited with the bored, the drunk with the sober—although there aren't so many of the latter. Clearly the bar help has been too generous during the cocktail hour.

In this flow, Jake, Chase, and I are like a boat offshore, bobbing along. Maybe Chase knows what comes next, but I am only interested in realizing that somewhere in this downhill walk of explanation I have somehow gained another glass of wine. It's a red one. I take a sip. Pinot noir, I think. It will go well with the abalone.

Then we stop, surrounded by the crowd, next to a standing microphone. Aubrey is introducing the star of the moment, Leon Fagatelle, the chef extraordinaire from San Francisco, son of a San Luis Obispo butcher shop owner. Leon has that three-day scruffy beard that is favored by the creative sort.

I feel free to take a bigger gulp of my wine. I know without being told that Leon's presence means my time on the stage is soon over. After all, people aren't here to meet me. They came for the food and for the bragging rights of eating obscure dishes in even more obscure places. They now need to be primed on what they can expect in the hours ahead. I see them let their fingers caress their smart phones in eagerness. I can tell they're eager to sign onto their favorite app, already anticipating the thrill of posting some food porn. I hope they won't be too disappointed. Cell phone coverage is rather weak on this bit of coast.

I attempt to move away, but Chase reaches out to hold me back. He throws a look suggesting I am a misbehaving puppy who must remain in place. So I stay. Aubrey speaks about the Long Table tradition and the desire to feature artisanal food. Polite clapping follows. Then Leon speaks about his roots to the coast and his love of this farm. I listen in wonder, in part, because I question if he really means it. I never thought he paid any attention to me or any of the purveyors who filed through his father's shop. As he goes on to describe the evening's dishes, he begins to lose my attention. I take another sip.

I look out over the crowd. I see Tiger and his wife. He is luckier than me. He found someone. Maybe I helped in that regard. He really was my friend in high school, but he scared me. I thought he was handsome, so tall and skinny, his skin always pale, as though he could never get a tan. I tried to get him to go swimming at my cove, but he never did. Maybe he was afraid of being sunburned. I didn't press too hard, because I had my own fears. I know full well I could have found a date that night for the spring dance. I set the whole embarrassing evening up as a way to destroy our friendship. He was beginning to mean too much to me, and I couldn't have that.

I didn't know that was what I was doing at the time, or if I did know, I certainly didn't know how to tell myself what was going on. But I knew I had to lose him, just as I lost Frank when he and Jessica moved on without me.

I look over at Frank, Jessica, and Otto. The old coot really is a charming fellow, and maybe I am a bit jealous of him. Otto, I mean. Frank likes him, I can tell. He's a neighbor who amuses Frank with his tales of times gone by. But isn't that what you want in a friend? Someone to share stories with? Someone who can make you laugh, without any expectation of more?

I always wanted more of Frank. Yet I was always afraid that Jessica would realize it. I'm not sure that she ever did. I don't think she has ever fully understood me, even after all of those years taking care of my sister and me. Sure, she probably knew things that my parents never realized. She was the one who found that stack of body builder magazines stuck under my bed. Even Jessica, the kind soul that she was, surely recognized that I held no interest in exercise or weightlifting. It couldn't have been a mystery. Still, she never tried to interfere with my attempts to lure Frank into our swimming jaunts. Even to this day she pretends to wonder why I don't have a girlfriend.

She's looking at me now, flashing a smile as though to say that she knows how much I dislike this evening but still wanting me to know that I have survived it. I have, and I can make it to the end. Leon says something about the dessert planned as the grand finale. His menu recitation must soon be over.

I feel the glare of Gina's anger. I'm a bit abashed. I wonder if I should go and tell her that I actually am happy to see her. As the evening has gone on, it has slowly penetrated my thinking that the woman with her must be a true companion. Is it possible that both of us are gay and that we have never discussed it? The woman is clearly looking out for Gina. I have no other explanation than to think that she and Gina are lovers.

Maybe it is only fitting, on a lovely fall evening that all these people should come back into my life. Maybe it is a reminder that things aren't over yet. I may still have the chance to live my dreams.

I start laughing. The idea is absurd. Aubrey and Leon stare at me. They clearly haven't stopped their spiel, but I can't control myself. The idea that I have any dreams to achieve is just too funny. I keep chuckling. I try to control it, and I move backward, away from their limelight. Chase is pulling me away as well, but when I look at him he seems to be smiling, as though he has been inside my head and knows what I have been thinking. Impossible, of course, but I like to think so.

The crowd returns their full attention to Aubrey and Leon. Then I hear a loud sound over the crash of the waves. It is the carillon of dinner gongs all being rung as Aubrey shouts out, "Dinner is served."

The actual Long Table Dinner is about to begin.
And over two hundred people rush to find their seats.

PART FOUR

THE SEATED GUESTS: DINNER

Saturday, 6:05 PM

Chaos. Over two hundred dash to their preferred seats at the table. A few lug their special chairs across the grass field. Bringing your own chair is a dying tradition lingering from the Long Table Dinner's earliest days when it was a requirement to supply your own seat. Most chair luggers are in no hurry as they staked out their claims when they arrived.

For the rest, it is like the Oklahoma land rush. Everyone has his or her own idea of what constitutes an ideal spot. Some want to gaze out over the ocean as they sip their wine. Others seek to ensure that the setting sun will be at their back. A few want to be where the table placements are angled in gentle curves to match the line of the bluff. Perhaps they think these seats will maximize their visibility of the entire dinner.

The truth is that none of this positioning really matters. Soon enough the servers will pour the wine and set down the family style platters for the first course. In moments, everyone will focus on eating, talking, and meeting their tablemates. The surrounding scenery soon fades from awareness, and the din of dining table chatter masks the crashing surf.

Aubrey always knew that there was no sense in alerting his guests to what will initially happen. Who would listen? Besides Aubrey revels in the initial flurry. It makes everyone feel they have entered into some grand pursuit.

For some people, specific seats are important. Leon reserved a spot nearest the kitchen tent for his father and sisters. But because neither Leon nor any of the kids even suspect the existence of Naomi, there is no spot for Michael's girlfriend. Naomi chose to drive separately and has yet to arrive. Michael wants to wait near the event entrance until Naomi arrives, but he's afraid that if he lingers, he won't be able to grab an additional spot near his reserved space.

Completely unaware of their Dad's discomfort, Lucy and Leanne view the table as a grand chessboard requiring strategic choices. They want to be sure their dates sit near their Dad. At the same time, they must seat their other friends along the table. Group dynamics are hard to predict, but their plans to ignite a flash mob serenade later on depend on multiple catalysts.

"Dad, why don't you sit down?" Leanne asks.

"I'm waiting for someone," he replies. Despite his best efforts to remain stone-faced, he smiles. The truth is that he is quite excited for his kids to finally meet Naomi. They will surely find her as adorable as he does. Anyone would.

Leanne looks perplexed. "What are you talking about? You're waiting for someone? Who?"

Lucy hears that. "Someone else is coming?"

Gina and Clem dart behind the Fagatelle family. The two women are scoping out the entire table length. For a moment, Gina contemplates stopping to say hello to Michael Fagatelle. She's been to his butcher shop many times and wants to be friendly, but she is concerned about how quickly the seats are being filled.

Clem is frustrated. "Why can't we just sit by your brother? Or by Jessica and Frank? You haven't even talked to them yet. You know how much you like them."

Clem makes sense, but Gina has something else on her mind. Maybe she can't articulate it, but there has been a purpose behind her need to drive all this way.

"Don't confuse me," Gina snaps. "I didn't come here to see them. I can be with them anytime."

"Then why did you come?"

Gina doesn't bother answering. She is scanning everyone she can see. Her roving stare stops. Clem follows the sight line. She recognizes the couple. It's Pedrag and his wife.

"I'm going over there," and she rushes off without allowing Clem a chance to argue. In her headlong dash, Gina nearly collides with Henry and Sylvia Metternich.

"Maybe we should go," Henry says to his wife.

"Don't talk nonsense," Sylvia replies. "I'm not made of glass."

"But tonight was supposed to be a happy occasion."

"And it is. I've always wanted to see this place."

"And now you have," Henry says quietly. He doesn't want to say the obvious.

"I'm a big girl. You just worry too much. Remember how happy I was when you told me about this dinner. You never surprise me and this was just the perfect thing. Think about it. My favorite part of California. This beautiful coastline. You know how I always linger over Facebook posts showing Long Table Dinners. I am not giving it all up just because he is here. So what if that man is part of this night? I never expected to meet him and I never wanted to. But now that I have, I can ignore it. Can't I still enjoy dinner?"

"Are you sure?" he asks.

She doesn't reply. She sets her lip in that purposeful way he has learned means her mind is made up.

"Let's sit there," he says pointing to an unoccupied point midway down the table. "We'll be able to watch the sun set."

He deliberately doesn't comment how Frank and Jessica are walking toward the opposite end of the Long Table. He hopes the distance is enough so that his wife won't be reminded of their lost son. As they move toward taking their seat, another slightly older couple head in the same direction. It's Elsbeth and Tiger.

"You'd think people would dress up more," Elsbeth sniffs. "This dinner is so damn expensive. I feel like I'm overdressed. These people can afford better clothes, and look at them. Well, I don't give a damn. I wanted this to be a special occasion and it is."

Tiger wisely doesn't comment. Personally, he thinks Elsbeth looks as though she were heading to her high school prom. No one dresses so formally any longer—and certainly not to an outdoor event. Her shoulders are bare and her cleavage exposed. When the evening wind comes up, his wife will be shivering. Lucky for her, she forced him into donning a sports coat, so he can hand over his jacket when she needs to warm up.

"How about here?" he asks. He doesn't care. He just wants to sit. He's afraid that if he doesn't get Elsbeth in a chair soon she will try to perch right next to Teddy. Already he found the way Elsbeth talked to Teddy on the tour embarrassing. He has no desire for an encore.

"It's so far away," she complains. Tiger doesn't ask just what is far away. He knows. Teddy and his party are heading toward the table nearest the kitchen.

Sylvia, already seated, speaks up, "Do you live in the area? You're so lucky to live in such a beautiful place."

The question distracts Elsbeth from staring at Teddy. She turns to face Sylvia. "If I could leave, I would," she snaps.

Sylvia colors. Henry's eyes dart about frantically. He might be desperately seeking another spot. But nearly everyone has taken a seat.

"Why would you say such a thing?" asks Sylvia. She is clearly astonished by the idea that anyone would want to leave this coast.

"I grew up here. I'm sick of the place. You know too many of the people. And too many of them know you."

"So do you know Teddy Mazzetti?" Sylvia asks.

Elsbeth blushes and can't help herself from glancing over in Teddy's direction.

Teddy is stumbling a bit as he attempts to follow Chase, who is trying to guide Teddy and his guests to the four seats that have been reserved. They are right next to where Leon's family is positioned.

"Can't we just sit here?" Teddy demands as they pass an empty chair. Some of his buzz is wearing off, and he desperately wants another glass of wine. Chase pays no attention.

Jessica smiles. "You are the guest of honor Teddy. You need to go where they assign you."

Otto laughs. "This long table reminds me of a time when I was still working on the cruise ships . . ."

Teddy rolls his eyes. Frank notices and makes a covert gesture that is meant to tell Teddy to mind his manners.

"Well, at least I'm done with the talking now," Teddy says. "Isn't that right, Chase?"

"Here we are," Chase announces. "A space for each of you. Just in time. Leon is about to introduce the first course."

Saturday, 6:09 PM

"Good evening, everyone and welcome to our Long Table Dinner featuring Mazzetti abalone and beef." Leon's voice is strong and steady. It shows no strain from a day spent in an ad hoc kitchen. Over the course of the day in that improvised workspace, Leon discovered that many of the items rented never made it to the ranch. But he has made everything work.

"Our first course this evening is a delicate serving of abalone pickled in an Asian-style brine and lightly dusted with fennel pollen. There are strips along the side made from leaves of local kelp smoked with scavenged driftwood. It should all come together in an intriguing juxtaposition of flavors. Enjoy."

A small platoon of servers marches out with large silver salvers. Each platter is covered with a drifting of pink Himalayan salt, which has nestled within beautifully polished abalone shells. Each shell holds Leon's appetizer, a set of abalone morsels beribboned with the smoked kelp.

Leon adds, "Here's the special treat. When you finish your appetizer, keep the shell as a souvenir. My thanks to Jake for polishing so many shells in advance."

Each of the dozen servers hired just for the evening carries two plates. They now set the first of those plates midway between each group of eight diners. It is left to the guests to dole out their personal serving and then pass the dish. Everyone needs to trust their neighbor to take only their share during the passing. Gauging by the crazed looks of some of the diners who seem unduly eager to pounce on these shells, there appears some danger of that rule being forgotten. But a snag pops up in the flow. The members of the enthusiastic Instagram-mad crowd are taking out their phones and snapping away. They are so eager to show their friends what they're about to eat that they forget about the guest next to them.

"Isn't that something? So pretty," coos Elsbeth over the platter of shells. Unable to see Teddy, her mood is lightening.

"Doesn't look like there's much to eat," grumbles Tiger.

Sylvia smiles indulgently. Being from the big city, she knows how these things work, and she is eager to give counsel. "Tonight's a tasting menu. So each course will be small because there will be so many of them. Treasure each bite. I know I will."

"You are so right, honey." Now that Henry can no longer see Frank, or—as he thinks of the man in his own head—the killing general, he is also relaxing.

Along the long table, all the abalone servings are in place. One tray serves Pedrag and Helena and the couple across from them, Gina and Clem—as well as the two other couples who are Leanne's friends. Those four have kept to themselves as they do not want to tip their hand about the evening ahead. A certain tension swirls around the young friends, which tends to place Pedrag, Helena, Gina, and Clem into their own small circle.

"Helena," Pedrag begins. "This is Gina. She grew up on this ranch."

"That was before your husband stole it from my family. My great grandfather created this ranch. Now your goons won't even let me walk on it."

Clem taps Gina's arm. It's one of Clem's tricks to get Gina to control herself, but Gina tends not to follow Clem's tapping hints for long.

Helena, for her part, has no interest in the introduction and doesn't care how rude her fellow diners might be. She's here to gather information, not to make friends.

"And your forebears did create a beautiful place," Pedrag responds. He's never deterred by a challenging conversation. For a while, he's been thinking that the only way to calm his wife's obsession over the abalone farm would be to buy the place and close it down. Perhaps there can be some purpose after all to his attending this dinner.

At the front of the table, Leon has turned off the microphone, but he lingers near his family. There are two empty seats between his sisters with their dates and Teddy's party. He asks, "Where's Dad?"

Teddy, further down the table, hears Leon's voice and looks up. "Michael's not here?" he asks. His words slur. A sparkling rose is paired with the abalone appetizer, and he did quick work of it.

Lucy jumps in. "He'll be here any minute. He says he's waiting for someone, and he asked us to make sure there was an extra seat next to him."

"Who else is coming?"

"I don't know."

Teddy is the first to notice the two figures walking up. He shouts out, "Here's your dad and mom." Teddy should know better. After all, he met Michael's wife many times while she was alive. He even attended her funeral. All the wine has befuddled his mind.

Teddy's words prompt Jessica to jump in. "Oh, Leon, are your parents attending? That must be so nice."

"It's Michael's birthday," Teddy blurts out. Someone told him that earlier, although he can no longer remember who.

Leanne replies with iciness, "Our mother is dead. I have no idea who's with him."

"Hey, Dad," Leon walks toward Michael. "Who's this?"

Michael smiles uneasily. "It's my date. Naomi, meet my son Leon. He's the genius behind all of tonight's menu. You're sure to love him and his food."

Leon shifts awkwardly from one foot to the other, not quite certain what to say or do. Then he recalls that he is the chef. He is needed in the kitchen. "Excuse me, but I have to start work on the next course. You're going to love it, Dad. Nice to meet you, Naomi."

And he scurries off.

Michael thinks one down and two to go. He takes hold of Naomi's arm and walks the few remaining feet. The eyes of his daughters are upon him and he doubts the wisdom of his planning. One of the boys (he thinks the kid's name is Dennis) stands up as they approach. Michael notices Teddy Mazzetti and nods to him. Another moment of reprieve, but he can no longer avoid what he has planned for weeks.

"Girls, I thought tonight would be a great opportunity for you to meet someone very important in my life. This is Naomi Cleveland. She and I have been seeing each other for a few months. I guess you could say we've been dating."

The girls are quiet. It's not quite clear just what they are thinking. Their dates are oblivious to any awkwardness. In fact, they are only moments from exchanging bro bumps with the dad in congratulations on his date.

"It's nice to meet you, Lucy. And you, Leanne. Did I get that right?" Naomi knows she is correct. The two girls are not identical twins, and Michael has shown her countless photographs. She was very careful to memorize each face. She wants to make this evening work, even though she tried to tell Michael that it was a bad idea to introduce her in such a public place, but Michael loves his daughters and is convinced they will be happy for him. Naomi is well aware that children can be more complicated.

"Your dad talks so much about both of you. Leon too, of course. He loves all of you so dearly."

"Well, since he never mentioned your name, I guess he doesn't love you." Leanne turns away. She has to. She's afraid she will start crying. She has spent weeks planning such a perfect evening for her dad. Now he's ruined it all.

The sun is lowering. There's less than an hour to go before sundown. Clouds have yet to appear on the horizon, but there is a settling chill in that final hour as daylight turns to dusk.

"Leanne, apologize. You're being rude."

"Hey, can I get another glass of sparkling wine?" shouts Teddy. Teddy is quite loud and many along the table notice.

"Your brother seems to be making a scene," Pedrag says calmly. "I think he's quite inebriated."

Gina sneers at the comment. She doesn't care if Teddy's drunk. She whispers something to Clem which neither Pedrag nor Helena can hear.

"What are you talking about?" Helena demands. She is finding the evening quite distasteful. Mostly vegan in her eating habits, she has grown accustomed to requesting exactly what she wants at her restaurants. Tonight is quite another matter, and she hadn't expected it. After all, she is a part owner of Leon Fagatelle's San Francisco restaurant. He should have known he would need to offer vegetarian dishes. There is no way she will let one of these detestable, slimy creatures go down her throat. The young man next to her eagerly scoops up the rejected serving of abalone.

The servers return. They move from group to group to picking up the empty appetizer trays. They set down baskets containing thin slices of toasted French bread. They uncork bottles of a coastal pinot noir from a local winery renowned for mastering grape growing so close to the coast.

"A red so early in the progression," sniffs Sylvia. "Are they bypassing the whites? Surely they're aren't serving a red with the next abalone course."

Sylvia does love her winetasting, and Henry debates whether to shut down his wife's conversation or egg it on. It would be one way to keep her mind focused on the things she enjoys. But he holds his tongue, even though he finds her a bit insufferable when she gets too wound up on nose, bouquet, and color.

"As long as it's got a high alcohol content, it's fine with me," jokes Tiger.

Elsbeth looks at him with affection. "Tiger actually knows a bit about wine. After all we live in wine country, and wine tasting is one of the things we like to do."

"So do I," sighs Sylvia. "So do I."

"Do you have any favorite local spots?" asks Henry.

Tiger answers. "Actually, I like this particular vineyard and its pinot. It's a family place located a few miles outside town. I think our cool climate makes for more interesting wines."

Sylvia nods in approval at Tiger's words, and Elsbeth looks at her husband as though seeing him for the first time. There's something novel in his appearing as the expert. Maybe she underestimates him a bit too often.

Sylvia accepts Tiger's pronouncement as the truth. Besides she is more interested in talking about the town. "This is such a lovely little village. Like I said earlier, it must be so nice to live here all the time. If we could afford it, I'd sell our place in Los Angeles and get a little cottage on the hill. I'd sit all day watching the ocean. Can you really see whales go by?"

"We like it here."

"And this ranch," Sylvia continues, "is the most beautiful place. I'm so happy Henry surprised me with tickets to this dinner. I've always wanted to go to one of the Long Table events. So romantic, don't you think? All of us eating together like we were one big family."

"I think these dinners are too expensive," says Elsbeth. "But since tonight's special, I guess it's okay. Officially, we're celebrating our fiftieth anniversary." This potentially tender moment is broken when Elsbeth adds, "We're only together because of Teddy. He was our matchmaker."

She glances at Tiger. "Or was he our pimp?"

Henry grabs the bottle of pinot noir to mask the awkwardness. He pours both himself and Sylvia more than their fair share. It seems politic not to add comment to that conversation.

Around the table, other conversations are equally awkward.

"You don't like your brother very much, do you?" asks Pedrag. Talking to Gina is better than sitting in silence, he figures, and an idea has occurred to him.

"About as much as I like you," replies Gina.

Clem jumps in. "You have to excuse Gina. We had a long drive up from Los Angeles this afternoon. And she's finding it stressful to be back on the ranch after such a long time away. After all, she grew up here. It's a very special place to her."

Pedrag smiles. "I guess it has been a while since you've been back. As far as I've heard, we haven't had to kick you off our land for a few years."

Gina takes the bait. "Your land! You and my brother stole it from me. You shouldn't even own one bit of this coastline. Not one bit. I never agreed to sell any of it."

"Well, it's too bad your brother didn't sell this abalone farm as well," snipes Helena. "What a horrible place. It should never be allowed to operate."

Gina says nothing.

The shadows inch longer; the air remains calm. For a moment the entire crowd of diners has either stopped talking, or maybe a particular large wave crashed against the rocks below. In any case, for a moment, everyone pays attention to the sound of the surf.

In the distance, a formation of pelicans flies low across the glow of the ocean surface. That image makes everyone recall the special locale of this dinner. More than one person pulls out a phone to capture a shot or two they can post to their friends.

Deena, Jason, Emily, and Clay—the friends of the Fagatelle girls—pull closer together for their own selfie. Then they huddle to talk of the surprise ahead. Putting their heads together also shields them from Pedrag and Gina's sniping. Soon, the friends start to gossip.

"Was that Leon's dad who came in late? The old guy with the woman?"

"Yeah, who is she? Didn't Leanne's mother die over a year ago?"

"Maybe he has a girlfriend."

"Leanne won't like that. She idolized her mother."

"It has to be a girlfriend. Who else could it be? The girls didn't mention anything about another guest."

"Well, it is his birthday. Guess he can do what he wants."

"I wonder if we should check with Lucy or Leanne and make sure the skit is still on. Maybe this changes things."

Back underneath the kitchen tent, Leon is involved with his own version of plans going wrong. While he wants to focus on finishing the garnish for the trays of beef carpaccio, he is foundering. He has an exact image in his mind on how the individual leafs of arugula should surround the edges of the plate, but it as though he has forgotten how to use his tweezers. Everything is a mess.

"Want my help?" Annabelle can see he needs it.

"Sure," he replies tersely.

"What's wrong?" she asks.

"I think I was just mean to my Dad for no good reason."

"How?"

"He shows up with this woman. None of us know who she is. We've never heard him say one word about dating anyone since Mom died. Then here's this woman. At least ten years younger than him."

"Is that what's wrong. She's too young? Hey, you're missing some arugula on this one."

"I don't understand why he didn't ask for me to give him another ticket if he wanted to bring a date. He must have planned it. The tickets were sold out weeks ago. The thing is that I could have given him another seat. It's like he felt he needed to ambush us."

"Maybe he just didn't want to put you on the spot for giving out another free seat."

"Why would he hide her from us? I don't like it."

Back at the table, Teddy is seated again. Jessica pours some of the pinot into his glass. She didn't give him as much as the others, and she certainly didn't let him pour for himself. She's careful, because similar to how there's only one platter for each grouping of eight, there's only one bottle to serve the same eight. Jessica thinks even a three ounce pour is more than enough for any of them, especially Teddy. She doesn't want him to pass out before the final cake is served.

She wonders if she shouldn't just let Teddy make his mistakes, but she dismisses the idea. Once a caretaker, she thinks, always a caretaker.

Saturday, 6:31 PM

Aubrey is pleased. Tonight is one of his best dinners ever: sold out, perfect weather, great menu, and a dynamite buzz. What more could one want? Maybe he'll give his staff a bonus. The idea flits through his mind and then disappears. The light evening breeze plays with the flaps of the hanging white tablecloths, and Aubrey worries things are about to change.

Leon and Annabelle stride out of the tent. Aubrey wonders why Annabelle is walking beside the chef. She was scheduled to be one of the servers. But Aubrey notes that the serving dishes from the initial course are all picked up, the initial wine bottles carted off, and the breadbaskets laid out. Maybe she's bored.

Aubrey has a theory about his events. People don't come for the food or the view, but to experience a moment of magic. To satisfy that desire, he and his team only need to ensure the food comes out, the wine flows, and no one contemplates anything sad. Aubrey thinks it should be a motto for life, "No sad moments." He tries to live that credo, which might be why he is successful at attracting his band of wanderlust kids.

Aubrey notices Teddy, which gives him a pang of concern. That man clearly has a different approach to life. He has been nothing but trouble from the beginning. Now Chase is pulling him away from the kitchen. Why isn't Teddy staying at his seat at the table? Maybe Chase should take the old man up to his house and convince him to sleep it off. Clearly he has been drinking too much. It's been a challenge to figure out how to curtail Teddy's drinks. That's always the problem with these dinners. With everything served family style, it's nearly impossible to cut off any single diner. The old woman who's staying with Teddy is walking toward Chase. Aubrey judges her a beautiful woman and wonders why she and her husband put up with Teddy.

Annabelle and Leon reach the microphone. She pulls it from the stand to hand over to the chef. Leon taps on the head, hears the reverb, and launches into his description of the next dish. Standing near the parking area past the far end of the table, Aubrey has trouble hearing more than bits and pieces, but there's no need for him to get closer.

Leon is boasting. "Notice how the wafer thin rounds of beef tenderloin line the platter to form a succulent film. I spilled the truffle foam over the top to mimic the tips of the waves hitting the beach below. If you like, think of the bits of arugula as an homage to the beds of kelp offshore."

Aubrey laughs to himself. Regardless of Leon's fanciful imagery, the guests are going to love this dish.

Then he spies some disquieting signs. Some people are not having a good time. One of the glum groups is Leon's own family. Leon was given tickets only to bring his father to the event, and then somehow he added two sisters and their dates. Aubrey argued with Leon over his insistence on serving a small birthday cake later, but eventually Aubrey gave in. He allows his chefs to always be right—as long as it doesn't cost too much. He doesn't recall Leon mentioning that his father would have a date. In fact, Aubrey thought the old man was a widower. The entire group looks tense, and it probably doesn't help that Teddy is sitting right next to them. Aubrey decides he needs to do something.

At the mike, Leon wraps up, turns, and strolls back to the tent with Annabelle close on his heels. She is excitedly chatting. It's not her usual style. Aubrey wonders what is going on, but Max who has just returned from the bus interrupts him. Even though the dinner still has hours to go, Max is already preparing for the wrap-up and has questions. He notices how Aubrey is watching Annabelle and Leon.

"I think our little girl has a crush," Max says.

Aubrey turns with an annoyed look. "Have you already started drinking?"

"Cool it, boss. Just one beer. I know to wait until everything's packed. Besides ain't this beach a perfect setting for a staff blowout? Ain't it?"

Aubrey doesn't answer He's back to scanning the table looking to isolate bad apples that could turn the evening's mood. It's an art, his ability to drop in on a conversation among strangers and nudge it into the party mode. He thinks people underestimate him.

He swoops in on a brewing trouble spot, his concern about Teddy forgotten.

"How are you enjoying the carpaccio?" he asks a couple looking a little too glum.

Henry answers for Sylvia, "Just delicious."

Sylvia smiles in agreement. She doesn't really know if she likes it or not. Everything tastes much the same to her, ever since she saw General Frank Mueller.

"Great. Just fantastic," Aubrey exudes. "And what about this lovely couple?" He swivels toward Tiger and Elsbeth. "I bet tonight's a special occasion."

Sylvia quickly jumps in, "They're celebrating their fiftieth wedding anniversary." Although Sylvia is quite proud of herself for announcing this fact, Elsbeth displays a slight grimace.

"And are your kids helping you celebrate?" Aubrey grandly gestures to the two couples sitting next to them. Jason and Clay, with their girl friends, look startled. They aren't expecting to be noticed, at least not until Leanne kicks off the singing tribute.

For some reason, Tiger finds the idea that these preppy-looking kids might be his offspring quite funny. "Are you kidding? Our kids wouldn't ever come to something as fancy as this. Too cheap. The only person my wife and I know here is Teddy."

"How's that?" Aubrey is feeling desperate. So far nothing he's doing is changing the trajectory of a downward spiral. If he isn't careful, the sour mood he detects will jump like a flu bug from person to person and infect the whole evening.

"We both went to school with Teddy," Elsbeth is quick to say. "He was Tiger's best friend. But he never had much to do with me. Always wanted to keep me at a distance. Even when he knew how much I wanted to see his famous old ranch he never offered. So I had to shell out a fortune for this fancy dinner just to get our chance. I can tell you this place is not so grand."

"You don't think so?" Sylvia asks. "I find it quite marvelous. One couldn't ask for a more beautiful evening. Everything truly is spectacular."

Henry notices a bit of pinot noir lingering in the bottle near them. He grabs it before the four college kids get a chance, and he pours the last into Sylvia's glass. A little wine always lightens the mood.

Aubrey notices such things. It gives him an idea. "Well, any friend of Teddy's is a friend of this dinner. It looks like you like that pinot, sir. Let me get a waiter over here and give this section an extra bottle."

At hearing that, the kids perk up. They give Aubrey extravagant mock applause. Clay jumps in to say, "We'll use it to toast this couple and their big day. What're your names?"

"I'm Elsbeth, and they call my husband Tiger."

"Tiger! Wow. Must be an animal in the bedroom, huh? Am I right?" Clay is quite pleased with himself for his stale joke, but Elsbeth takes an appraising look at her husband, as though it took some stranger's joke to let her see her husband with fresh eyes.

"He's not so bad," she admits.

The server delivers the extra bottle. Aubrey pours enough into each of the glasses to empty the bottle.

"Well, then, here's a toast to Tiger and Elsbeth. May tonight be the best dinner you've ever had in your lives. May tomorrow's be even better than tonight's."

Young and old clink their glasses together. Those around the eight, seeing the motion, start to raise their glasses as well. The faces seem less strained, and the smiles more genuine. Aubrey thinks to himself, "My job here is done."

Saturday, 6:42 PM

Under the canvas marquee, Leon's staff finishes the thirty-two platters that will hold the next course. It's a return to abalone. Leon yearns to step out of the tent, head toward the bluff, sit and watch the waves, maybe smoke a cigarette, and let his mind clear. It's hard to think about cuisine when his Dad is out there with some unexpected woman.

"Aren't you forgetting something," Annabelle asks. She doesn't want Leon to abandon his plans, and that is what seems likely to happen. She is dismayed that he hasn't asked for the small dishes needed for the palate-cleansing dish—the course she earlier predicted he wouldn't actually serve. After this day together, she wants him to prove her wrong.

Leon knows what Annabelle is talking about, but the dinner is already running late. He never listed the sorbet on the menu. No one but Annabelle and his staff will even know it's missing. The intermezzo course was planned as a surprise for Aubrey.

"There isn't time," he says.

Leon is deflating before Annabelle's eyes. She doesn't understand his attitude, and she won't accept it in someone so young. "You're wrong. There certainly is enough time. Everything is already made. We only have to serve it."

"But the presentation is too fussy," he counters. "Time matters."

She fears his hesitancy has something to do with his family, but she doesn't know what. She senses a mood shift ever since he met his father's girlfriend. She doesn't understand why that bothers him. What she does understand is how important this dinner is to him. She is not going to let Leon destroy the very thing he is creating.

"You're right. Time does matter," she says with determination. "You need more time to finish the meat course. Leave everything to me. I can plate the sorbet. That will let you do what you need to do with the short ribs. You know there actually is no option. You have to serve this surprise ice because your timing for the next course counts on the distraction. You know I'm right."

Where did this conviction come from? She has no idea, but even he knows that she is absolutely correct. She can see the respect in his eyes. She doesn't normally get any acknowledgement of her skills at these dinners. She likes it. She could get used to it.

"You win. Get the bowls out. So you know what to do?"

She smiles. "Yes. A slice of the heirloom tomato, a scoop of the tomato gazpacho ice, and a sprig of fresh celery."

"You have to do it fast. That ice has vodka in it. There's reason I call it a Bloody Mary surprise."

"Got it, boss!"

She heads off to the supply shelves. The rest of the servers move out with their abalone Louis salads. Leon muses that maybe this dinner will work after all. He lingers a moment more than necessary to watch Annabelle begin to assemble the sorbet course.

The first server with the salad platter stops in front of Michael Fagatelle and his girls. He recites his spiel. "Our salad course is a take on the famous West Coast dish, crab Louis. Only instead of crab, our chef is featuring a special preparation of abalone in a fresh mayonnaise, paired with local greens and Morro Bay avocados. Enjoy."

"I thought Leon was supposed to describe each dish," Michael remarks. Neither of the girls says anything. Michael thinks they are deliberately ignoring him.

Naomi breaks the awkward silence, "I'm sure he's very busy in the kitchen. I can't imagine how so few people put on such an elaborate event. And I'm told they do it several times a week, going from farm to farm. Can you imagine the planning that must be involved?"

The girls ignore Naomi and that makes her want to slap these two. How can they be so rude to their father? Especially on his birthday. It's not as though she didn't warn Michael that it was a bad idea to surprise his children. Further, she doesn't understand why it was so important to him that she appear unannounced. It would have been far better for each of the girls to be prepared.

Naomi had seen the pictures of the whole family together at various events. The Fagatelles clearly were a tight-knit bunch. For any family, but especially theirs, it would have been a shock to suddenly lose their mother so young. It is hard for Naomi to tell Michael anything about family interactions. She and Charlie never had children and Naomi had been an only child. What can she claim to know of brothers and sisters or being fathers and mothers?

Well, damn it, she knows more than Michael gives her credit for. She can see petty jealousy and selfish pride when it is right in front of her. That's what is going on here. Even the girl's boyfriends, as clueless as they seem to be, are uncomfortable. The question is: what is she going to do about it?

"Your Dad and I met at a survivor's group," she begins. She carefully watches the girls' faces. She wonders if they even know that he participates in such a group. "It's hard when the most important person in your life leaves. I don't know which is harder. When the person dies unexpectedly like my Charlie. Or when you know it's coming. No matter how much time you have to prepare, it's never enough."

Leanne's face displays no sign of sympathy.

"Do you know how much your father is hurting?"

"Of course I do," Leanne snaps. "I lost my mother too you know."

Lucy squirms a bit, "We love Mom and Dad very much. But it hasn't been very long."

"It's been almost a year," says Naomi gently. She doesn't wait for a reaction, she just continues. "I know, because Charlie died almost at the same time. Michael and I were both very new to the survivor's group when we met. Maybe that's why we found a comfortable space with one another."

"Naomi is a lot like your Mom," Michael says.

"Really? She's twenty years younger."

Dennis wants to change the conversation. "I hear it's your birthday, Mr. Fagatelle?"

Leanne cuts him off. "Don't bring that up. I think Dad has other things on his mind than his birthday."

"But . . . " Dennis sputters. He's thinking of the grand event ahead.

"We should just let him enjoy the day however he wants to. He doesn't care what we think."

"Baby, don't say that. I invited Naomi because I thought this would be a great chance for everyone to meet one another. You're spoiling it."

Dennis stands up. "Look. Mr. Mazzetti is coming back. Should we talk to him?"

Teddy has been wandering as he tries to escape Jessica's control. She's keeping his wine glass empty. When the most recent bottle, a lovely chardonnay intended to be paired with the crab Louis came by, she motioned the fellow along. At that, Teddy stood up and started walking around without any real purpose in mind. Perhaps he holds some inchoate thought of trying to find Leon and talk to him. When he glances at Michael and his family, his course shifts. He recalls there's something he needs to say to the butcher, but he can't quite remember what it is.

"Hey Michael, there's something I want to talk about," Teddy says. "But damned if I know what it is. Maybe another glass of wine would help."

"We got some left," Dennis shouts out. He stands, walks over to Teddy and pours the rest of the chardonnay into Teddy's empty glass.

Through this, Naomi watches Lucy and Leanne. There's something she should talk to them about. She just isn't sure when to do it.

Saturday, 6:53 PM

By this time, the salads are cleared, and the tomato ices are set in front of each guest. The sorbet is already beginning to melt. Gina discards her frothy twig of celery from her bowl and slurps the small serving as though it were an icy oyster on the half shell. She has other things in mind.

Clem reaches out, "What are you up to?" She knows this woman well. She recognizes something has changed.

Gina doesn't bother to answer. Instead, Gina pushes back her chair, stands, and marches toward the two older couples. Her eyes are set on one specific individual—Tiger. Thinking of her brother's high school days, she plans to get to the bottom of something. Seeing no recourse, Clem stands as well. She mutters a soft "excuse me" to Pedrag and his wife and then dashes after her friend.

"That's a bit rude, don't you think?" Helena says. Her husband shrugs. He's glad to see Gina disappear. He's working on an idea, and her absence lets him stay focused.

The four friends of the Fagatelle girls look at each other. They're beginning to recognize the challenges ahead if they are going to try to jumpstart a mass sing-along. No one thought in advance of what distractions might be going on in other guests' minds.

Gina reaches her target and says with unusual energy, "Hi, Tiger and Elsbeth."

Tiger, Elsbeth, and their two newly found friends across the table, are feeling the effects of the extra bottle of wine provided by Aubrey. There's an unusual giddiness to Elsbeth. She is finally feeling as though coming to this dinner has been a really good thing.

"What's up, Gina" Tiger says, although it is a bit hard to be sure exactly what he slurs out. Elsbeth smiles indulgently. Sylvia has been very interested over the last ten minutes in hearing everything Elsbeth has to say about the small town. This has placed Elsbeth in the unaccustomed pleasure zone of being the focus of someone's favorable attention.

"Hey, I just wanted to come by and say hello. It's been so long and I thought 'what were the odds that we would both be sitting here having dinner together after all these years,' although I must admit back in the day, I sometimes thought you'd end up living here with Teddy."

"What?" Tiger says. He's looking more befuddled than the extra wine calls for. Elsbeth's eyes narrow.

Clem reaches the table. "Gina, let's get back to our table." She emphasizes her suggestion by tugging on Gina's sleeve. Gina is in a mood all her own.

"Tiger, you should meet Clem. She's my lover."

Now Henry and Sylvia are watching the interchange. Just starting to feel good about the evening, this threatens to spiral everything out of control. Neither Henry nor Sylvia has anything against lesbians or any other alternative lifestyle. But the growing tension in Elsbeth's face radiates its own signals.

Back at the table's end, Teddy remains standing, albeit a bit wobbly. He grabs the back of Michael's chair. It's not quite clear whether he plans to make some major point or just needs the extra support. Naomi is about to stand and help Teddy back to his seat before he falls. Before she can, Chase reappears.

"Mr. Mazzetti," he says. "Your tomato ice is going to melt."

Teddy, who is fond neither of Bloody Marys nor intermezzo courses, remains focused on his empty wine glass. He wonders how that happened.

"I was going to go talk to Michael," he says. "I think I should wish him a happy birthday. He's my best customer."

Michael blushes at hearing that. He can't help but think about the stack of unpaid bills back in his office.

Down the table, Tiger is blushing too. He has no idea about how to respond to Gina's unexpected aggressive stance. He's still trying to work his way through her crack about his living at the ranch. What did she mean by that?

Gina eagerly helps him out. "Well you know, the way you and my brother were so into each other, back in the day. I just figure things run in the family."

Suddenly a light bulb goes off for Sylvia. "Oh, are you the sister of Mr. Mazzetti? Is this your ranch too?"

Clem decides to end this conversation. She becomes more forceful in prompting Gina back to their seats, but Gina, as always, has her own idea.

"It should be my ranch," she sputters, "but my brother is a treacherous little snake. Stole it from me, that's what he did, and then he sold half of it to that asshole over there, the guy that we're sitting with."

Henry sees the target of Gina's gesture. He is suitably impressed by who he sees. He prides himself on his ability to pick technology stocks (about which he displays an unfortunate habit of acquiring in small quantities at their high and later selling at a low), and so he recognizes the subject of Gina's scorn.

"Isn't that Pedrag Miles?" he asks with some awe.

"The one and the same. He built a big house next door. His goons won't even let me walk on the bluffs that used to be mine. Now tell me, is that fair?"

"You said he owns the place," Henry points out.

"He stole it. By conspiring with my brother." Suddenly she spins toward Tiger. "You should have fucked my brother in high school. Maybe then he wouldn't have fucked me later in life."

During this short exchange, an incredible range of emotions crosses Elsbeth's face like a bad movie in fast forward. The innuendo that her husband might be gay doesn't disturb her. They've spent enough decades in the same bed that she knows the charge isn't true. Even if it were, it would hardly matter. She has the family she wanted, and she's never felt neglected in that regard. But something is bothering her.

Hearing Teddy, the love of her teenage life, slandered by his own sister, is unsettling. How could she have worshipped someone who wasn't even into girls? She isn't about to buy a word of anything spouted by this annoying sister.

On the other hand, Sylvia is quite intrigued by this turn of conversation. Unlike her husband (who is considering ways to go over and introduce himself to Pedrag), Sylvia has no interest in famous technologists or real estate misdeeds. An old man's sexuality is just as dull. As far she's concerned it's just fine that Henry's libido dialed back to simmer some five years ago. The occasional quick Saturday night tussle to prove they can still do it is more than enough to satisfy her urges. But this angry woman might tell her something she simply must know about the couple that's been around Teddy.

"So you must be Teddy's sister. You probably know the people eating with your brother. What can you tell me about that couple? I feel like I should know them."

Seeing a chance to reset the mood, Clem jumps in. "Of course, Gina knows who they are. Jessica and Frank Mueller are old family friends."

Clem's ploy actually works on Gina, who looks over at the elderly couple. By this time, Jessica has managed to lure Teddy back to his seat. Even from this distance Gina can see the care and concern on their faces. They are emotions she recalls from her preteen years. While she may detest her brother, she still cares for Jessica and Frank.

"Oh them. Jessica and Frank. They're the best things that ever happened to my life. Always took care of me and gave me love when nobody else ever did."

Gina smiles at her thoughts and wants everyone to share in her good memories. Then she notices tears streaming down the woman's face. Even Gina can tell that they aren't tears at hearing a happy story. They seem tears of anger and hatred.

Sylvia doesn't wait to be asked about her tears. "Well, that man killed everything that mattered to me."

Saturday, 7:00 PM

Leon is back on stage. Annabelle stands at his side. At some point during the evening, she transformed and became his needed sidekick. Without any words exchanged, the two somehow mutually agreed that she would join him for his short introductions.

"We're pouring the wine for this next course a bit early," Leon says. "I want it to enjoy a little extra time to breathe in this beautiful evening air. You should find that this extra time will open it up and round out its luscious tones. This is a lovely, peppery, and spicy wine. You will be able detect hints of blackberries and plum in this local syrah. The grapes are actually grown very close to the cooling fogs of our coast, just a few miles from here. Like Mr. Mazzetti, the family of the winemaker has been part of this community for over a hundred years."

Michael eyes his son. He senses something is going on. He catches the eye of Naomi. She in turn slightly arches her eyebrows because they both detect the spark passing between Leon and Annabelle. Neither of the sisters notices anything. They still stew over the unplanned guest in their midst. Their festering anger is no secret to Michael and Naomi.

"Let the wine breathe in the aromas of the sea for a moment. Then give it a good swirl when your next dish arrives. Take a sip and allow it to coat your mouth. Then taste a bit of the braised short ribs. Follow that with the potato gnocchi and fresh grilled corn. Then I suggest you should sip the wine again. I guarantee that the wine takes on a whole new flavor. Try it. If all goes well, your taste buds will explode with the flavors of the harvest."

Down the row, Helena Miles pays no attention to the culinary gobbledygook of her young chef. While she may hold an investment in his restaurant, that funding was never a result of her having much interest in food. Her pursuits are generally marked by higher callings. Nevertheless, at the moment, she is trying hard to garner more than her fair share of the gnocchi. It's not that she particularly likes the pasta-like dumplings. It's just that she will not allow a gelatinous chunk of short rib to pass through her well-defined lips. This dinner is leaving her uncomfortably hungry.

"I've been thinking," Pedrag starts. He wants to air his idea before the Mazzetti girl returns, and he has noticed that both Gina and Clem just turned from the couple they darted toward earlier. Pedrag can't be certain but it appears that the woman of that couple is now crying. No doubt Gina has uttered something horrible.

"What?" his wife asks.

"We could have this all."

Helena looks at him and lays down her folk. She senses something is about to break her way. "You know that's all I ever wanted. But how?"

"Listen to me carefully. Before that woman gets back. Then just follow my lead."

The servers are out with their bottles of the purple inky syrah. As they make each small pour, that area of the table is engulfed with a whiff of intoxicating aroma. Among the guests, the fanciful even imagine they see a light violet hue in the colors on the Western horizon. It is as though the wine and the sea and the sky are beginning to merge. Along the ridge of the hill next to their setting, even a few cows seem to appear as sentinels to the lowering sun.

The platters of short ribs with gnocchi are rapidly depleted. Some admire the deep crusty brown of the meat's glaze, a direct result of Maillot principles at work with the wine of the braising liquid. Others like the way the meat stands out against the fluffy white pillows of gnocchi dotted with the charred tips of yellow kernels recently sheared from their cobs. Still others just eat.

At the table, Michael turns his attention to his daughters.

"The kid's knocking it out of the park tonight. Don't you think?" He hopes complimenting one sibling might open a path to discussing what's really on his mind.

"Yeah, it's a great meal," murmurs Lucy.

Naomi thinks enough is enough. "Listen girls" she begins.

For some reason, Teddy finds great interest in this family drama, so much so that he doesn't even notice that Jessica is again preventing his wine glass from being filled. Meanwhile, Otto regales the guests on his right with a story from his old days on passenger ships. That leaves Frank and Jessica time to talk to one another.

"Sixty years ago, did you ever imagine that we end up here?" Frank whispers to his wife. "Still babysitting the boy."

"Hush," she says. "We just need to get him through the night. Teddy has never done well with stress."

Back at her chair, Gina blurts, "Did you miss us?" She and Clem sit facing Pedrag Miles. One of the millennial kids looks up and gives Gina a warning look. She pays no mind.

"So I had a thought while you were gone," Pedrag says.

Clem looks at the man with curiosity, but Gina is already distracted. She stares toward the end of the table where her old babysitters dine. It looks like that crying woman is walking over toward Frank, even though her husband is clearly trying to pull her back.

"I think I have something to suggest that you might like," Pedrag continues. "As I understand it, you still own half this ranch."

"Technically forty-nine percent. But you know Teddy controls it."

"Still I don't think the courts will allow him to ignore your wishes entirely. At least not if you had a good attorney on your side."

Clem's face darkens. She isn't trusting where this might head. She reaches for the platter with the remaining bits of short ribs. Helena has left very little in way of the accompanying gnocchi. Clem decides to distract Gina with food.

"Let's taste this," Clem says and proceeds to spoon some onto her girlfriend's plate. For the first time, she notices that at the center of Gina's plate there is a painted decoration of a small hive encircled by a few flying bees.

"What's your point?" Gina asks. "It didn't stop him from selling you half my ranch."

"But I've been thinking that he's kept the best part for himself. Did you know that my wife and I hold major investments in a number of restaurants, including the one run by tonight's chef? We could really use this whole place. For the beef, you know, and the abalone. Why let your brother keep the parts he loves? What about you?"

"Again, what's your point?"

"Helena and I were thinking we should reunite this historic ranch. We could bring the parts back together like they should be. It would let us supply our restaurants with our own artisanal beef and abalone. I can assure you that we would be responsible stewards of the place. Face it. I'm not sure how well your brother takes care of the ranch. Just look at the way he resorts to renting out the place for an event like this."

"He would never sell."

"But maybe you would. And maybe, just maybe, we could convince a judge to override the provisions of the trust, especially if we could show Teddy's mismanagement. Think of what this land is worth today. Millions. Imagine what you might do with your share."

Clem whispers to Gina, "He's playing with you. Don't listen."

"I'm quite serious. You know I can afford to buy what I want, and nothing would make me happier than to keep this place going, supply abalone to my own restaurants, and use your family home as a guest house. Well, you can see how well it all fits together."

Gina looks down the table in thought. She sees that a nearby platter still retains some gnocchi and roasted corn. To buy herself some time, she says, "Hey, guys, if you're not going to eat that, would you mind passing it down."

The platter is passed. Finally, she returns her attention to Pedrag. "No, I can't. I don't want to do that to my brother."

Helena is fidgeting and staring intensely at her husband with an aura of betrayal. Suddenly, she screams at her husband. "What the fuck are you saying? I don't want this damn abalone farm to exist one more day. You're supposed to buy this place and tear it all down."

She turns to Gina and Clem, "It doesn't belong on the coast. It should never have been built. And I want it gone. There's no way I need to use your ramshackle childhood home as a guesthouse. Teddy acts so high and mighty the way he loves this place, but it's a pestilence, a disgrace. I want it gone."

She sputters to a stop, spent.

Gina looks at her, and a smile creeps over her lips. Even a twinkle might be appearing in her eye. She turns to Pedrag.

"You should let your wife talk more often. She's far more persuasive than you. She's right. My precious brother doesn't deserve any of this. So, I agree. Let's cut a deal."

At that very moment, two of the Long Table crew suddenly come running through the grass to opposite ends of the long table. They shout, "They're out. They're out. Cattle broke through the fence."

Saturday, 7:13 PM

One couldn't exactly call it a stampede. About a dozen dark brown cows amble down the hill heading straight toward the Long Table. As cattle runs go, this isn't one to write home about. To the majority of the guests—who have little experience in such matters—the lumbering beasts seem dramatic. After all, a few at the table are still dining on the well-braised ribs of some former relatives of these very animals.

As a rule, Teddy's farmhands diligently keep things in repair. The grounds of the abalone fishery had been fenced off from the main pastures by multiple strands of barbed wire for decades. Perhaps the more gregarious of the cows noticed the arrivals of so many vehicles. Perhaps the dust along the gravel road lured them to the crest of the hill and to the grazing pastures closest to the Long Table Dinner. No diner saw the breakthrough. Exactly what happened is a mystery.

Clay whispers to Emily that he noticed that some cows earlier were munching along the fence line with their eyes turned toward the ocean. He claims that he worried about a break, but he is a person prone to fanciful displays of playacting. The group's unannounced rendition of "The Best of Times" is not that far away, and so none of his friends pay him any mind.

Regardless, the warning cry sets the crowd in motion. Folks push back their chairs, women grab their purses, and still others pull out their phones. Capturing a bull rampaging through the china of this cloth-bedecked table would be quite the social media triumph.

Once standing, none of them quite knows what to do. Should they make a dash to the parking lot and zip away from the dinner? That's not really practical, since the cows are between them and the parked cars. Should they back down along the cliff to the safety of the beach? Surely cows couldn't—or at least wouldn't want to—scramble down the gravelly cliff. But what if they did? People might be forced into the surf. The calmer among the crowd note the slow pace of the cattle.

The cows seem much more interested in the green grass at the edge of the abalone troughs than in attacking any tables. The guests decide that it's more prudent to finish dining. They return to their chairs and sip the remaining wine in their glasses.

"Oh, for God's sake," mutters Teddy. Even in his inebriated state, he knows this must be taken care of. "Where the hell is Jake?"

He turns to Frank and Otto. "Let's go herd them back where they belong."

"Need some help?" Michael asks.

Teddy nods and the four of them set off. Aubrey rushes up as well. The man is actually trying to find Chase. He doesn't see his assistant, so he demands of anyone in earshot, "What are you going to do about this? I need to get everyone seated before the dessert course."

Michael turns to the guys sitting quietly beside his daughters. "Get up. Teddy needs our help." He doesn't really know whether or not these town boys will be of any use, but the way they allow his two daughters to behave has begun to annoy him. They need to sweat a little.

"This should be interesting," Leanne jokes. "Dennis might step in a cow pie. Can you imagine how he'll react to that? He didn't even want to set foot on a working ranch."

Lucy manages a weak smile. She doesn't like the fact that she and her sister will be left behind with Naomi. "Maybe we should help too."

"Stay here. There're some things we need to discuss." Naomi has a steely air.

"Like what?" Leanne demands.

Jessica hovers near the space vacated by Michael. She's uninvited, but she's feeling abandoned. "We should let the men be the men. Sometimes they just need to prove a point. Besides it will do Teddy some good to move about. He's been drinking too much, too fast."

The girls quickly welcome Jessica with smiles. They expect her presence will force Naomi into some polite state. They underestimate the woman. "I'm sorry, but with Michael and your boyfriends gone, we're going to talk about your behavior this evening."

Jessica realizes she is in the wrong place. Not knowing how to extricate herself, she simply remains silent. Naomi isn't bothered by Jessica's presence.

"You've treated your father like a pariah all evening. He doesn't deserve it. Neither do I. I know I'm not your mother. No one can be. But she's gone. Don't you want your father to be happy?"

"But you're too young," Leanne sputters.

At that, Jessica decides retreat trumps awkwardness. She pretends as though she is going to go see what her menfolk are up to and backs away. She's one of the few leaving the safety of the table. Most guests, seeing a group of men head off to wrangle the cows, feel sufficiently reassured to reseat themselves. Only a handful still stalk after Teddy and his draftees. Some have their phones ready to capture some hoped-for drama.

Pedrag is one of those who sat down as soon as it became clear that Gina is not leaving. He's got a deal to close.

"Do you mean it? If we can figure out a way, are you willing to let me buy the rest of this ranch?"

"Think about what you're doing," Clem warns her friend.

Gina pays no attention to Clem. "Of course, I mean it. Look at Teddy. The way he pretends to run this place. But even now, he needs Frank at his side to take care of his own cattle. That's my useless brother. Let it all go."

The line of men spreads out. Newly arrived on the scene, Jake takes control and points toward where the fence is broken. The group starts to close in on the cows, which accustomed to being directed, stop grazing. The first to break is a mother with a young calf near her side. She starts retreating; soon the whole group heads back toward the gap in the barbed wire.

Back at the table, Tiger is feeling unsettled. He doesn't understand why, but he wishes Gina had never stopped by the table.

"Maybe I should go help out," Tiger muses.

"Why? Do you need to go talk to your boyfriend? It looks like he has plenty of help."

Elsbeth is trying to process a new thought that never occurred to her these past fifty years. In her day, people didn't talk about other folks being gay or different. She never wondered about her husband. She always thought Teddy was so handsome that even now she can't allow herself to imagine that he might not have been interested in her. What kind of fool wastes decades imagining that she threw away her chance at true love with Teddy? Why feel a need to spend hundreds of dollars on a bizarre dinner with portions too small for any sensible person? Is that what it took to see what was really going on? Was any of this a way to celebrate fifty years of marriage?

"Just go," she says again. "He might actually need you."

Henry also stands, "I'll join you."

The shadows lengthen as the sun dips lower in the sky. The offshore breezes remain at bay. It's that time of day when the most mundane of objects pick up an inner glow. Even the cows seem slightly luminescent as they plod toward their home fields.

Jake has appeared beside Teddy. "My guys are on the way. There's a break near the creek. We can do a fast fix to the fence. Don't worry about the rest of your fancy dinner."

Otto is a bit winded. After all, he's well past the age of wrangling. Frank motions to him, "We should head back. Let Teddy and Jake take it from here. We're just in the way."

"It's exciting though," Otto says. "Reminds me of a time during the war," and Frank tries to hurry the old man along as a way to prevent him launching into yet another tale. He's afraid it will be the same recollection that he heard last night about the German soldier hiding in the barn.

"Are you General Frank Mueller?"

It's Henry. He was left behind when Tiger scurried forward to join forces with Teddy. Nevertheless, Henry has achieved his target. He is exactly where he wants to be. He is standing beside the general who commanded his son. Having reached his target, he isn't quite certain what he wants to do. Frank seems equally perplexed by the unexpected question.

"I guess you could say that. Once a general, always a general. But I've been retired twenty years. Not used to strangers calling me by that title."

"And were you stationed in Kuwait during the first Gulf War?"

Otto senses something is amiss. He completely drops whatever story he was planning to tell. He doesn't like the feel of this situation.

"I think we need to get back to Jessica," Otto says in an attempt to keep moving, but Frank stops. He looks quizzically at his questioner.

"Were we stationed together?" he asks.

"Do you remember Lieutenant Matthew Metternich?"

There's a visible start to Frank. He remembers the name. Only a few hundred American casualties occurred during the Persian Gulf military action in the Nineties. The numbers in the Air Force were quite small and only a couple were under Frank's command. There were unusual circumstances about Matthew's death.

"So are you Henry Metternich?" he asks.

"I guess you remember my name? But do you remember my son?"

"Yes." Frank pauses. "I remember the letter I wrote you and your wife the night your son died. It was a tragic time."

"It was an event that should never have happened. And it was your fault. You were in command. You should have prevented it."

Frank thinks how it is hard to say what might have happened if things went differently. It's not as though life is some contraption designed by Rube Goldberg in which one mechanism directly sets off another, where the instruments are bizarre and the path is long. If a voice had been raised a bit louder here, or if someone had understood faster there, or if the machine hadn't sputtered in that unexpected moment . . . so many ifs. In the end, what happened, happened.

Frank is not particularly philosophical. But he realizes people only know how to look back across their own lives and the elements that they saw and participated in. In their rear view mirrors, they create a meaning that may have nothing to do with the way the universe works.

He is right. Like tonight: If that new ranch hand hadn't left for lunch early, he would have remembered to tighten the barbed wire. If there hadn't been the backfire of a car, the year-old heifer wouldn't have rubbed against the fence and caused it to tilt. If the diners hadn't made so much noise, the curious cows might not have broken through. If Frank hadn't been so responsible, he would never have volunteered to help Teddy round them up. If Tiger hadn't been so disturbed by Gina's rant, he might not have jumped up to find Teddy. Then Henry would never have joined him and might not otherwise have found himself face to face with the man he spent more than twenty years hating.

Who can say what really happened in Iraq nearly a quarter of a century earlier? But under the setting sun, each of these men realizes they don't know how to move on to reach a common truth. Indeed, Henry now wonders if there would be any point in discussing it more.

"Well, I just want to say my wife and I blame you," Henry is soft spoken. Frank says nothing. "Our lives have never been the same since the day Matthew died. Your letter didn't help. Nothing helped. And seeing you at this dinner . . . well, it only makes me realize how much we've wasted. All the time we thought about you, blaming you. You're just an old man. Knowing that won't change anything for us. I still hope you rot in hell."

Henry doesn't say another word. He only turns to return to his wife.

Otto looks at his neighbor and friend. He has no story for the moment.

After a long silence, Frank speaks, "I wish I could blame myself. But then where would it end? I just need to look forward. "

He sees Jessica in the distance watching them. He can tell by her stance that she realizes something has happened. But even Frank isn't sure how to describe what just occurred nor does he know what he will tell his wife. He only knows that at this moment, he wants to be next to Jessica more than anything else in the world.

So he goes to her.

Saturday, 7:25 PM

Jake takes the lead in guiding the cows back toward the break in the fence. It won't be hard to herd the cows through the gap. Because Jake and his helper Miguel are clearly in control, Teddy happily leaves. At the same time, he is rather glad about this diversion. It got him up and moving about. His level of inebriation has dropped at least two notches. Maybe he can make it through the rest of the evening.

Someone else has different plans. Good old Tiger finds Teddy. He has been tracking him through the long dry grasses, dodging a few recently dropped splotches of dung. There is a bit of a wild look about Tiger. But Teddy finds the bedraggled look endearing. It reminds him of why years ago he liked hanging around the boy.

"I want to talk to you," Tiger says.

They're alone on a patch of grass. The farmhands steadily move the herd along and are already restringing the wire. Guests who jumped into the roundup are ready to eat once more. Teddy notices for the first time how strings of incandescent lights strung between the trees are creating a canopy of a sort over the long table. It puts him in a good mood.

"What about?" he asks Tiger.

"Your sister just said something that kind of pisses me off. She said you're gay. Are you?"

Now Teddy has never really ever talked about being gay to anyone, not even to the occasional man in his life. But he feels caught up in the evening. If even his cattle can break free, then why can't he?

"Maybe." He pauses. "Hell, yes, I am. What's it to you?"

"Did you know back then?"

"Does it matter?"

"Yeah, it matters. You were the only person who ever paid any attention to me in high school and the only guy who ever treated me like a human being. I thought it was because you liked me."

"Well, I did like you."

"I don't mean like that."

"I didn't say it was like that." Teddy stops. It's a time for honesty, he thinks, and besides, this man is asking for the truth. Maybe it's time he got it.

"And what if it was? What's wrong with the fact that I thought you were cute and I felt giddy whenever you were around? What does it change now? Did you ever come out here and go swimming with me? I never even got close to getting you stripped naked on my beach. Let alone doing with you what I really thought about doing.

"So, yeah, I was like 'that' back then. I guess I knew. I guess I just didn't want to admit it. Still don't. But remember you asked."

It might be all the wine, but Teddy has never felt so alive. He never realized how liberating it was to be truthful. Without thinking, he reaches out, pulls Tiger in, and kisses the weather-beaten lips of this grizzled face.

"There. Now you got something to complain about."

For the longest moment, Tiger stares at the rancher. Then he starts laughing like a braying mule.

"You know," he says, "Elsbeth would have enjoyed that kiss a hell of a lot more than me. It's all she dreamed of these past fifty years."

"So what? You want me to come back with you now and give Elsbeth a smack on the lips. I will. All you got to do is ask." Teddy means it. In his drunken state, he just might do anything.

"Tell you what. If you do that for me, then I'll be civil to you whenever you come into the store."

"It's a deal."

Teddy thrusts out his hand and the two shake on it. They start walking toward the lighted strands and the white draped tables.

"Just so you know," Tiger says. "I never thought of you that way. But I didn't worry about it. The reason I wouldn't come out here was because I didn't know how to swim and I didn't trust the ocean. I didn't want you to think less of me. But don't think that means I ever wanted to do anything funny."

"I don't know. You always seemed pretty horny. You did get Elsbeth pregnant quick enough."

"Yeah. Well, think what you want. I guess we can never know for sure what might have happened."

With that, the two are back in the light of the dinner canopy, just feet from Elsbeth's chair.

Saturday, 7:31 PM

The cattle revolt is over. There are no casualties. Frank is the first to limp back to his seat. Otto tails behind. "What happened?" Jessica asks, fearful that some animal bulldozed her husband. She sees Otto's hand motion, and she drops the topic.

The three are seated again. The servers have taken advantage of the fracas to clear the table. They now place a small cordial wine glass by each seat.

Otto picks up his glass and rolls it around in his long skinny fingers, staring at the simple vessel as though it were the key to some great secret. The glass prompts him to starts another story. There is something different this time. He speaks with tentativeness almost as though he has not honed this particular tale into his usual and often-repeated clarity.

"I remember a day during the war," he starts. "I think it was early fall, because the wind was so cutting, but there was no snow. I was still a boy. I was probably with my mother to carry home whatever groceries she could find.

"Mother wasn't a strong woman. I don't mean physically. She probably was strong enough in that regard, but my father easily cowed her. Still, she had great respect for authority, which was probably a good thing because by this time the Nazis controlled Amsterdam. They were everywhere."

It wasn't at all clear, not even to Otto, where he was going with this memory. Frank senses that his encounter with Henry is the spark for this tale. Jessica still wonders what happened. She is convinced she missed something important, but there's such earnestness in Otto's face that she is reluctant to interrupt him.

"To get to the main market, we had to go by this railway station. The place was very crowded. I remember all these frightened people. Parents. Children. Old grandparents. Not so old as me now, I suppose, but I didn't expect to see so many people out with their suitcases, or see the Nazi soldiers herding them toward the train.

"I remember how Mother stiffened and grabbed my hand. I was so embarrassed by that. You see I thought I was too old to have my mother hold my hand. The soldiers were yelling. I remember that. They were so loud, and I guess they just wanted to be done with pushing those people into the rail cars. They weren't even proper train coaches. I remember some were boxcars and others were cattle cars, and I thought people aren't allowed to travel in those.

"Mother just kept walking forward trying not to catch their eye. I know she just wanted to be inconspicuous. But when a soldier ahead of us, a boy not that much older than me, used his gunstock to push an elderly man forward, then Mother's resolve broke.

"'Stop that,' she shouted. As she rushed toward the soldier, she dropped my hand. But suddenly four of those soldiers were facing my mother. As much as their guns, I remember how heavy their coats seemed. I still remember how I wanted to be wearing one myself, because the wind was so brisk that day.

"'Treat these people with some decency,' she said. Her voice trembled. It must have taken great will for her to speak up. I don't know why she did it. By that point, I was next to her. This time I took her hand, because I wanted to pull her back. Back to sanity, you know.

"'Move along,' one of the soldiers grunted, 'or you and your boy will be joining this shipment.'"

Otto set the glass down. Servers were coming by with a local late harvest riesling, but he waved his hand to shoo them away. "And with that, Mother's momentary bout of heroism disappeared. She hurried me along and we didn't look back. After the shopping was done, she found another route home. We never spoke of that day.

"But I think about it. What should I have done? Did any of those people survive? When was Mother braver? When she spoke up or when she walked away?

"You can never know."

Otto stops talking, looks at Frank, and smiles. Jessica reaches out to take Otto's hand, but it is her husband that she watches most carefully. Lucy and Leanne have been listening to this story, anything to avoid paying attention to Naomi. They look a bit shaken but then Leanne mouths to her sister, "It's nearly time."

Mid-table, Teddy and Tiger stop in front of Elsbeth. Henry, already sitting next to his wife, is holding her hand. He is whispering something, but Teddy is too energized to pay any attention to that. He reaches out, pulls Elsbeth up from her chair, and delivers a loud, ostentatious kiss to her lips.

"What the hell?" she says.

"Tiger says I owe it to you."

She looks crossly at both of them, but then a flush sneaks into her cheeks. Like Teddy, she has had more wine this evening than is her custom.

"Do you think that makes up for missing our prom dinner?" she asks.

"Well, I am forgiving you for taking Tiger away from me. Now I can move on."

The funny thing is that Teddy means it. It as though some strange weight has been lifted from him. Maybe he needs to go find Leon in the catering tent and give him a kiss too for old time's sake. He's never felt so free.

"You're just crazy," Elsbeth replies. She's not sure if she wants Teddy to stay or to leave, but she decides. "Tiger, why don't you come and sit next to me. They'll be serving dessert soon enough, and we don't need your old friend hanging around."

The words sound snappish but Tiger knows his wife is actually feeling pleased.

Elsbeth turns to look directly into Tiger's eyes. "Happy Anniversary dear. This just might have turned into the dinner I always wanted.

Hearing Elsbeth's words, Teddy is also happy. Then he sees that his sister is standing with Pedrag near the Fagatelle family. Maybe while he's feeling so high, he should make amends with her. No need for a kiss there. Just saying "I'm sorry" should be enough.

He saunters up. For the moment, he feels like he just passed fifty instead of being on the verge of hitting seventy.

He smiles, "Hey, sis."

Gina turns to Pedrag. "Can I tell him?"

Saturday, 7:38 PM

"Tell me what?" Teddy asks.

The last remnants of setting sunlight disappear at the horizon. Only the most discerning of eyes can still decipher a touch of orange in the deep blue-black. The sun fully sank, without a green flash, beneath the horizon over twenty minutes ago. Most guests failed to notice it. There was food to eat and wine to drink and conversations to be had. By now everyone is a bit sloshed. The combination of beef and syrah served to rev up the group energy.

The friends of the Fagatelle girls are getting antsy. When Leanne signed them up for this impending lark, they each imagined how an impromptu song mob might seem entrancing under a darkened sky. No one gave a thought to what the individuals around the might think or want.

"This has been a weird night," Clay begins. "The way Mr. Fagatelle showed up with that woman. Do you think Leanne will even still want to do this stunt?"

"Why wouldn't she?"

"Didn't you see the way those two girls glared at their Dad and the date? I don't think they like him very much at the moment. We should go check with her. Just to be sure."

He stands, and realizes just how dark it has become. He steps outside of the canopy of lights and looks upwards. The stars dazzle him. For a moment Clay forgets what he wants to do.

Near the head of the table, Jessica leans in toward her husband. "What happened back there?"

Frank smiles back, but to Jessica it feels more like a grimace. And she knows that he doesn't want to talk about it. She and Otto exchange glances, and she wonders why her old neighbor seems so subdued.

Meanwhile, Teddy is outside of the glare of the lights. In the shadows just outside the serving area, he stares down Pedrag and Gina.

For the past few moments, he has felt the king of his world. For once, he has done what he wanted to do. Everything didn't come crashing down around him. Quite to the contrary, he feels like a hawk soaring over the plains of the ranch. Now these two show up like hectoring crows trying to destroy the pleasure of his flight.

"You have something you want to tell me?" he demands.

He looks up and sees Leon walking toward the head of the table. The chef carries a birthday cake bedecked with dozens of candles. Their flickers echo the stars above, and Teddy is tempted to ditch his tormentors, stride over, and kiss this young chef. He should kiss everyone he ever longed for. It's time to take control. Maybe even find Chase. Who cares what happens?

But Gina ruins it. "Pedrag and I have an agreement that I will work with him and force you to sell the ranch. He wants your land. I want his money."

Michael looks up to see his son with the birthday cake. Naomi smiles broadly. Steeling himself to grin through all that's ahead, he braces himself for a wobbly rendition of "Happy Birthday."

From the corner of his eye, Clay catches the flickering of the candles. It's about to begin. It is too late to ask. He stops and hurries back to his friends.

For a beat, it seems as though Leon is about to begin the traditional birthday song, when suddenly his sister boldly stands to face her father. She begins singing in a loud voice, "The best of times is now."

She's a bit off-key, and she seems more angry than happy. Then her sister stands and together they're warbling about some faded rose. Michael doesn't really know what they're doing. Clearly Leon is equally surprised. He seems in danger of dropping the cake. Annabelle saves the day by taking it away, and setting it on the table.

Up and down the long table, everyone stops talking. Already surprised by seeing the cake, the guests don't know what to make of the sisters' loud voices which carry to the far reaches of the table. Then, unexpectedly, one of the young men in the middle stands and joins in, and they can hear his words more clearly. Above the food, the lyrics talk about the need to live and love. Only a few have any idea this song is playing off an old Broadway musical.

Three others stand and join in the song. Two more young men rise to their feet at the head of the table. And is it possible? One of them holds a concertina. Some of the guests find this unexpected performance entrancing. Others fear that they are going to be forced into participating.

Already the young people are trying to get everyone to stand and join in. Two of them have managed to get Henry and Sylvia up on their feet. The couple link arms, start to sway, and attempt to follow the unfamiliar lyrics.

Leon is appalled. What have his sisters done? Michael just wants to leave. First his daughters behave horribly to his girlfriend. And now this.

"There's no fucking way!"

Jessica starts. She knows that strident voice as it rises above the song. As Teddy's babysitter for so many years, she recognizes Teddy's voice when he feels hurt, pinned, and vanquished. She can't help herself. She stands. She wants to protect him.

It is too late.

"You can't have it!"

Teddy is pummeling his sister and screaming. Gina is forced to back up hurriedly, retreating into the light of the dinner, trying to raise her arms in reflexive self-defense. All she can get out is "Teddy, stop."

Pedrag remains in the darkness. He smiles. Things are working out just fine. He is quite confident that he will soon get his wife off his back.

The flash mob performance sputters to an unplanned stop. Guests at the far end of the table stand trying to see what is going on with Teddy's fight. They hear the shouts, but are too far to see the details.

Most aren't certain if this is somehow connected to the surprise song. Nothing makes sense.

In the kitchen, the workers look down at the beautiful quince tarts, each already sliced into segments of eight. Some of the tarts are already graced with dollops of whipped creamed. The staff wonders, "Will we even get to serve the final course?"

Taking advantage of the hubbub, Tiger grabs the bottle of the dessert wine. He pours Elsbeth and himself a hefty portion. They toast one another. Internally, both thank the gods that they avoided getting more entangled with Teddy years earlier . . . although each of them is also secretly thinking about their unexpected kisses.

"The ranch is mine. It's mine. You can't have it," cries Teddy.

He pushes Gina in the chest with both of his hands. She stumbles backward and falls into Leon. Leon loses his footing and tips backward. The chef reaches back to catch himself. He places one hand firmly down into the mass of lit candles and mounds of icing atop his father's cake.

It doesn't stop him. He falls completely into the cake. The end of the table tips up and everything slides to the ground.

Naomi bursts out in laughter. All she can say to her man is this, "Your family sure throws you a hell of a birthday party."

Leanne glances at Lucy and both girls smile at the remark. Leanne whispers, "You know she does remind me a little bit of Mom."

Teddy stands in dismay. What has he done?

PART FIVE

TEDDY:
AFTER DINNER

Saturday, 7:42 PM

Betrayal. What else can you call it? I know it in an instant. My sister just thrust a sword into my stomach and twisted it until my guts spill out. My friends stand by and watch as everything that ever meant anything to me is wrenched away. In a flash, I understand it all.

I may be drunk, but I recognize family treason when it happens. Gina has always been out to get me, never liked me as a brother, and now she can wreak her revenge. I see no way out of her plot. It is so ironic. For a moment tonight, I falsely believed in the power of redemption. I hoped that a moment of honesty could wipe clean a lifetime of living a lie. It truly seemed that everything was possible.

If I believed in the Bible, I would know that to every thing there is a season. I want to believe that. After all, as a rancher I know nature. Every winter I see how the rains evoke the glorious possibility of life. The parched ground eagerly sucks up new water. While little seems to change, it does. There's a different smell to the earth that suggests new possibilities. The hills turn green. Sprouting tips of grass break through brown thatch. Seasonal streams flow again. Low-lying patches form small short-lived ponds. Larvae of long-gone frogs somehow hatch again. Tiny tadpoles swim once more. Bright orange California poppies dot the green hillsides. The invasive wild mustard, which is no good for my cattle, emerges in beautiful bands of color that grow taller than the cows. Hints of scarlet pimpernel and patches of violet lupines color the landscape.

It's renewal. Even the cattle and their calves seem to have a bounce as they seek out fresh grass. The redwing blackbirds return to the rushes of the creek. The swallows grab daubs of mud to build their nests beneath the eaves of the barn. All things seem possible in spring.

But I know better. The rains always stop. The grasses dry. Everything mutes back into a palette of browns, tans, and oranges. As summer goes on, even the morning fogs lessen. As days become warmer and in some ways more beautiful, everything around you is drying away. Finally we trod through autumn and await the winter rains.

At this moment, autumn is underway, but change is not yet here. Let's face it. I am in the autumn of my life. For me, the rains were never bountiful, not even during my spring. Now they will never come. Gina has only accelerated the reality. She lit a match to my seventy years of dryness.

Someday, perhaps, the embarrassment of this last course may vanish but just as likely I will never stop reliving it. When Leon falls into that cake and his hand lands directly on top of the lit candles, he looks at me, not Gina, with astonishment.

"What's wrong, Mr. Mazzetti?" Leon sputters out.

I have no answer. My only consolation is that no one is hurt.

At that very moment from the kitchen tent, Aubrey watches me. I don't need to see him to know that to be the case. No doubt he is determined to save what he can of this stupid dinner.

Already he is sending out his minions with their dessert platters. That recaptures the fickle crowd. Everyone forgets the shouts between my sister and me. The performing kids sit down. My more dramatic performance has snuffed out whatever they were planning.

Almost no one watches as Leon stands up. White icing still covers his hand. He puts that sweet arm around me and consoles me.

"Mr. Mazzetti, everything will be all right."

I pretend to believe Leon. Yes, of course, everything will be all right.

Everyone is eager to hurtle toward the evening's close. Something in the eyes of Frank and Jessica makes clear their disapproval. I know that at last their babysitting days are over. Otto stands silently beside them like a guard. He seems to forget that he is my guest. Everyone is here only because I allowed them in.

No one cares about facts or me. They just focus on eating their slices of tart. For all two hundred and fifty people, I have become a shade of the night.

Chase comes up to my side. "The night's nearly over," he says.

I laugh bitterly, "Is that so?"

"There's one more thing we'd like you to do." He says it tentatively. I can't decide if it's because he's afraid I will refuse or because he judges me long past the point of doing anything that's expected. "Normally, we ask the host, you know the owner of the place, to stand with Aubrey to say goodbye as people leave. Could you do that?"

Of course I can do that. I will be happy to do that. The sooner they are gone, the happier I will be. I never wanted one of them on my ranch. Goodbye to foolish people trying to feed off my memories, sucking up the abalone that I grew, the cattle that I raised, and the ranch that I preserved. Goodbye to all those dregs of my past who I thought meant something to me, to those who could have been friends. Goodbye to all those greedy people who only wanted to use my ranch. Goodbye to my sister who doesn't care about me or our home. Goodbye to my perfect bluff and my ranch. Goodbye to it all. Fall is here.

Chase adds, "I will stay by your side. I'm here to help you."

I play the big man and stand next to Aubrey for the next half hour. I say farewells and accept compliments over the beauty of this piece of coastline. The guests don't know that it is slipping from my grasp, not that I care what they think. Their stories don't matter to me. This is my dinner, not theirs.

Michael Fagatelle and his entourage are among the first to leave. His arm is wrapped around his girlfriend, and his daughters no longer wear scowls. There's a whole gaggle of twenty-something kids walking with them. With great excitement, they are all over one another as though trying to strengthen some fragile truce.

"I don't even know what you guys were singing," Michael laughs.

"It doesn't matter," one of his children says. "We just wanted to make the night special."

"Well, it was that. That's for sure."

Lucy laughs, "We certainly didn't need to worry about putting on the show, did we?" She catches Naomi's eyes, and they both smile.

None of them really pays any attention to me. Which is just as well.

Tiger and Elsbeth also walk by. They also smile warmly at me. It is as though the coldness of the past decades has melted away in the flash of two kisses. At least Elsbeth got to see this ranch that was so important to her.

Tiger suddenly turns back toward me. "I gotta say Teddy, after tonight, I'm really glad you didn't show up at our prom dinner."

Elsbeth giggles.

"Yeah, you might have ruined everything."

Elsbeth throws a playful punch at her husband. "Don't go harassing the poor man. We need to get home. We still got some celebrating to do."

Pedrag and Helena stroll by and speak softly to Aubrey. Neither looks at me. Even though Pedrag almost whispers, I hear what he says. "Next year, if you want to, host it here again because I'll own the place. I'll even let you use my other stretch of the beach."

Perhaps Aubrey thinks the man is giving him what he originally wanted, but I suspect it's really Pedrag's way of reminding me of his pact with Gina. Pedrag looks up and grins.

"Sorry about getting you so worked up," he says. "Maybe I won't listen to my wife, and I'll keep the abalones."

When Otto, Jessica and Frank go by, I want to pull them aside. I need to apologize for embarrassing them in any way.

"Jessica, Frank," I say. But it's not loud enough. They don't hear me. It's just as well. I never have been good at saying I'm sorry. I let them walk on. All remnants of last night's *gezellig* seem lost.

Besides, the two of them are engaged in an earnest conversation with an out-of-town couple. I know I chatted to those two earlier in the evening, but I don't remember anything about that talk. I just hear a snippet of the conversation.

"I want to apologize. Tonight makes me realize we need to let the past go," the man says to Frank. Then they are out of earshot. Maybe when I go back to the house, I can utter my own apology.

So many people walk by. When your life is spent in a town as small as mine, and when you have sequestered yourself on an out-of-the-way seaside ranch with just a few workhands, two hundred and fifty people seem a multitude. The stream feels endless. While most give Aubrey and me effusive thanks for a wonderful evening, I want to move on. The buzz of all the wine consumed earlier in the evening is slowly ebbing away. My back aches. I am thinking about what I need to say to Frank and Jessica.

The evening is almost over. Once more, I can hear the breaking of the waves below. There is a clang from the washing of metal utensils in the kitchen tent. For a moment, I feel blessed. Gina and her gal pal Clem must have snuck out.

But I am not so lucky.

Gina walks up close. Clem is holding back. "Maybe it is wrong of me to work with Pedrag, but you have to admit it's time we both moved on. This ranch isn't good for us. It's become your prison."

I think she means her comments as an overture of good will. I want to accept them as such. But I don't have much practice in being the gentleman. I stand there silent for a second too long. I don't even look at my sister.

I start to think of all the reasons why I shouldn't welcome the beginnings of a truce. Besides, I tell myself, she has yet to win. My father had pretty good lawyers. Just because she's tapping into the might of Pedrag's legal team doesn't mean that she can break through the intent of Dad's trust. I could still triumph.

Then I feel foolish. She's right. I need to escape this ranch. I turn to look her in the eye and be her brother, but I am a moment too late.

"It's time to head out," Clem says to her lover.

But first Gina has one more thing to say. "I really do think that this will be the best for both of us."

After enduring a few seconds of my silence, she decides not to push the conversation further. She and Clem resume walking. Then she turns her head and throws me a disappointed look.

Was it my last chance? I just know one thing. This is the autumn of my life. Fall is a dangerous time in California landscapes. Everything dries out, and just one spark can explode the sere hills into flames. Maybe that's good. Many native plants propagate only in fire. While the ground squirrels may escape the flame in their underground tunnels, and hawks may fly overhead while fox outrun the flames, not everyone can be so lucky. Some things must always perish before the rebirth is possible. Fire demands it price for rebirth.

I reckon that I should be that sacrifice.

Saturday, 9:06 PM

I walk up the hill. Chase is at my side. Behind us, the Long Table crew is hard at work. They are tearing down everything that was erected over the day. I can hear the clang of metal as pans are loaded into the trucks and the snap of table legs being pushed back into place. That is followed by clunks as the flat surfaces are loaded one atop another in the back of the truck.

I am not certain why Chase feels a need to walk me home. A moment ago, as the last of the guests entered their cars and started to drive up the gravel road, Aubrey motioned the young man over. Nothing was said, but I can guess what was conveyed between them. "Make sure this drunken old man makes it to his bed."

I'm not so drunk anymore. If there is reluctance in my uphill walking, it is only due to what I know awaits me. My trio of overnight guests is clearly already in the house. They walked away from me more than a half hour ago. We haven't spoken since the embarrassing fall into the cake, but a conversation cannot be put off forever. I have to make things right.

"Tonight was one of our better dinners," Chase says.

I can't help but laugh.

"Really?" I ask. "What do your hosts usually do? Jump up onto the table and do a strip tease? Steal all the wine?"

"Are you worrying about Leon and the cake? No one's going to remember that tomorrow. All people will recall is how beautiful this weather was. They'll talk about how the temperature was perfect and how the breeze was just strong enough. They'll marvel about the way the stars came out to shine down on them driving away. And they'll tell everyone about the food. It's why these people come. Tonight every bit was delicious. Believe me, everything doesn't always come together. At least not in a moment of perfection."

"I didn't know that it did tonight," I mutter.

"That's because you don't let yourself see it. You're like one of your abalone. All hard muscles and an even harder shell. You move along the sea bottom and don't look at what's around you."

"Then I get snatched up and eaten," I break in.

"Mr. Mazzetti, that's exactly what I mean. You got the wrong outlook. Things aren't so bad. After all, what's wrong with your life? You're healthy. You're good looking. You have friends. I can tell those folk waiting for you at the house love you. Plus you own this beautiful ranch."

"Now you stepped in a mess," I warn.

I don't know where to go with all this prattle. When you're young, everything still seems so possible. Every word Chase said about me applies more to him. He truly is beautiful. The people he works with admire and like him. Why shouldn't they? He's a decent kid. But he has time. He can still make of his life what he wants from it.

That's the thing he doesn't understand. Time doesn't stand still. Life is so tantalizingly brief, like the mist that sprays up when the waves hit the beach. It hangs for a moment in the air with sunlight shining through it. But then it falls. It always falls, and before you know it another wave has washed over the first. That rhythm never ends, but the individual rainbow in the mist, a particular fragment of light, one brief second of reality . . . those things are gone forever.

Why even think about this nonsense? No one young knows any of this. Not one of them can foresee what lies ahead. Certainly not a young man whose shorts are too short and whose legs are too long. They live their lives behind some gauze—a veil that prevents them from seeing the harsh reality ahead.

It's just like that band of youngsters who tried to serenade Michael Fagatelle. They think life is a musical in which they write their own song that will bring them applause. When you're young, you think you can attract everyone's attention. You plot out your heading, enjoy a rip-roaring finale, and still anticipate plenty of time for an encore.

That's not the way it is. There's always something. Or, there's someone like me who lumbers into the scene and destroys it. Before you know it, lights are struck, the curtain is drawn, and the audience—these people you care about so deeply—sneaks out the front door.

When you're young, you only see the shiny object that lures you forward. You want it to be yours. It's like Aubrey's girl helping out Leon in the kitchen. Maybe they're both each other's shiny penny. I saw how they looked at one another. They may think that they are saying the first lines from the beginning of their scene, but in the theater of life, they're probably just bit players in a third rate farce.

So many shiny pennies in one's life. How easily they fall through the fingers. Then one night you find yourself standing on a darkened hill breathing dust from scores of cars driving away, and you look at a boy who could be your grandson—if you ever had had a life—and you stand and patiently listen to him try to tell you that life is beautiful.

But you know better.

Indeed I do. Does it matter what Frank or Jessica think as they sit inside my own living room? They may be waiting for me to finish this walk up the hill, but why should I care? Just like my ranch, this life won't be mine much longer.

It's been a long one, but not particularly a good life. Eventually you must face the music.

"We're here," Chase says.

"So we are," I reply and I open my front door. I tell myself that I must be prepared to make amends.

Saturday, 9:08 PM

Otto speaks first.

"Well, well, the wandering minstrel has reappeared." The man seems back to his storytelling self, and I know his comment is meant as a joke. Standing just inside my own front door, I don't appreciate his feeble attempt at humor. Frank seems to smile at it. Chase is already walking away.

"It's been a long night," says Jessica, "but we wanted to wait up and be certain that you arrived home safely. I thought maybe we should talk."

She places an unneeded emphasis on the word "safely." I'm not certain what she is suggesting, but this overall atmosphere reminds me too much of my childhood. I recall a night when I was just sixteen. It was one of those many weeks when my parents were off on one of their gallivanting trips, and Gina and I were left in the hands of our sitter. That night I sauntered into the house long past my curfew. By the time I arrived back to the ranch Jessica was alone. Maybe Frank was working at the airbase or was off in the kitchen getting a sandwich. In any case Jessica wasn't pleased.

That was unusual because she was seldom cross with either Gina or me. She possessed an equanimity that should have been an inspiration. That night I wasn't really thinking about her feelings. I was walking on a cloud. I had achieved something that I thought was a great new beginning. I had managed to get Tiger naked.

Now it wasn't skinny-dipping on my own favorite beach, which maybe was just as well. My success happened far up the local creek at a shallow swimming hole. This pool didn't dry up in even the worst of droughts. Since it was still spring in a wet year, the water was deep. That part of the creek belonged to a rancher who didn't like trespassers, so we were renegades. We had snagged a six-pack and wanted a private place to party. We drank all six cans while spinning tales of what we hated about school and what wonderful things we might do one day. In the slightly alcoholic haze of a full spring moon listening to croaking frogs, everything seemed possible.

The night air stayed warm. When I suggested that we should go for a swim, Tiger didn't hesitate. He just stood and started stripping off his clothes. I remember how he wore a shirt with a Henley collar, which seemed an unlikely mod touch for our little town. As Tiger threw that shirt to the green grass lining the creek, I realized I was getting behind. I quickly stood to follow his lead.

It was little more than seconds before our pale bodies stood on the creek's edge, and we jumped in. God, it was cold. I can still remember how excited I was. Admittedly, there was nothing remarkable about Tiger. Tall and lanky with no chest hair. I knew what I would see. There wasn't a boy my age in town that I hadn't seen naked in the high school locker room and its group shower.

But this was a different moment. Fifty years later, I wonder if Tiger even remembers that it happened, or if it meant anything to him. Earlier this evening, he acted so pure when he stated that he never came to the ranch to go swimming with me. Could it be that he didn't remember our going out that night?

We stayed in that water only for moments before we hurried out and dressed. Sobered by the cold, I nevertheless drove home elated.

When I walked into the house, Jessica was waiting. Her worried face deflated me. I didn't wait to hear what she was thinking. Yet I still remember that night.

I should have told her then what I was feeling, just as I should tell her now. I want to, yet it seems easier to take a different path.

"You should go to bed," I say to my trio. "I'm doing just fine. I don't need anybody."

I look at the three of them in the warmth of my living room. It is lined with all my favorite plein air paintings. Damn that art. If I hadn't been eager to own those oils and watercolors, maybe I would never have sold half the ranch.

Frank steps over to put his arm around me. "You don't know how things will turn out. Your sister's just angry with you. By morning, she will likely regret everything she said. Even if she doesn't, your dad employed clever lawyers. You can fight to keep this place."

"Why?"

"What do you mean? You love this ranch."

"It's nothing but trouble. What good ever happened here?"

Frank was having none of that, and he removed his arm. "Are you telling me now that I went swimming on that cold beach of yours for no good reason? If nothing else, I always thought that our moonlight dips would be one of your good memories."

"I don't know what you mean."

Of course, I know exactly what he means. Now is the time when I should tell both of them how much they mean to me. I should tell them that I don't need the ranch. I can go out on my own.

"Listen, son, don't think you ever kept secrets from us. Maybe you thought you hid things, but you were one open book. Don't get me wrong. I liked being your hero. Maybe your parents always thought you had a crush on Jessica, and but she and I knew better. Maybe we coddled you too much, and maybe we should have forced you to break free sooner. We thought we achieved that after you followed us to New York. But I guess you weren't really free to be you. You just bounced back here. Like a tetherball tied to its pole.

"We wanted to think you were happy on this place. But maybe you weren't. We thought we understood the workings of little towns, so we assumed you had someone special hidden away. But God, Teddy, it's the twenty-first century. If you can't tell Jessie and me that you're gay, then what's going on?"

"I'm not gay."

It came out without thinking. All of us in the room know that my statement is not true. Still, part of me really wants to believe that is it. I closed off so much of my life. I don't even know what's true and what isn't. I have to start somewhere. Why not now?

Frank doesn't sense my inner turmoil. Instead, he has a pensive air. "Something odd happened to me tonight. I was reminded of the ways things can go terribly wrong in life. People get hurt. And yet you can't stop moving ahead."

Otto nods as though Frank has uttered some great profundity.

"And maybe you drank too much tonight. And maybe you embarrassed yourself by fighting and causing Leon to fall into a birthday cake. Yes, and let's admit that your sister blindsided you. And we all know it happened in front of hundreds of people you don't know."

"But none of that matters," Jessica breaks in.

I just look at her. It does matter. Suddenly I realize just how much it matters that I will lose this ranch. Don't they realize it? They look at me like they really care. I could try to explain, but I don't. The night has been too long. I have drunk too much. I wouldn't know where to begin. I have to leave.

"You are so wrong. It matters a great deal."

I back out my own front door, and I slam it closed behind me. But I stand there for a moment, unwilling to fully walk away. I eavesdrop. Maybe, I even consider going back in.

I hear Jessica say to Frank, "I'm glad that we came."

"Why?"

"I finally feel we can let him go. We need to let him grow up."

That hurts. Am I just a spoiled teenager? I walk off my porch. I need some time.

Saturday, 10:08 PM

Outside, I sit for the longest time on the hill's dry grass beneath the towering eucalyptus. The tree's smell reminds me of those nights when the camphor oils of a humidifier would permeate my bedroom to cure a childhood cold. There's something comforting in that, and it keeps me from thinking about why I should not have walked out.

From my vantage point overlooking the abalone fishery and the dark sea beyond, the world seems shadowy. Not really so dark. There is the shimmering light on the ocean of the rising moon. The water reflects a cloudless sky mottled with millions of stars. The smear of the Milky Way feels muddled even as it glows brightly.

Some people are moving about down below, a bit like ants after a broken stick is pushed into their hill. The moonlight isn't quite bright enough for me to identify the individuals. I guess their identities by their actions.

Surely that larger figure beneath the tent is Leon. I never got my chance to confront him this evening. What would he have done if I had walked into that kitchen and smacked him on the lips? Would I have found it as gratifying as kissing Tiger? Could a quick buss wipe away my two decades of mooning over a teenage boy? I know it's a foolish obsession over a memory of a wisp of a lad. If I go back into the house and talk to Jessica and Frank, maybe I can finally admit that I have led a wasted life. For scores of years, I have sat in this spot, worrying about the cracking plaster on a fake Spanish hacienda. I have spent money cheated out of my sister to fill the walls with the paintings of lesser California impressionists. I have worried if the price for abalone would continue to rise or take a dive like my paintings.

I am exhausted. I am not at all industrious like those below. Leon efficiently directs his staff to repack everything. Already the majority of boxes have been loaded back onto the delivery truck. Some of Aubrey's men are preparing to dismantle the tent.

Where is Aubrey? Maybe he's already gone. I don't know anything about the schedule of this crazy cooking band, not even if they have another dinner somewhere tomorrow. How far away might it be? Does Aubrey stay with the others for these events?

I am clueless. I know no more about Aubrey and his colleagues than I do about most things. Honestly, I have managed to slide these many decades over the surface of almost everything that could be meaningful. Life has been little more than a game board. I think about those youthful concoctions that I forced Jessica and Gina to play— elaborate fabrications of what I thought were the pitfalls and opportunities of life. I smile at how my perception of the game of life was so limited. I should go back into my house, tiptoe down the hall, and sneak into the bedroom closet to dig out my invented games. I've kept them all. Most have never been played by anyone but me and my imagination.

One could ask: if no one played them, did the game even exist? I long to drag out my Santa Lucia mountain game, force Jessica and Frank to sit around the dining room table, and roll the dice. We'd wend a path through the old ranches. We'd face droughts and fire, spring rains and bonus calves, and everything else that existed in an eleven-year-old's imagined world. I forced my entire universe onto a single folded board.

With a roll of the dice, we might create a different life for me. In my games, no spinner ever causes you to land on an obnoxious technocrat with too much money or a sister who despises you. In my games, everyone has a chance to win.

Why retrieve the board? Even if I could convince my houseguests to play along, we would soon realize that such a simple vision of life is uninvolving.

By now, I should know more. I also know that I should confide in the people who are close to me. Still, I resist.

Below, the crew is making quick work of the takedown. All the linens have been removed from the table. They are folded and ready to be loaded. The chairs are placed on special carts ready to go back onto the truck. Someone walks around and picks up the occasional stray piece of trash. By morning, no one will realize that a horde of people once dined here.

The driver of the truck carrying the kitchen deliverables revs the engine. The driver is ready to leave. Not much is left. The cars of the guests have long since gone. Most of Leon's workers have also departed. Now that my eyes have grown accustomed to the light, I am better at identifying the individual players. Leon is still down there. He opened one of the extra bottles and is sipping a glass of wine. He is with that young woman who shadowed him throughout the evening.

The only other people left are Aubrey and his crew. None of my ranch hands are about, but then they are neither needed nor expected to be there. In the morning, they have a fence to repair and abalone to tend.

Although I was introduced to all of Aubrey's team, at the moment I cannot remember anyone's name other than Chase's. I don't see him. Aubrey is standing beside that garishly painted bus his team uses as a dormitory.

Then I see Chase. He steps out of the bus. A couple of terry cloth towels are thrown over his shoulder. He holds a bottle of wine and some plastic glasses. He heads toward Leon and the girl. They exchange some words. I can't tell what they're saying, but from Leon's body stance I get the impression that he isn't very taken with Chase's idea. On the other hand, the girl seems keen.

Chase sets down his wine and glasses. He reaches out and grabs the hands of both people and pulls them toward the water, toward the bluff, and toward my perfect beach.

He has a way about him. He can lead people to their destination. He can make people move forward, achieve their destiny, and live life like they are supposed to.

Leon and the girl cannot resist. They stroll forward, each step drawing them closer to the edge of the cliff. Chase steps back. He picks up his wine and glasses and follows the party he set in motion.

Saturday, 10:37 PM

I must have fallen asleep for a few minutes, or maybe much longer than that. I can't tell from the sky. The back of my shirt is damp from lying flat against the ground. Something wet and slimy is crawling over my hand. Just above me I see a shooting star. Or maybe it is a jet flying from San Francisco to Los Angeles. Whatever it was, in my groggy state I can't focus enough to detect the difference between the celestial and the mechanical. I prefer to think I glimpsed some bit of heaven crashing to the earth.

There's laughter in the distance. Not from behind me, which would be toward the house. That place is dark except for the front porch light. I think it unlikely that any of my guests have stayed up late worrying about me. I wince thinking that I missed my chance to go in and apologize.

I hear more laughter. It is definitely drifting up from the beach. It flows from younger folk who are fueled by alcohol or weed.

I force myself to sit up. Below me on the pebbled shores of the ocean, Aubrey's kids have scavenged dried driftwood. They have piled it up and lit a bonfire. The flames leap about. A few sparks dance heavenward. In autumn the grasslands are dry, but tonight there is almost no wind. The fire itself is well guarded by the bluff and there is little danger in an errant spark. I find something entrancing about the risky fire. It changes the whole complexion of the evening. Its flames make the night sky darker by comparison. The stars become more luminescent, and the waves shimmering in the distance seem more silvery.

All the workers appear to have joined the beach party. Aubrey stands beside the fire and stares into it. The flames and his red hair are just different shades of the same bit of the rainbow. He seems pensive. The others sit or recline on the beach. Some rest against a few big logs that washed up in last year's spring storm. The others sit on a large outcropping of grey rocks. All hold drinks of some type. They look toward the fire and lean in toward the heat.

I still can't retrieve their names, even though I recall seeing all of them at some point during this horrible day. Some now hold long neck beer bottles. I hope they don't drop them. Shattered glass would foul my perfect beach. I only want bits of glass to appear after they were washed out to sea for months or years and are returned as wave-smoothed sea glass.

Leon is down there. He's still with that girl. Annabelle. That's her name. He must be ten or fifteen years older than her, and yet from this distance they seem so relaxed with one another. I wonder whether she will board Aubrey's bus in the morning, or will she join Leon's car to start a different chapter?

How many times have I needed to choose between one path or the other? I am not like that person in Robert Frost's poem. I can't even remember the roads not taken. But there must have been some. Surely, at times, there was more than this place, this ranch, and this beach on the California coast. But if this is all that there ever was, then what in the world is wrong with me?

Frank. Tiger. Leon. The names are the signposts to my unattainable destinations. If I am honest, there were a few other persons over the years. There was Daniel in New York—that Columbia student with the perfect ankles who preferred Topsiders with no socks. Years later, there was Shawn who couldn't figure out how to make a small bookstore profitable in our nearby village. Funny how I tend to skip over the names of two men I actually touched. Maybe that's because half the time I didn't even know the names of my encounters. Truth be told, I didn't want to know their names. Ignorance made me safer.

Always that beach below was where my true dreams lay. It is the spot where as a little boy I thought everything I wanted could be possible. I believed the beach was all I ever needed. If my sister has her way, that strip of sand will be just another trophy in the vast gallery of Pedrag's life.

Yet tonight it seems alive. Someone brought a guitar to the shore. Another name comes back to me. I think the man with the guitar is called Max. He's lightly strumming a soulful tune. The two who are a couple are now dancing. As though my memory is returning, I am sure that they are called Cat and Hillary, although I am not quite certain which name belongs to whom. The woman lays her head down on her partner's shoulder, and they slowly shuffle across the sand.

The sound of the fire crackles above the guitar music. There's another burst of laughter. Leon, Annabelle, and Chase are in an animated circle. They are egging one another on, but the snippets of chatter rising isn't crisp enough to decipher.

Something seems familiar. I recognize the scene. Chase is convincing them to go swimming. It is September, and while the sea is never warm around here, it's about as warm now as it will ever be. Still I understand their reluctance. To most, the waves will be too cold.

From his gestures, Leon appears to be protesting that he doesn't have a suit with him. Annabelle doesn't seem concerned. All of them have been drinking. Inhibitions are lowered. Chase's argument is clearly persuasive. I wish I had known his approach years ago. Soon all three begin disrobing.

Of course, they are more modest than I would prefer. Maybe people see too much nudity on the web and can't embrace it themselves anymore. I hear kids don't like to shower in gyms, and the gym shorts worn by basketballs team players just get longer and longer. These three stop once they have stripped down to their undergarments. They're still laughing.

They don't know I'm up here, and yet I don't feel the least bit prurient. After all, this is my ranch, and their coworkers surround them. Besides the guys' boxer shorts aren't as revealing as Speedos.

They dash into the water with great shouting. Chase forces them into the surf. They dive beneath an oncoming wave. Gentle as that wave is, it's enough to break their spirit. All three bound out with water streaming from their hair.

Aubrey walks toward them with a stack of towels. Someone planned ahead for this possibility. They quickly wipe themselves down and wrap themselves in the towels.

I watch the scene. Nothing much happens. They indulge in a few more bottles of wine and beer. Max continues to play the guitar for a couple of additional songs. They worked hard this day; their fatigue is catching up. Slowly they peel off one by one.

When Leon leaves, Annabelle walks beside him. As Leon reaches his car, he stops, cups Annabelle's face, and gives the young woman a long kiss. Limited by the darkness, I can't see their expressions, but somehow as she turns to walk toward the Long Table bus, I detect a spring in her walk. I am convinced that this will not be their final kiss. I want to believe that this is the beginning of their story.

Only one person still remains by the fire. It is beginning to die down. Chase still stands in his wet boxers. His back is toward me and his eyes face the western horizon. Out there, there is a dark line where the calm sea meets the night sky. It is an impenetrable point. I wonder what he searches for, but I hope he finds it. Indeed, I hope that every one of these kids finds whatever they seek, whomever it might involve, and wherever it may lie.

Chase turns. He picks up his towel from the ground. Now he looks eastward, toward where the sun will rise in a few hours, and toward where I am sitting in the darkness beneath my eucalyptus trees.

I know he can't see me, and I don't want him to know that I am watching. I sit as quietly as possible, barely breathing. Finally his eyes turn away. At last, he too walks toward the painted bus.

I am glad that Chase didn't realize I was here. He has been at my side most of the night keeping me on track. But my world is over. What lies ahead belong to the Chases and the Annabelles. They don't need to worry about me.

No one needs to worry any more.

Saturday, 11:03 PM

For a long time I sit in the darkness and gaze toward the dying fire. Part of me thinks I should walk to the beach and completely douse the flames. There's no sense risking that unexpected breeze flinging glowing embers into the dry grass. My abalone troughs would crack in the heat of a fire.

I don't do anything. Maybe I am a bit hypnotized by the evening, or perhaps I have been drunker than I thought. It seems wiser to simply sit on the ground and contemplate the night world.

Behind me in my own house, everyone is settled. I suspect all are asleep although no snores escape the thick walls. Down below, the lights have gone out in the school bus. Tomorrow, early in the morning, the team will no doubt head toward their next destination. Alone in the stillness, I hear sounds emerge. My sense of hearing seems to have improved and reclaimed two decades of disappearing sounds. The croaking sounds of frogs rise up from that point where the seasonal stream reaches the ocean. The flow hasn't actually reached the ocean for the past few months, but there are still pools of water there, and I guess frogs thrive.

There is also the sound of crickets. Overhead rustles the nearly soundless swoop of a bat, or maybe some night bird. And there remains the lulling tone of the quiet ocean. As for mankind, I might as well be the last person alive on this stretch of land.

I overcome my torpor to walk down the hill. I try to step carefully and avoid making noise. No one needs to know that I am stirring. As far as I can tell, no one does. The fire is dying, but the coals still emit a pleasant warmth. Standing over that rising heat, I peer into the lingering flames.

I realize how deflated I feel and how much I have lied to myself for this past year. All that time I complained to anyone who would listen about my fears concerning this upcoming dinner. I never acknowledged that I was also equally excited by its possibilities.

When Aubrey suddenly appeared on his motorcycle months ago, I loved the burst of potential that he blew into my life. For the first time in many years, I felt the world opening up.

I know I've entombed myself on this ranch. Maybe someone could tell me why, because I don't know. Especially after my trick of selling half the ranch, I have the money to explore the world. I could spend time wherever I want to. And what do I do with that freedom? Other than my excursions to San Francisco to bid in an auction house's annual sale of early California art, I seldom venture more than thirty miles. I write or call almost no one. Jake, who actually runs this ranch, doesn't need me.

Aubrey opened a door to a broader world. He provided me a chance to interact with hundreds of people I never met. It suggested a world where somehow my life would seem relevant again. I needed to say yes to Aubrey's request because I knew time was running out.

I don't know what miracles I expected to happen. While I feared the possibilities of strangers, I can't say exactly what I thought they might do to me. Maybe what I feared more than the strangers were the people I knew best.

So why did I seek out that unexpected pleasure that came with luring them back into my life? Seeing Leon at that planning dinner in San Francisco started it. He was never more than a teenager I thought cute—a teenager I only noticed when I was already middle-aged. I never expected something to happen with Leon. Most of all, I took pains to ensure he wouldn't realize how I always watched him when I made deliveries to his father's butcher shop. Yet, like too much in my life, he became an obsession. Somehow, Leon embodied something missing in my life. He seemed the spirit of physical attractiveness. He brought to life the part of me that I never wanted to accept. Of course, I imagined him to be something that he wasn't. I wanted him to also be a conflicted gay boy. I wanted everyone to be like me. But there's only one me.

When I joined Aubrey and Leon for dinner, it was the first time I really talked to Leon. He wasn't anything at all like what I imagined. I was forced to cast aside a veil that had somehow cloaked my real understanding of his youth. While I didn't like losing that memory, it was at the same time both exhilarating and dangerous.

Maybe that was the moment when I truly started to fear the night of the Long Table Dinner. What if through the eyes of hundreds of strangers, I realized that my beach and bluff weren't at all that special or perfect? What if the judgment of others forced me to cast away my entire life and confront the mess I had made of it?

So many possibilities. That's why I wanted Frank and Jessica at my side. They understood what this place meant. They were my charms against disillusionment.

The veil, once pulled back, keeps exposing realities. I see clearly now that Frank is an old man. Across these decades there was never any possibility that he would be my adolescent boyfriend. I thought those desires were my secret, but now I know that wasn't the case. Both Jessica and Frank always understood my emotions.

There was no good reason to maroon myself on this deserted bit of ranchland. I could pretend it was some island that no one could reach, but of course anyone could if they bothered to try. Even Tiger and Elsbeth finally breached my defenses. For fifty years, we have bristled with one another in this small village. In another timeline, we might have been friends. That possibility has passed.

While I liked to think that I was the only one stranded in my particular situation, tonight I discover my sister is also gay. How could I not know that? Why have I been so focused only on myself?

All of these people. They've lingered in my life, and I dressed them up in the roles that I wanted them to play. Somehow, tonight, I feel as though we have all been stripped naked. I see everyone as he or she really is. Maybe for the first time ever.

There's only so much that one should endure. Maybe it's time to end this farce. Maybe it's time to strip myself.

Saturday, 11:24 PM

Too many memories. Too many thoughts. When you're young, the runway ahead seems so long. As fast as you motor forward, you hope to gain enough speed to let your feet leave the ground. Then, at some point, the ground just drops away and you're soaring through the life that is yours. Whether it's cloudy or clear, stormy or calm, you're aloft and the world stretches ahead. If you're wise, you look around and enjoy the scenery. Sooner or later, the gas will run out, the engine will sputter, and the trip will end.

Maybe there comes a moment when you should announce that you're ready to land. The journey is finished. There's nothing left to see. Maybe you've kept your eyes so tightly closed through it all there's no longer an opportunity to open them this late in the game.

Am I the only one who feels this way? Last night in my house, I was the youngest one at my table. Surely each of my guests had snuck a look over the edge of mortality. I wonder what they saw and what they think about. But then, who cares? They are not the ones who must live my life.

I pace around the dying fire without knowing why. Little heat is still being emitted. Besides that I am not at all cold. The evening is almost balmy. Both the sky and sea are calm. This is such a rare thing along the coast. Over the water, the moon casts its long reflection. The moon will be setting before the sun rises, or so I think.

But I also think that this is the perfect night. This is the kind of moment I wanted when I thought about luring the objects of my affection down to the water's edge. It would have made it so much easier to convince them that it wasn't too cold to go for a swim.

Tonight, maybe I only need to persuade myself. Why not go into the water one last time? To swim naked under the moonlight. To float on the icy water. To stare up into the starlit sky. I've heard it said that when you look at the stars, you are actually peering into the past. Distant light has traveled so many years that some of those dots were already blazing hundreds and millions, even billions, of years ago—and this light is that long ago moment. Surely somewhere among all that light streaming down, there are a few dots representing my nearly seventy years. That expanse must hold a few glimpses back into the time when my desires were still possible. Now I am standing at the edge of the water. The sand is wet. The tide is coming in and slowly reclaiming more and more of the beach.

What the hell. There's no time like now. I take off my bow tie and unbutton my dress shirt. After I take the shirt off, I neatly fold it and the tie before setting them on a large rock. I pull my white t-shirt over my head and take equal care in folding and placing it atop the blue dress shirt with its thin white stripes. I step out of my loafers, peel off my over-the calf socks, and add them to the pile. My bare feet dig into the sand. It feels colder than I expected, but I'm nearly there. I unbuckle the leather belt. It was my grandfather's belt. It is made from the tanned hides of one of his own cows. It always seemed special to me, so I take extra care to roll it tight. The last things to remove are my linen slacks and the Lycra boxer shorts that are beneath them. Together they create a tidy pile perched on that rock.

There is something liberating about standing naked on this beach. I don't think I have done it since my twenties. I step into the edge of the water. It is just in time for another wave to rush forward across the beach and fully engulf my ankles. The water is cold, but I don't care. This is where I belong.

If I were standing in a lake, the water around me might act as a mirror to my soul. This seawater is not calm enough to reflect anything but the light of the moon. I have no possibility to see reflected the reality of the old man who stands naked in this water. I don't have to reflect on my sagging chest, the white pubic hair, or the crepe-like texture of my mottled skin. I can still be what I always wanted to think of myself as being. I can be that heroic Greek god stepping off a marble plinth into the reality of the common man—my muscles beautifully chiseled, my hair in unmoving curls, and my face suffused with dignity.

This is the man who walks into the waves. It's not the person who for nearly seventy years avoided any meaningful relationship with another man. It's not the rancher who's betrayed his family legacy. It's not the person who once cared about Jessica or Frank or Gina or any of the people for whom I could be standing strong.

Into that chilling water, I stride like the god I want to be. The waves are higher than I expected. One breaks and swamps my genitals. I feel them shrink inward, but still I stride forward. The cove may be shallow at first, but I know it has a sharp drop off not far ahead. I know where I am headed.

But before I leave forever, I want that final look. I want to stand in the sea that gave man life and view the sand, the bluff, and the ranch that gave me much of what I sought. I stop. I turn to face the coast.

There on the beach, in front of the embers, stands one lone person. The tide is coming in quickly. An errant wave has already swept over my carefully stacked clothes, but the waters have yet to reach the fire or the person standing in front of it. It is Chase.

I know he sees me, but so far he hasn't reacted. He's standing there, mere feet from the encroaching water. He's wearing flannel pajama bottoms and an oversized sweatshirt. Just seeing him in those clothes makes me realize how cold the water is. I start to shiver. I should never have looked back.

Now, because I have, I feel lost. I am a strong swimmer, so I know I could turn, dive into the waves, and swim out as far as possible. I could go past the drop-off, and let all of this end. There would be no way he could reach me in time.

I hesitate.

He waves. It is a motion that suggests he is just out for a walk and has happened to see me in the water, with no understanding of what is about to happen. It is as though he is just being friendly. I can't help myself. I wave back.

Suddenly, I understand what's he doing. He's pulling that dark heavy sweatshirt over his beautiful head and he's tossing it far up the slope. Now he steps out of his pajamas. He is completely naked. He has become the statue I wanted to be.

And he steps into the water.

Saturday, 11:31 PM

Chase treads slowly but surely into the water. It is as though he doesn't feel the chill, not even when he reaches the point where the water rises toward his waist. He is closer now and I can make out his features. He smiles, as though it is the most natural thing in the world for an old wrinkled crank and a young smooth-skinned man to stand naked in a cold ocean as the clock ticks down toward midnight.

He stops in front of me and looks directly into my eyes. I know he understands.

"Hello, Mr. Mazzetti," he says. "What are you doing?"

"I felt like a swim," I lied.

"Is that wise. All by yourself? So late at night?"

"Well, dinner is over, so I no longer have a guardian angel to tell me what to do, or not to do."

I don't know why I said that. Chase is not my guardian angel. If the preceding hours have taught me anything about Chase, it is that he is my taunting devil. He forced me to play the role of host. Besides, I don't want anyone watching over me. I'm old enough to take care of myself.

"Then maybe you can be mine," he says—and without warning he leans backward to hit the water, his feet rising and his face turned toward the stars. There's still enough moonlight for me to admire his body but that feels presumptuous. I don't know why. I didn't ask him to strip and join me. So I look away, and then I decide I should also float.

I have never been in a sensory deprivation tank, but I think this moment might be close. I am touched only by the water and cooling night sky. In my ears thrums the sound of the ocean, and the more I look skyward, the more the universe shows itself.

"Do you know what I like about my job," Chase asks. His voice sounds oddly muffled by the water filling my ears.

"I don't," I reply. My voice too seems different, as though it belongs to another person and I think just for a moment, "Why don't I be that person?"

He continues talking, and I feel as though I'm in a dream. His tone is soothing, but I try to listen carefully. There's another part of me that wants to fall asleep.

"I meet so many people. I guess you would expect that, the way we travel around the country and feed hundreds of new people each night. You'd expect all those guests to be so happy. After all, the settings are always beautiful and the chefs are among the best. The food is fresh. Every night is meant to be a celebration.

"And yet, I feel so much unhappiness. Know what I mean? I don't understand why, but I connect with people. I can always tell what they want and what they fear. Sometimes I can feel as though I see their future. It's kind of a curse the way I can anticipate what people will do, say, and give up.

"Maybe that's why Aubrey keeps me on. He doesn't really understand his own workers, and he's terrible at planning ahead. For me, life is just one giant chessboard, and I can map out all the potential possibilities ahead. I'm always trying to be ready for the next move.

"But it's sad when you see so many people who won't ever place one of their pieces in a dangerous new position. Sometimes I think people just want to fashion their own prison."

I don't respond. How can I when I am almost certain he's really talking about me? Moreover, I don't understand his point.

"We all have fears, Mr. Mazzetti. When I saw you out in the water all by yourself, I didn't know what would happen if I joined you. For all I knew, you might just swim away into the darkness and get lost in the night. And that would have been very painful to think that I caused you to flee.

"Then I thought, maybe that isn't the way this story goes. Maybe there's another way things could end. Actually in my head right now I am holding on to dozens of different threads of storylines, wondering whichever will eventually be reached. They're all possible universes. I can't be certain which one comes true, anymore than I can name all those stars above us. I just don't know. We never know."

I feel I owe him a response. Surely, I must at least give him that. "But which path would you like to see happen?"

A wisp of a cloud is coming in from the west. Maybe the normal evening fog banks are finally showing up and will force this picture perfect evening to an end.

"I don't think it's up to me to write your story."

"Isn't it your story as well?" I respond. Just then the swell pushes my floating body into his. He feels warm which only reminds me how cold I am becoming. What do I do next?

"I guess no one's story is just theirs. But I don't think you should simply abandon yours. A lot of people tonight know you and judge you and want things from you. Isn't it time to claim what you really want?"

I say nothing. Even at this warmest time in autumn, the ocean waters are usually no higher than sixty degrees along the coast. There's something seeping out of me. The funny thing is that I find the chill comforting.

I sense a disturbance in the water beside. Chase is back on his feet. He reaches out to grab both my floating hands and he pulls hard.

"Stand up," he commands, and I do.

"I think it's time," he says. "Mr. Mazzetti, it's time to leave this beach."

And I make my choice.

Sunday, Before Dawn

I wake with a start. The small pebbles beneath me are pushing against my bare skin. There's only a modicum of heat emanating from the coals of the bonfire. But I am warm. I feel myself held by the arms of a naked Chase.

I must have fallen asleep. For a long moment, I feel confused. Then I remember those minutes before I fell asleep. They're like a strange dream and I can't be quite certain any of it is true. I try the usual tricks to be certain one is awake. It all confirms that I am, even though I can tell Chase is still asleep. His slow, low breathing soothes me. I replay how I left the ocean.

Chase insists that I walk out of the cold water, and as I did all evening, I follow his instructions. I do it willingly. We have been chest deep in the water, and as cold as that is, as I emerge into the still night air, wet and dripping, I begin to shiver. By the time we reach the shore, I am chattering violently.

"We need to get you warm," Chase says. He guides me toward the few remaining embers, makes me sit, and then, from directly behind, wraps his arms around me. "You'll feel warmer soon," he promises.

That's all I ever wanted really. Just for someone to reassure me that I will stop shivering and get warmer, and the promise that everything will be all right. I can't do it by myself. I am sure some people can. They have the inner strength to weather whatever life throws at them. I have always needed someone to hold me and be my guardian. I am such a child, but I feel too old to change.

I don't know how long we sat there. Time simply stretched into the vastness of the sky, and there was no need for either of us to say anything. I didn't even bother worrying about what might be on Chase's mind. I simply was. Maybe it was the alcohol that still controlled my thought. Maybe it was the spirits of my ancestors who built up this ranch. Maybe it was me, but everything in the moment seemed right.

And I guess I fell asleep.

Now I am awake, and I know that it is time to move on. But I am reluctant to break this moment. I know that however much longer I might occupy this ranch or this planet, there will always be a part of me that will remain on this perfect beach in this perfect moment. Nothing has happened, yet everything has changed.

Chase stirs. The change in his breathing tells me that he is awake. I choose not to say anything. I want this moment to stretch for another beat. But then I know it's time.

"You should go," I say.

He rubs his hand across my arms. "You're still too cold," he answers. "And you have to walk up to that house."

He stands and walks over to where he placed his pajama bottoms and sweatshirt. It happened in another life, or so it seems to me.

"Put these on," he says.

"Don't be silly," I reply. "My house is only a few hundred yards up that hill."

"And my bus is right over there. You're the one who's cold. And you know at your age . . ."

I laugh.

He doesn't finish his sentence. He doesn't need to because I already am pulling up the flannel bottoms. They're loose enough to fit comfortably, but the sweatshirt is a bit tight on this flabby body. I probably look like an idiot, but already I feel so much better.

"I think it's time I headed back," Chase adds.

I need to say something, but nothing seems appropriate. I mumble, "Thank you."

I'm not sure what I am thanking him for: is it coming into the ocean and preventing me from swimming away? Because I would have. At least that's what I want to think. Or is it for holding this old body and letting me reclaim for a moment the wonders of human touch? Maybe it's thanks for looking at me and actually seeing the flawed person that I am and yet not walking away.

Within me there rages nostalgia deep and dark. I won't speak about what this young man means because I know he's just the momentary symbol of a life of fantasies and dreams. Yet somehow I feel that at this moment I have been blessed with a newfound clarity. Maybe he was the catalyst, but I think a little of bit of it was me. I have changed.

"What about your clothes?" I ask.

"Keep them," he says. "We'll be leaving early in the morning, and I don't need them. It's been an interesting night, Mr. Mazzetti."

"That it has."

He is walking away. His naked feet gingerly make their way up the rocky side of my perfect bluff. His bare back is turned toward my perfect beach. In the waning light of the dying bonfire and the soon-to-set moon, there's a reflection of his white behind and the tan lines that frame it.

Soon he is lost in the darkness. He is just a shade moving through the grass. I am alone in the place I have always wanted to be. I consider lingering for another moment, to take in another view of my sea, but I know the night has passed its peak and is now hurtling on toward another dawn. I know I must change. I need to turn my back on the vale of my youth. I must walk up my own hill.

I can do it. I am ready to stride into the east, to view a new world, and to await the dawn.

The Long Table Dinner is over.

ABOUT THIS BOOK

People are often interested in what inspires my novels. There's a backstory to *The Long Table Dinner*. It began when a good friend named Patrick claimed he had the perfect title for a novel about one's past—*The Veil of Youth*. About that same time, I attended an extraordinary dinner put on by an organization called Outstanding in the Field; it was held at the Ocean Rose Abalone Farm.

I had been working on a different novel but was facing severe writer's block. Suddenly, prompted by these events, a whole new story came to mind. It was about a different type of vale of youth. In some ways, the story became an alternate universe vision of what my life as a gay Wisconsin farm boy might have been if I had grown up instead on a California coastal ranch and never met my husband of 35 years.

So, in short, this is not a story about an actual dinner I attended, nor the people involved with that evening. Nor is it actually about me. Rather it is about an imaginary group of people with interconnected lives, and how a single night could upturn the entire world of a single person.

But one character is definitely inspired by a real person. A few years ago, I met a charming Dutch storyteller named Otto Witteveen. Over a lengthy cruise, he regaled my husband and me with a vast array of amusing tales of his youth, and he insisted I needed to include him in my next novel. Well, Otto, as you know, I added a character named Otto and with your permission even gave him a chance to tell a couple of your favorite tales. Please know my fictional Otto is nowhere near as wonderful and delightful as both you and your wife Aida.

The story of Happy's unfortunate burial as told by Frank in this book is also inspired by an anecdote I heard from Troy Underwood, who met his wife DeAnn under circumstances similar to how my characters Frank and Jessica met. Otherwise their life story is completely different.

My thanks to Patrick for helping to inspire the concept—and to Otto, Aida, Troy and DeAnn for letting me borrow a few stories. I would also like to thank our Dutch friends Riet van der Ploeg and Wim Boogaard; they first made us aware of the concept of *gezellig* and also shared some details of life in the Netherlands during World War II.

As always, I greatly appreciate the initial readings of the drafts of this book by two individuals who truly help me identify flaws and disconnects—Dixie Walker and Tina Masiak. Any remaining mistakes are entirely my fault or a result of my stubbornness about listening. I would also like to thank Dena Kuhn for another great book cover design. Finally, my appreciation, thanks, and love to my husband Robert who has to put up with a lot during my creative bouts.

ABOUT THE AUTHOR

Dennis Frahmann currently resides on the Central Coast of California in a small town called Cambria, but he grew up on a dairy farm in Wisconsin, became a food critic in Minneapolis, and worked for more than 30 years in high tech marketing. This is his fourth novel.

www.ingramcontent.com/pod-product-compliance
Lightning Source LLC
Chambersburg PA
CBHW020637260626
47157CB00008B/2780